CHERUB

DIVINE MADNESS

ALSO BY ROBERT MUCHAMORE

THE RECRUIT

THE DEALER

MAXIMUM SECURITY

THE KILLING

CHERUB

mission 5
DIVINE MADNESS

ROBERT MUCHAMORE

Simon Pulse
New York   London   Toronto   Sydney   New Delhi

This book is a work of fiction. Any references to historical events, real people, or real places are used fictitiously. Other names, characters, places, and events are products of the author's imagination, and any resemblance to actual events or places or persons, living or dead, is entirely coincidental.

SIMON PULSE
An imprint of Simon & Schuster Children's Publishing Division
1230 Avenue of the Americas, New York, NY 10020
First Simon Pulse hardcover edition October 2012
Copyright © 2006 by Robert Muchamore
Originally published in Great Britain in 2006 by Hodder Children's Books
Published by arrangement with Hodder and Stoughton Limited
All rights reserved, including the right of reproduction
in whole or in part in any form.
SIMON PULSE and colophon are registered trademarks of Simon & Schuster, Inc.
For information about special discounts for bulk purchases, please contact
Simon & Schuster Special Sales at 1-866-506-1949
or business@simonandschuster.com.
The Simon & Schuster Speakers Bureau can bring authors to your live event.
For more information or to book an event contact the Simon & Schuster Speakers
Bureau at 1-866-248-3049 or visit our website at www.simonspeakers.com.
Designed by Mike Rosamilia
The text of this book was set in Apollo MT.
Manufactured in the United States of America
2 4 6 8 10 9 7 5 3 1
Library of Congress Control Number 2006922520
ISBN 978-1-4169-9944-7

WHAT IS CHERUB?

CHERUB is a branch of British Intelligence. Its agents are aged between ten and seventeen years. Cherubs are all orphans who have been taken out of care homes and trained to work undercover. They live on CHERUB campus, a secret facility hidden in the English countryside.

WHAT USE ARE KIDS?

Quite a lot. Nobody realizes kids do undercover missions, which means they can get away with all kinds of stuff that adults can't.

WHO ARE THEY?

About three hundred children live on CHERUB campus. JAMES ADAMS is our fourteen-year-old hero. He's a well-respected CHERUB agent, with four successful missions under his belt. James's eleven-year-old sister, LAUREN, is a less experienced agent.

James broke up with his girlfriend KERRY CHANG a while back, but they're still on good terms. Among his other friends on campus are BRUCE NORRIS, GABRIELLE O'BRIEN, and KYLE BLUEMAN, who recently turned sixteen.

AND THE T-SHIRTS?

Cherubs are ranked according to the color of the T-shirts they wear on campus. ORANGE is for visitors. RED is for kids who live on CHERUB campus, but are too young to qualify as agents. (The minimum age is ten.) BLUE is for kids undergoing CHERUB's tough hundred-day training regime. A GRAY T-shirt means you're qualified for missions. NAVY—the T-shirt James wears—is a reward for outstanding performance on a mission. If you do well, you'll end your CHERUB career wearing a BLACK T-shirt, the ultimate recognition for outstanding achievement over a number of missions. When you retire, you get the WHITE T-shirt, which is also worn by some staff.

WHAT IS HELP EARTH?

Help Earth is a well funded and highly secretive terrorist organization that aims to *"Bring an end to the environmental carnage wreaked on our planet by global corporations and the politicians who support them."* More than two hundred people have died in Help Earth attacks since the organization surfaced in late 2003. James Adams foiled a major Help Earth operation in his first CHERUB mission.

CHAPTER 1

GAS

It was half seven in the morning, but James had already been in the dojo for ninety minutes. Six pairs of kids were spread over the padded floor, wearing sweaty kit and a mass of protective padding.

Exhausted from a brutal twenty-minute sparring session, James bowed to his training partner Gabrielle, before grabbing a plastic bottle off the floor. He tipped back his head, opened his mouth wide and squeezed out a jet of high-energy glucose drink.

As he tried to swallow, a palm slammed into his back and he stumbled forwards, crashing into the springy blue floor with juice dribbling down his chin. Miss Takada ground James's head against the mat, using a sixty-year-old foot with gnarled yellow nails and sandpaper-tough skin.

"Wa ru one?" instructor Takada shouted. Her English was awful, but luckily she stuck to pet phrases that James knew by heart.

"Rule one," James replied awkwardly, as the foot squished his lips out of shape. "Always be alert; an attack can come from any direction at any time."

"Be alert, stay alert," Takada tutted. "Drink quick, not glaring at ceiling like fool. Get off my floor. You dishonor my floor."

James dragged himself up, keeping a wary eye on his teacher.

"OK!" Takada shouted, clapping her hands to get the attention of the whole class. "Final exercise. Speed test, little balls."

A few of the shattered teenagers mustered enough energy to moan. There were only ten days of CHERUB's six-week advanced combat course left, so everyone knew how to play: six students lined up against the wall at each end of the dojo, Miss Takada would throw out ten mini soccer balls and the two who didn't make it into the changing room with a ball had to forsake breakfast and run twenty laps around the outside of the dojo. It was a violent game and even wearing protective gear, broken bones weren't out of the question.

Takada reached into a net filled with balls and threw out the first three. Twelve teenagers charged forwards, as they bobbled across the floor.

James sighted one rolling fortuitously towards him, but Gabrielle was faster and bundled him out of the way. As James plowed into the floor for the hundredth time that morning, Gabrielle ripped the ball out of reach.

She managed three gangly steps, before coming under attack from two boys who'd started from the other end of the room. One hit Gabrielle headfirst, butting her in the stomach, while the other slid in with a two-footed tackle. Gabrielle groaned in pain as she hit the deck, but managed to hold on to the ball by tucking it under her chest.

The boy who'd butted Gabrielle tried to lever her into an arm lock, but caught a padded elbow in the face for his trouble and crumpled backwards in a heap.

While battle still raged over the first three balls, Miss Takada tossed in two more. James was exhausted, but the prospect of laps around the dojo gave him enough motivation to spring up and take a lunge. This time he judged it right and plucked the ball from between his legs without breaking stride.

James was thrilled to see less than fifteen meters between himself and the archway into the boys' changing room. He leapt over a flying kick, picked up speed, and could almost taste a cooked breakfast in the campus dining room. But three paces shy, the dream was shattered by a bulky sixteen-year-old called Mark Fox.

Mark had ham-size fists and a twenty-centimeter height advantage over James, who got bundled into the padded wall before spinning out and adopting a fighting stance. It didn't seem fair facing off an opponent who was so much bigger, but advanced combat training was meant to be realistic and the real world isn't fair either.

James tried to visualize himself as the plucky underdog, who could come off best like in some kids' movie. But the illusion didn't last. Mark moved ruthlessly, spraying James with flying sweat as he landed a left-right punch combo, followed by a knee in the ribs. James crumpled up as Mark tore the ball from his grasp.

"Later." Mark grinned, looking smug as he swaggered towards the archway.

The padded blows had only knocked the wind out of James, but he'd landed awkwardly and bent back some fingers. He stood as soon as he'd caught his breath, but his face was screwed up in pain. Six kids had now made it into the changing rooms; three more were almost there with no opponent in sight. That left James and two girls fighting over the last ball.

Dana Smith currently held it. She was a fifteen-year-old Australian, about the same height as James, muscular for a girl and an excellent athlete and swimmer. Gabrielle O'Brien had just turned fourteen and was the youngest on the course, but she could hold her own and had Dana penned into a corner looking for a way out.

James positioned himself a couple of meters behind Gabrielle. He figured Dana would make a break for it. Hopefully, Gabrielle would take her down, and he'd be able to wade in and grab the ball while the girls tangled on the floor.

But Dana showed no sign of moving and Miss Takada was growing impatient. She had a queue of red-shirts outside waiting for their beginners' karate class.

"You got one minute, or all three of you run," Takada said, drumming on the face of her watch.

Gabrielle backed away from the corner, trying to lure Dana out. James was backing up too, as Dana made her move. Gabrielle lashed out, but Dana dropped down and skidded beneath the flying kick on her knees, sweeping away Gabrielle's leg in the process.

4

James sensed an opportunity to snatch the ball, while Gabrielle was falling and Dana was on her knees. He plowed into Dana, grappled her around the neck, ripped the ball out of her hand, and clasped it to his chest, ignoring the pain in his fingers.

Dana yelled as she broke out of the choke hold and flipped James on to his back, before straddling his waist. She pinned his shoulders under her knees and batted him across the face. As she did so, James's weakened fingers lost their sweaty grip on the ball. It bounced between his legs and began rolling across the mat.

Gabrielle spotted the ball and dived in. By the time Dana realized that James had let go, Gabrielle was sprinting triumphantly towards the girls' changing room.

James was still pinned to the floor as Miss Takada made a circular motion with her finger. "OK, you two. Round and round, twenty time. You know the drill."

As the instructor stepped out to yell at the rowdy group of red-shirts outside, James looked up at Dana with a hint of desperation. Her beefy thigh muscles loomed over him and her entire bodyweight pressed on his shoulders.

"Let us up," James gasped. "It's over."

Dana gave him an evil smile. James didn't know Dana all that well. She was a loner, still a gray shirt after five years of CHERUB missions, and notoriously bitter towards younger kids like him who'd achieved better things.

"This is because I'm a navy shirt, isn't it?" James said. "Well maybe you've been unlucky, or whatever, but you can't blame me for that."

"It's not that." Dana grinned.

"C'mon, let me up," James said, getting angry as he

tried to wriggle out. "Takada's gonna have a right go if she comes back and sees we're not running."

"She'll be a few minutes helping the little kids get changed. I've got long enough."

"Long enough for what?"

"You'll see," Dana said, shuffling forwards so that her bum loomed over James's head.

James heard a rumbling sound from inside Dana's shorts and felt a blast of warm air.

"Oh, Jeeeeeesus," James whined, screwing up his face.

Dana started laughing as she rolled off and found her feet.

"You're an animal," James groaned, wafting his hand in front of his face. "That's putrid. I'll get you back for that."

He couldn't help seeing the funny side. He liked Dana, even though she was an oddball.

Dana shrugged. "Don't expect me to lose any sleep."

James's laughter dried up as he staggered towards the dojo exit, grabbed his trainers, and began stripping off his padding. Twenty laps around the dojo takes half an hour when you're knackered, and it was freezing outside.

CHAPTER 2

CLYDE

The Echelon security network is
the world's most sophisticated
electronic surveillance system. It
is jointly run by the United States
National Security Agency (NSA) and
the intelligence services of several
friendly nations, including Great
Britain and Australia.

Echelon monitors communications,
including telephone calls, e-mails,
and faxes passing via microwave
links, communications satellites,
and fiber-optic cables. The system

currently scans nine billion private
messages and conversations per day.

Every hour, approximately one
million messages containing trigger
words such as bomb, terrorist,
napalm, or phrases such as Help
Earth or Al Qaeda are picked out
and stored by the system. These
suspicious messages are run through
logic analyzing software that is
capable of determining the emotional
state of a person from their voice,
or the likely context of suspicious
words in an e-mail or text message.

Of the million messages stored
each hour by Echelon, about twenty
thousand will be flagged by the
computer and read by one of two
thousand monitoring staff on duty at
any given time.

In late 2005, an Echelon station
in southeast Asia intercepted an
e-mail message between two unknown
parties. The e-mail mentioned a
possible Help Earth attack in
Hong Kong and the involvement of
a sixteen-year-old environmental
campaigner named Clyde Xu.

Rather than arresting the young
suspect, it has been decided to
infiltrate Xu's family in the hope

that more senior figures within Help Earth can be uncovered.

(Excerpt from a CHERUB mission briefing for Kyle Blueman, Kerry Chang, and Bruce Norris.)

HONG KONG, FEBRUARY 2006

Kerry Chang broke into a jog when she spotted Rebecca Xu leaning against a lamppost waiting for her. The two thirteen-year-olds wore the school uniform—blue blouse, navy skirt and pullover, white tights—and were mixed up with hundreds of others dressed the same way. Some were heading home alone, some stood in groups gossiping, while others cut precariously into four lanes of snarled up traffic, trying to catch a double-decker bus parked at a stop on the opposite side of the road.

"Good day?" Kerry asked, speaking in Cantonese.

Rebecca shrugged. "School's school, you know how it goes."

Kerry knew how she felt. When an undercover mission drags on, the person you're pretending to be starts getting mixed up with who you really are. She'd now been attending Prince of Wales school for six weeks and had settled into a rut.

Rebecca started walking.

"Aren't we waiting for Bruce?" Kerry asked.

"Detention." Rebecca smiled. "I thought you knew. Your brother's such an idiot."

"*Step*brother," Kerry said. "No shared genes, thank you very much. What's he gone and done now?"

"Oh, just him and his stupid mates yapping all through

9

math class. Mr. Lee chucked a mental and told them to come back after school."

Kerry shook her head, "I wish I was in your class. I've got nobody to talk to all day."

Rebecca smiled. "But we'd probably get in trouble for chatting all the time."

The air-conditioned school was always chilly, but it was sunny out and Kerry got hot as they headed home. She loosened her tie, then pulled her sweater over her head and knotted it around her waist. The fifteen-minute walk took the two girls through a maze of high buildings, cramped streets, and elevated walkways choked by fumes from speeding traffic.

Home for both girls was a recently built tower block, twenty stories high. It had five identical cousins, the last of which was still under construction. Hong Kong's sea air and tropical climate eats buildings, and despite its newness, the balconies stretching skywards already looked tatty.

In most wealthy countries, cramped apartment blocks like these would house the poor, but Hong Kong is one of the most densely populated cities in the world and this accommodation was mostly home to professional types. Rebecca's family was typical: her father was a dentist and her mother part-owned a jewelers shop in an upscale mall.

The doors parted automatically as the girls passed into a muggy lobby. The security guard gave them a friendly nod from behind his desk.

"Have you got much homework?" Kerry asked, as they waited for the elevator up to the ninth floor, where they both lived.

"A fair bit," Rebecca said. "We can do it together . . . or surf the Internet, whatever."

"Cool," Kerry said. "But I'm gonna go in my place and lose the uniform first. I'll see you round yours in ten minutes."

The front door of the cramped apartment led directly into the kitchen. Kerry yawned as she stepped inside. She dumped her backpack on the floor and skidded her keys across the dining table. Assistant mission controller Chloe Blake leaned through the doorway leading into the living room.

"Hiya, Kerry. Where's Bruce?"

"Detention."

"Oh, *great*," Chloe said, looking stressed.

"What's up?"

"Are you doing homework with Rebecca tonight?"

Kerry nodded. "As soon as I'm changed. Why, what's going on?"

"You'd better look at this."

Kerry moved through to the living room. Sixteen-year-old Kyle Blueman—Kerry's other stepbrother for the purposes of this mission—was sitting on the couch dressed in shorts and a T-shirt.

"No school?" Kerry asked.

"Clyde Xu skipped out of our English class this morning," Kyle explained. "I followed him down to the harbor, but I had to keep my distance and lost him at a busy crossing. John picked up a couple of mobile calls in the surveillance suite back at the hotel, but they didn't tell us much. All we know is that Clyde met with someone at an Arby's in the business district around lunchtime."

"Any idea who?" Kerry interrupted.

"Not even a name," Kyle said. "But after the meeting, Clyde came back here to the Xus' apartment. We've got it on video."

Chloe flipped up the lid of her laptop, which was connected to a satellite antenna on the balcony. She double clicked, opening up a video file which Kerry leaned in to watch. The fisheye image was from an ultra-wide-angle camera that Bruce had sneaked into the light fitting above Clyde Xu's bed four weeks earlier.

"When was this recorded?" Kerry asked.

"A couple of hours ago," Chloe replied.

The screen showed Clyde Xu walking into his tiny bedroom. He sat on his bed, then pulled off his trainers and school shirt, revealing a muscular chest.

"He's *so* fit," Kerry said.

"Totally," Kyle grinned. "Cutest little terrorist I've ever seen."

Chloe tutted, "Can you two keep the raging hormones under control and concentrate on what you're watching?"

Clyde Xu pulled a small, cellophane-wrapped package out of his school backpack, then leaned forwards. He opened a chest of drawers and tucked it under a pile of socks.

"Any idea what that is?" Kerry asked.

"Impossible to tell," Chloe said. "But you don't go to all that trouble to meet someone and come back with something you could have bought from the Seven-Eleven, do you? Can you try and get a look at it, maybe take some photos?"

Kerry looked uncertain, "Couldn't we wait until tomorrow and go in when the Xus are out at work and school?"

"It would be easier," Chloe said. "But that's fifteen or sixteen hours away. Who's to say Clyde won't have passed the package on to someone else by then? Knowing what's in that package now might be the difference between foiling an attack and hundreds of innocent people losing their lives."

"Well," Kerry said, shaking her head, "it's gonna be tricky without Bruce there keeping an eye out. He's *such* a knob, getting himself in trouble on the one day we need him."

Chloe clicked a few icons on the laptop screen, making the display switch to a live feed from the Xus' apartment. Between them, Kerry and Bruce had managed to place a miniature camera and microphone in every room.

"Well," Chloe said, as she flipped between the live pictures from six different cameras, "Rebecca is in her room, Clyde is on the computer in his parents' room, and we can rely on Mum and Dad not being home before seven o'clock."

Kerry nodded. "You can't get Clyde off that PC once he's online. Rebecca always has to fight with him when she wants to go and play Sims Two."

"Do you think you'll be safe going into the room without Bruce covering you from outside?"

Kerry shrugged. "I can probably talk my way out if they catch me in the room, but if I'm sitting there taking pictures of whatever he's got hidden in that drawer, our cover's totally blown."

"What do we do if the package turns out to be a bomb?" Kyle asked. "If it is, Clyde could be planting it at any time. In just a few hours, or something."

"I doubt it's tonight," Chloe said. "Don't forget the second meeting."

"What meeting?" Kerry asked.

"Something John picked up in one of Clyde's mobile calls," Chloe explained. "He's got a meeting tonight at eight o'clock."

"Where?"

"No idea where or who, Kerry. But groups like Help Earth keep information on potential attacks separate. One person deals with the device, another knows the target, and the attacker is only given the whole picture at the last minute. That way, the plan isn't compromised if anyone is caught."

Kerry nodded. "So, all these meetings mean the attack has to be coming soon."

"Almost certainly within the next seventy-two hours," Chloe said.

"What if Clyde isn't the attacker?" Kyle asked.

"We've had this discussion," Chloe said, a touch wearily. "Xu is a sixteen-year-old with no specialist knowledge. His only use to Help Earth is as a lightning rod: an unlikely suspect who can take some of the risks that more senior people don't fancy."

"Right," Kerry said. "I'll hook a two-way radio up under my T-shirt. As soon as I get in Clyde's room I'll fix it in my ear. You guys watch on the video and speak to me if you see someone coming."

Chloe gave Kerry a friendly rub on the back. "You'd better hurry up and get changed before Rebecca starts wondering where you've got to."

CHAPTER 5

PLASTIC

Rebecca's bedroom was a windowless box, so the two girls always did their homework in the Xus' living room. Kerry lay on the floor, with her books spread over a sheepskin rug, while Rebecca sprawled on a smart leather couch with one eye watching MTV.

"Oooh, Busted," Rebecca said, grabbing the remote and then turning the sound up loud.

Kerry looked up from her math exercise book and shook her head. "I can't believe you still like them. They're so last year."

"Last year, next year, Matt Jay is still hot."

Kerry giggled. "Not as hot as your big brother, Clyde."

Rebecca screwed up her face. "*Kindly* keep your

warped fantasies about my brother to yourself, Kerry. Besides, he's only interested in saving bluebottle dolphins, or standing outside the American embassy with some dopey placard. I don't think he'd know what to do with a girl if you gave him one."

"Bottle*nose* dolphins," Kerry corrected as she stood up. "If you're listening to that racket, I'm going to the loo."

Kerry guessed the Busted video lasted three-and-a-half minutes. Rebecca wouldn't budge while it was on, but she needed to know what Clyde was up to as well. She cut out of the living room, took two paces down a hallway and stepped through the open door of Mr. and Mrs. Xu's bedroom. Clyde sat at a desk between two wardrobes, totally wrapped in a game of Doom III, with gunfire roaring out of the speakers.

"Ahem," Kerry said, noisily clearing her throat as she stepped up beside Clyde.

"What?"

Kerry smiled, with a hint of flirting, as she pushed a strand of hair away from her face. "I like that T-shirt, Clyde. It always looks nice on you."

"I can't pause this game," Clyde said irritably as he switched weapons and unleashed a barrage of rockets. "I'm playing an online death match. What is it you want?"

"We won't be getting our Internet set up until my dad finishes his old job and moves in with us. I was hoping I could do an e-mail to my old mates back in London."

"They've got Internet in the library at school, you know," Clyde said.

Kerry backed off a step and made herself sound

wounded. "OK," she said weakly. "I'll do it at school, I suppose."

Clyde sensed that Kerry was upset and briefly snatched his eyes away from the screen. "Look, after this game, OK? It'll be ten minutes or so; I'll give you a shout when I've finished."

Perfect, Kerry thought as she brushed her hand against Clyde's shoulder. "Thank you, Clyde."

She turned on her socked feet and passed through the kitchen, confident that she had two uninterrupted minutes to get a look at the mysterious package. There was a short hallway leading from the kitchen towards Clyde's and Rebecca's tiny bedrooms. The bathroom door was directly opposite.

Kerry leaned into the bathroom and tugged on the light cord to make it look like she was inside, then cut a quick glance over her shoulder before slipping into Clyde's room. Her heart rate bounced as she pushed open the door, flipped on the light switch, pulled a tiny earpiece from inside her T-shirt and plugged it into her ear.

"Chloe, can you hear me?" Kerry whispered.

Chloe's reply came through the earpiece with a soothing tone. "Don't worry; I've got your back. You'll know the second either of them moves."

"Mind's gone blank," Kerry said nervously. "Which drawer was it?"

"Second one down."

Kerry quietly slid open Clyde's drawer and slid her hand amongst the balled up socks until her fingers touched the package. She made a mental note of its exact

17

position before pulling it out and placing it on top of the cabinet.

"OK," Kerry whispered, as she unraveled the plastic bag wrapped around the package and glanced inside. She immediately recognized the contents, having used identical equipment during basic training. "Looks like four bars of plastic explosive—probably C4—and two self-contained detonators. I can't tell what type they are just from looking."

The explosives looked like gray plasticine and the two sophisticated detonators would make turning it into a bomb a snip: simply mold the explosive to shape, put it where you want to—inside a car, under a desk, whatever—push in the detonators and your bomb is complete.

"Someone paid a lot of money to get their hands on these," Kerry said.

"Whys and wherefores later, Kerry," Chloe warned, deliberately keeping her voice calm. "Just take some photographs and get out as quickly as you can."

Kerry slid a tiny digital camera out of her jeans. She placed the two detonators, which looked like tiny fireworks, on the top of the drawer and took a picture. While the flash recharged, she set out the explosive ready to photograph.

The doorbell rang.

"Dammit," Kerry gasped into the microphone. "Chloe, who is that?"

In the flat five doors along, Chloe sat at the laptop clicking through the different camera feeds until she came to the one positioned in the corridor outside.

"It's Bruce," Chloe said.

Kerry snapped the picture of the explosive and started putting it back into the bag in a state of panic.

"What the *hell* is he playing at?"

"I don't know," Chloe said frantically. "He must have got out of detention and decided to come straight over there."

"Didn't you ring him to say what was going on?"

"Oh . . . ," Chloe said, sounding choked. "I should have, shouldn't I?"

Kerry was annoyed, but she didn't have time to let it fester. She quickly wound the plastic bag around the package, shoved it back under the socks, and pushed the drawer shut.

"Clyde and Rebecca are in the kitchen," Chloe said.

Kerry tried to think as she heard Rebecca answer the front door. The kitchen was less than two meters away; there was no way she could emerge from Clyde's bedroom without being seen.

"Hi, Becks," Bruce grinned, speaking in stilted Cantonese that had improved rapidly over the six weeks of the mission. "I thought you and Kerry would be doing homework. Is she here?"

Rebecca nodded. "How was detention?"

"Oh, nothing major." Bruce shrugged. "Just wasted half an hour of my life staring at a clock with my arms folded."

Clyde looked put out at having had to answer the door. "Might as well go for a pee now I'm up. I was kicking that guy's butt till you got here."

"You can't, Kerry's in there," Rebecca said.

But by the time the words were out, Clyde had the bathroom door open.

"Not unless she's flushed herself down the toilet she isn't."

Rebecca looked mystified, as Bruce had the horrible realization that he'd probably blundered in and disturbed Kerry when she was up to something.

"Maybe she went home," Bruce said edgily.

Back in Clyde's tiny bedroom, Kerry realized she needed to do something desperate as she ripped out the earpiece and tucked it back down her T-shirt.

Rebecca opened her bedroom door and leaned inside. "Kerry?—Well, she's not in there."

Kerry plunged her little finger deep into her nostril, then dug her nail into the soft tissue and ripped it out. The pain was horrendous, but she managed to snatch a wad of tissues from Clyde's bedside table and bunch them against her face as he stepped into the room.

"What the *hell* are you doing in here?"

As Kerry turned to face Clyde, she blew out the drips of blood that had collected at the base of her nostril. Clyde looked shocked as it dribbled over her lips and down her chin.

Rebecca stepped in behind her brother. "Oh my God, Kerry. What happened?"

Kerry didn't need to fake anything, the injury she'd inflicted upon herself was bloody and extremely painful.

"I get nosebleeds quite a bit. I was coming out of the toilet and it started up really bad. I ran in here to grab tissues."

If Rebecca or Clyde had stopped to think in great depth, they might have wondered why Kerry didn't go back into the bathroom and grab some toilet tissue, or grab a paper towel from the kitchen rather than enter a room she wasn't familiar with. But neither of them could think beyond the bloody face and pained expression standing right in front of them.

"What do you want us to do, Kerry?" Clyde asked.

"I think I'd better go home," Kerry said, close to sobbing. "My mum's there. She knows how to stop the bleeding. She's done it loads of times before."

Bruce opened the door of the flat. Kyle and Chloe had watched Kerry's escape plan unfold on the laptop screen, but they weren't prepared for the torrent of blood pouring down her neck as she stumbled towards the table and slumped into a dining chair, glowering at Bruce.

"Moron!" Kerry screamed. "You nearly blew this whole operation."

"I'm sorry; I didn't think," Bruce said, wrapping his hands over his head, totally unable to look Kerry in the eye.

"You *never* think."

Chloe stepped in to calm them down. "Kerry, it was my fault. I should have phoned Bruce."

"It wasn't you that got a detention," Kerry said.

She grabbed her camera out of her pocket and banged it on the table, as Kyle grabbed a first aid box from under the sink.

"Bruce," Kyle said, trying to be diplomatic, "why don't you go in the other room and e-mail the photographs to John. I'll stay here and patch up Kerry."

Bruce and Chloe walked through to the living room, as Kyle handed Kerry a damp flannel to wash her face.

"The old nosebleed trick," Kyle said. "I learned it in espionage training, but to be honest I'd totally forgotten it."

Kerry appreciated Kyle's bedside manner and managed a tight smile as she dumped the bloody flannel on the table in front of her. "I won't be in any hurry to use it again."

"OK, tip your head back. I need to take a look up there."

Kyle took a small torch out of the first aid box and shone it up Kerry's nostril. The flow was already slowing, as the blood darkened and clotted.

"Fingernails pick up a lot of dirt and bacteria, Kerry. I'm gonna squirt antiseptic up there so you don't get an infection."

Kerry couldn't nod with her head tipped back, so she made a little *uh-huh* noise as Kyle flipped the top off of a pump spray.

"This might be a little bit cold. Hold your breath; I don't want it running down into your throat."

Kerry clenched her fists in pain as the mist of antiseptic burned the inside of her nose.

"Sorry," Kyle said. "I'll make you an ice pack from the fridge. You'll have to hold it against your nose until the bleeding stops."

Chloe came back into the kitchen from the living room.

"I spoke to John at his hotel and told him about the plastic explosive. He says it's critical that we find out where Clyde Xu's meeting is tonight and what's being said."

CHAPTER 4

meet

Every breath reminded Kerry of the dried blood caked inside her nostril. She was in a packed shopping street, walking briskly alongside her mission controller, John Jones. It was dusk and the greens and reds of hundreds of illuminated signs reflected off his silver-framed glasses and bald head.

"Can you still see Clyde?" Kerry asked.

She could only see the backs and heads crammed around her. John was taller, with a view over the crowd.

"I think I can," John said. "But straight dark hair isn't exactly uncommon around here."

There was a brief gap in the crowd and John caught a glance of the yellow baseball jersey attached to the head he'd been watching for the last two minutes. Clyde Xu was wearing a green bomber jacket.

"Dammit," John said. "Wrong guy."

"You're joking," Kerry gasped, as they stopped walking and anxiously turned into the frontage of a shop selling tacky jewelry.

John pulled a smart phone out of his pocket and dialed Chloe. She was back at the apartment, sitting in front of the laptop.

"I've lost Xu," John said. "What are you getting?"

MI5 had connections inside Hong Kong's telecommunications industry and they'd managed to set up a trace on Clyde Xu's mobile phone signal, without having to tell the Chinese authorities about the CHERUB operation.

"According to this he's right on top of you, John," Chloe said. "Mobile tracking isn't pinpoint, but he should be less than fifty meters away."

"Which way is he moving?"

"Nowhere fast. Maybe he's gone into a shop or something."

"Thanks, Chloe," John said. "Call me back if he starts moving."

John snapped the phone shut and looked across at Kerry. "Any sign?"

"I'm too short," Kerry said. "I can't see a thing."

"Chloe said he's stopped moving."

"We passed a Starbucks twenty meters back," Kerry said. "We could check that out."

"Right," John said.

As the pair turned away from the display of cheap watches to head for Starbucks, Kerry spotted a green jacket, hands buried in pockets. It flashed past less than a meter in front of them. Luckily, Clyde Xu had things on his mind and his eyes were glued to the back of the person walking ahead of him.

John and Kerry exchanged shocked expressions, before stepping into the crowd and resuming the chase.

"How did we manage to get in front of him?" Kerry asked.

"Must have dropped into a shop to buy something," John said as he craned his neck, desperate not to lose his fix on Xu for a second time.

Kerry looked at her watch. It was three minutes to eight, which either meant Clyde was running late, or that the meeting was going to take place somewhere nearby. They closed right up on their target as they waited to cross a road. As soon as the green walk sign lit up, Clyde jogged forward behind the first line of stopped cars, then bounded across the pavement and into a noodle bar with a grubby white sign and a plate glass frontage steamed up with condensation.

They wanted to give Clyde a few moments to settle into the restaurant. John and Kerry crossed the road at a sedate pace, then made themselves look busy at a news-stand. Kerry bought a *Hong Kong Times* and some sweets, while John called Kyle on his mobile phone.

"Kyle, where are you?"

"Me and Bruce saw you crossing the road," Kyle answered. "Don't sweat it."

"OK," John said. "Stay close to the restaurant, but don't let Clyde see you and don't make any moves before I give you the all clear, you understand?"

"You're the boss," Kyle answered.

John snapped his phone shut and looked at Kerry as she slid a tube of mints into her jeans. "Ready?"

Kerry handed John the newspaper and nodded. "As I'll ever be."

"OK, go and win yourself an Oscar. I'll follow you inside in three minutes."

Because of the condensation, Kerry wasn't sure what she'd find as she pushed open the glass door. The kitchen was at the front of the restaurant, with a muggy soy-sauce smell rising from steaming tubs of noodle and rice dishes.

A sweaty face popped up from behind the counter. "Hi, do you want a table, or take-away?"

"Table," Kerry said tightly. "I think my friend is already here."

The man waved his hand towards the rows of plastic tables at the back of the restaurant. Kerry felt queasy as she passed a short line of customers waiting for take-away. The restaurant was 70 percent full and the decibel level was pretty high. She spotted Clyde at a table and was relieved to see that the person he was meeting hadn't arrived. He looked tetchy, jiggling his ankle up and down and fanning himself with a laminated menu.

"Hi," Kerry said as she sat opposite.

Clyde's chin dropped so fast it practically hit the table-top. "What . . . ? What are you doing here?"

"I followed you," Kerry confessed.

"Par-don *me*?"

Kerry started to babble, "Clyde, I know this probably sounds dumb, but I really wanted to talk to you. I've been meaning to for ages, but I kept chickening out. You see,

I can't stop thinking about you. All the time. I just *need* to know if you like me. You know, not like a friend. Like a girlfriend."

"Well, um . . . Kerry, I'm flattered."

"Oh . . . this feels so dumb now," Kerry said, screwing up her face like she was about to cry. As she did, she reached into the pocket of her jacket and pulled the sticky backing away from a small listening device.

"Are you even allowed out this late on your own?"

"Not really." Kerry sniffed. "I should have realized you didn't like me."

"Kerry, there's nothing wrong with you. I bet we'd get on really well if we were the same age. But I'm sixteen and you're thirteen. Be sensible, that's never gonna work, is it?"

"I'm nearly fourteen," Kerry said, as she stuck the bug to the underside of the table.

Now the initial shock of Kerry's presence had worn off, Clyde put some thought into how embarrassing it was going to be if the person he was meeting found a girl sobbing at his table.

"And I'm nearly seventeen," Clyde said, snatching Kerry's wrist and squeezing it hard.

"You're meeting another girl here, aren't you?"

"Now you listen, Kerry," Clyde snapped, pointing a finger. "I'm here for a meeting. We can talk about this some other time. But right now, you have to get out of my face."

Kerry had no reason to stick around now she'd planted the bug. She snatched her arm away from Clyde and sobbed dramatically as she stood up. A group of women with lots of shopping bags sitting a couple of tables away craned their necks around, slightly concerned.

"I'm sorry, Clyde."

Clyde raised a hand in front of his face, as if to say he couldn't listen to any more. "Just *get* out of here."

As Kerry strode out of the restaurant, pretending to be in tears, she swept past John heading in the opposite direction.

John passed between the rows of tables and settled in a few rows behind Clyde Xu. He pulled open his newspaper, placed a wireless headset over his ear that looked exactly like the kind that get supplied with upmarket mobile phones and switched on the receiver unit. He heard the sound of Clyde anxiously jiggling his menu.

It was nearly quarter past eight when a heavily built Australian man carrying a large sports bag slid into the plastic bench facing Clyde Xu. He reached across the table, shook hands with Clyde, and spoke in English.

"How's it going, pal? Sorry I kept you."

Clyde had a nervous touch in his voice, like a first date or a job interview. "No worries."

"OK, mate, nothing goes in writing, so prick up your ears," the Australian said, too quietly for anyone in the noisy restaurant to overhear, but easily picked up by the tiny microphone half a meter away from his mouth.

"The bag is for you. There's a security pass and cleaner's uniform inside. The pass is for an office block called the Pacific Business Center, in Kowloon. The real cleaners work from eleven at night until two in the morning. You sneak in just after they arrive at eleven tomorrow night. Tell the security on the front desk that it's your first night on the job and you got lost. Act nervous."

Clyde smiled. "I probably will be nervous."

The Aussie smiled back. "Only natural, son. When you arrive at the office, you stay the hell away from the other cleaners and hide out until they leave."

"Where do I hide?"

"Toilets. Not the ones in the offices themselves, but the ones outside by the elevators. They're maintained by a different contractor that only works during office hours.

"At two a.m., you use the security pass in the bag and enter the offices of Viennese Oil on the sixth floor. It's a small Italian oil exploration company. At the back of the office you'll find the chairman's suite behind a set of double doors. In the washroom off to the side will be a Samsonite overnight bag. It'll be packed with clothes and toiletries. Open the bag and place the explosive at the bottom. Insert both fuses, in case one goes wrong. You activate them by snapping off the heads and twisting the two wires together.

"When you've finished, you go back to the toilets and strip off your cleaner's overall. Then you leave the building via the stairs. You'll set off an alarm when you open the fire door. The security guard is no spring chicken, but he might call the cops so I wouldn't hang around, OK?"

Clyde nodded. "What happens then?"

"You're a teenager, so my guess is that you go home and play with yourself before falling asleep."

"No, I mean what happens with the explosive. Why are we putting it into an overnight bag instead of under his desk or something?"

The Australian shook his head slowly, "Come on, you know how this works. We don't tell you what you don't need to know."

Clyde felt stupid. "Of course. Sorry."

CHAPTER 5

FOLLOW

John was troubled as he sat behind his newspaper in the noodle bar, listening to Clyde Xu's meeting with the Australian. He was operating nine and a half thousand kilometers from home, without the knowledge of the Hong Kong authorities, and he was a couple of bodies shy of what he really needed to run his operation.

In the UK, a CHERUB mission controller can call in extra cherubs, adult intelligence officers, or police at short notice, even bringing in a team by helicopter if necessary. Out here, there was nothing except a couple of deskbound MI5 officers at the British embassy, who John wouldn't have trusted to carry his luggage, let alone reveal the existence of an ultrasecret organization like CHERUB.

John's team had spent six weeks building up to the moment when they could successfully identify Clyde Xu with a more senior member of Help Earth, but that would all be for nothing if the Australian walked into the crowd and disappeared before being identified. Someone would have to follow him.

It couldn't be John himself, he'd be recognized after sitting opposite the Australian in the restaurant. Chloe was back at the apartment coordinating the phone tracking and there was a chance the Australian had been watching the restaurant for some time and had seen Kerry.

That left Kyle and Bruce as the only ones who could do the job. John had told them both to wear protective body armor under their clothing, but he still wasn't comfortable about sending two boys after a man who might be carrying a gun. There was also a chance they'd bump into Clyde and get recognized as he left the restaurant.

John studied the physically imposing Australian, looking for any obvious sign that he was armed. But he'd been in the intelligence game more than twenty years and wasn't fooling himself: Unless your target is stupid enough to let a weapon bulge through their clothes, there's no way to tell if a man is carrying a gun.

At least the potential problem of Kyle and Bruce bumping into Clyde solved itself. The Australian threw a HK $100 note on the table as he stood up to leave and told Clyde to stay back and pay the waitress.

John grabbed his mobile, dialed up Kyle, and kept his voice low. "Where are you?"

"We're lurking by a cash machine fifty meters down the road."

John's brain tried to turn a dozen contradictory factors into a decision.

Kyle spoke tautly. "Come *on*, John. We've been waiting six weeks. Me and Bruce can handle this."

John took a deep breath. Help Earth had killed more than two hundred people since they first surfaced. This was an exceptional opportunity to crack the organization open and the boys were keen to go.

"All right," John said, running an anxious hand around the back of his neck. "You're going for it, but no stupid risks, OK? Your mark is tall, two hundred centimeters. Big shoulders, squashed up nose like a rugby player. Blond hair, side parting. Smart suit, rectangular glasses with an orange tint."

"Just eyeballing him now," Kyle said. "He's stepping out. How far are we taking this?"

John had no basis for making a decision on how dangerous the Australian was. "Kyle, it's down to your training and common sense. There's nothing I can say."

"Do we just follow, or do you want us to take him down?"

"Yeah," John said. "If you think you can do it, take him down."

He snapped the phone shut and hoped he'd made the right call.

Kyle grinned at Bruce as he pocketed his phone. "John's got the jitters, but we're on."

"Mission controllers always get the jitters." Bruce grinned. "I think it's in their job description."

"And we've got ourselves a nice, easy mark."

The Australian's blond head stood out in the crowd, and because he didn't know Kyle or Bruce they could follow more closely than John and Kerry had been able to follow Clyde. Still, the boys couldn't get cocky: two teenaged Europeans stood out, wandering the streets of Hong Kong after dark.

After walking a kilometer, the bobbing blond head ducked into an underground MTR station, down a flight of steps, and into a gloomily lit ticket hall. The Aussie had a pass and entered through the electronic turnstile. The boys didn't.

"Shiiit," Kyle said, as he headed up to the ticket machine with a hand burrowing down his pocket looking for change.

An elderly man stood in front of them, trying to feed in a twenty-dollar note. It was agony watching the note whirr in and out, with a red LED flickering above the slot. Finally, the note got sucked in and a paper ticket and a flurry of coins clanked into the dispensing drawer.

"Come on, granddad," Kyle murmured impatiently, as the old codger scooped up his change.

Bruce pushed in and began feeding his coins. As soon as the first ticket popped out, Kyle grabbed it. He raced through the turnstile and began sprinting down an empty fixed staircase that ran between two crowded escalators. Bruce was fifteen seconds behind him, but there was no sign of the Australian when they met up at the bottom.

"Which way?" Bruce gasped, as the crowds bustling around them divided off towards platforms for trains heading east and west.

"We've gotta split," Kyle said anxiously. "You try east-bound."

The boys headed through the crowd on to separate platforms. The metro was packed out and Kyle got jammed into a slow-moving crowd on a short flight of steps leading down to the westbound platform. The crush made it impossible to see anything beyond the head of the person in front and no amount of pushing was going to help.

Bruce had an easier time making it on to the other platform, but a distant rumbling and rush of air meant a train was arriving at any second. If the Aussie was on the platform, he had to identify him fast.

Bruce scanned the platform, but couldn't see the distinctive blond head. To get a better look, he pushed through to a drinks vending machine at the back of the platform, wedged his trainer in the drawer where plastic bottles dropped out and used it as a step to raise himself above the crowd.

It only took a second to spot the blond head, fifty meters down the platform. Meanwhile, the wind coming through the tunnel was blowing back Bruce's hair and the two lamps on the front of the incoming train lit up the tunnel.

There wasn't time to fetch Kyle. Bruce stumbled forwards as he stepped down, clattering into the back of a rough-looking dude with punkish hair and slashed-up jeans. He turned on Bruce with an angry face.

"Watch it, you piece of shit."

Bruce ignored the remark as the train doors slid open. He plowed into the crowds of people getting off, but only managed to move fifteen meters along the platform, before having to cut into a carriage as a recorded voice told him to *mind the doors*.

The air-conditioned space was cooler than the stifling interior of the station, and Bruce felt a hint of relief as he grabbed a pole and the train began to move. It was standing room only, but the carriages weren't packed out, so he began moving towards the front of the train, politely asking people to make way.

"Sorry, I've lost my auntie . . . 'Scuse me . . . Coming through."

The design of the Hong Kong metro gave Bruce a huge break: Instead of separate carriages, the train was made up of an unbroken tube, with a bendy section every thirty-five meters to enable it to turn corners. The train was slowing up for the next stop by the time Bruce made it to the front section, which was less crowded than the center.

The Australian had found an empty seat, and as people stood up to get off, Bruce grabbed one for himself, squeezing between two fat ladies twenty meters away from his target. It was close enough to eyeball the Australian, but not so close that the Australian would pay any attention to him.

Bruce took out his phone, hoping to contact Kyle, but there was no signal in the tunnel, so he grabbed a discarded newspaper off the shelf behind. The text wasn't English and while six weeks in a Hong Kong school had brought his conversational Cantonese close to the level of a native speaker, he still found the weird little squiggles the language was written in hard work. After a couple of lines, he gave up and stared at a car ad.

• • •

The Australian stood as the train slowed down for its fifth stop. Bruce had been watching him out of the corner of his eye and nothing seemed to suggest that he was suspicious.

When the train stopped, Bruce and the Australian exited through separate doors. Awkwardly, Bruce was nearer to the exit, so he rested his trainer on a bench and fiddled with the shoelace until the Australian was in front of him. Before giving chase, he pulled on a Nike baseball cap to alter his appearance slightly.

At this end of the line the train ran just a few meters below street level. After passing through the turnstile, the station exit was a short flight of steps up from the platform. They were on a four-lane road, lined with office blocks and hotels. The sky was now completely black and the evening breeze had some bite. Apart from a few bars and restaurants, the shops all had their metal shutters pulled down for the night.

If he'd had the chance, Bruce would have contacted Chloe back at the apartment to say what was going on, but within fifty meters of the station the Australian pushed his way through a revolving door and into the lobby of a smart hotel.

Bruce followed a few meters after him. The place looked expensive and modern: moody lighting, abstract art, a slate floor, and black marble columns. There was a rowdy scene in the bar off to one side, as a bunch of tanked-up businessmen watched a horse race on a big-screen TV.

The Australian headed through the lobby and straight

for the elevator. With no idea what floor he was staying on, Bruce had no option but to stand alongside his target and wait. He felt nervous, but if the Australian remembered him from the train, he wasn't showing it. Or maybe he did remember, but wasn't sweating over the presence of a thirteen-year-old boy.

The elevator made a *bing-bong* sound and the doors slid, revealing a glass sided car with a marble floor. Bruce let the Aussie step in and press the button for the nineteenth floor. As the door closed, Bruce reached towards the buttons and made an *oh* sound, as if to say, *my goodness, we're on the same floor.*

This was easily the most suspicious thing Bruce had done, but again the Australian took it in his stride. As the elevator moved slowly up the outside of the hotel, both passengers stared out of the glass sides at the surrounding skyscrapers and the view over Hong Kong harbor. A giant cruise liner heading for the ocean terminal was ablaze with yellow light.

"That's one *beautiful* rowboat," the Australian said, leaning his giant hands on the leather-padded railing.

Bruce was tense and got thrown off balance by the sudden outbreak of conversation. "Um, yeah. Probably stuffed with fat old people though."

The Aussie laughed. "You're probably right. Whereabouts is that accent from, London?"

Bruce shrugged. "My parents came from Wales originally, but my dad works for a bank and I've lived all over the world."

By the time Bruce said this, the elevator had slowed and the doors were splitting open.

"Well good night, son. Enjoy your stay."

Bruce stepped out of the elevator and pretended to be confused by the sign with the different room numbers and arrows pointing in three directions. The Australian strode past a line of massive cacti and purposefully onwards down a thickly carpeted corridor towards his room.

Unfortunately, he didn't have far to walk. Bruce panicked as he looked around and saw that the Australian had stopped outside the second room along and was already pushing his door open.

"Hey, mister!" Bruce shouted. "I think you dropped this."

The man looked mystified as he backed out of the doorway. As Bruce strode quickly towards him, holding out the first random scrap of paper he'd found inside his jacket, he reached into the opposite pocket and slipped a brass knuckleduster over his fingers.

The Aussie was a big bugger and Bruce wasn't taking any chances.

CHAPTER 6

BRASS

As he closed in, Bruce glanced inside the Australian's hotel room. The lights were off, so it looked like he was alone.

"Did you just follow me up here, kid?"

The man's expression was curious rather than fearful. If Bruce had been an adult, he would have instantly suspected the Hong Kong police or Chinese secret service. But he assumed that the slim thirteen-year-old with a mass of tangled hair was just a lonely kid who'd taken the casual conversation in the elevator for more than it was worth.

"I don't know what your problem is, son, but—I'm really sorry—I've got things to do."

The man put up no defense as Bruce landed a quick jab with the brass knuckle. It sliced open the side of the Australian's head and sent him stumbling backwards into the room.

Unfortunately, it wasn't the knockout blow Bruce had hoped for. As the door of the hotel room slammed shut behind him, Bruce landed a roundhouse kick in the man's stomach. But when he closed in to take another swing with the knuckleduster, the dazed Australian kicked back. Bruce dodged and the kick only glanced across his ribs, but his opponent was twice his weight and it sent him slamming against the doors of a wardrobe.

The Aussie wiped his mouth on his jacket before facing Bruce off in a serious-looking fighting stance.

"So, you know some moves, eh?" He grinned, as blood trickled down his head. "What are you, the world's titchiest mugger?"

"Something like that," Bruce said, trying to sound more confident than he felt.

Now he'd lost the element of surprise, Bruce was worried that he'd be outmatched by a significantly larger opponent who'd clearly done martial arts training.

"Why don't you back out the door and we'll forget about this?" the Australian asked. "I won't call the cops on you, I don't want any trouble."

Bruce considered the offer while his heart banged in his ear. His opponent was huge, fit, and knew how to fight. The most important thing you learn in combat training is that you should never bite off more than you can chew.

"Right," Bruce said, backing gingerly towards the

door and even managing an uneasy smile as he grabbed the handle. "Even stevens."

Bruce tugged at the heavy door, keeping one eye on his opponent. As he was about to step out, the Australian suddenly jerked forwards and began spewing up on to the carpet. Realizing that the blow to the head had taken more out of his opponent than he'd thought, Bruce let the door go, then used it as a kickboard to gain explosive speed. He crashed into his weakened opponent with a powerful kick to the head.

The Australian collapsed backwards into a writing desk, clutching a dislocated jaw as Bruce knocked him out cold with another jab. After being momentarily revolted by the chunks of puke all over his hand, Bruce's CHERUB training kicked in.

Priority one was to defend the room in case someone else turned up. Bruce twisted the lock and then flipped across the manual bolt. It's tricky to judge how long someone is going to stay unconscious, so step two was to secure the victim. Bruce grabbed the desktop lamp and ripped it out of the wall socket. He grabbed a multitool from his tracksuit bottoms and cut the plastic flex from the base of the lamp. Then he folded the free cable into equal lengths and sliced it in two.

The unconscious Australian was slumped backwards over the desk. Bruce slid off the knuckleduster and pulled on a pair of disposable gloves, before grabbing the quilt off the bed and throwing it down to cover the puke on the floor. He knelt in front of his victim and began tying his ankles with the flex.

After binding ankles and wrists, Bruce realized his

victim was struggling to breathe. He prised open the mouth and was rewarded with a dribble of sick. Bruce turned his head away from the nauseating smell, then plunged two gloved fingers down the Australian's throat to clear out the muck.

Once Bruce was certain that his victim was breathing properly, he used all his strength to lower the unconscious body to the floor on top of the quilt. Then he adjusted the limbs into the recovery position so that his victim didn't choke while he was unconscious.

Now the room and victim were secure, Bruce switched the soggy gloves for a fresh pair before pulling his mobile out of his jacket.

"John, it's me."

"Bruce, where are you?"

It was only as he stood with his mobile to his face, staring at his giant victim trussed up on the floor, that Bruce got a realistic sense of what he'd just achieved. There *had* to be a navy shirt in this.

"I've got him good," Bruce said jubilantly, almost laughing. "I'm at the Crowne Residence, room nineteen-eleven and our oversize friend is tied up at my feet."

John sounded pleased. "Good job. Was he armed?"

"Nope," Bruce said. "He didn't seem the type, so I risked it."

"Are you OK?"

"Except for the dude's puke all over my jacket, yeah."

"Right," John said. "Do you feel safe up there?"

"I think," Bruce said. "I haven't had much chance to look around, but it seems like he's the only person staying in this room. Are you gonna send in the cavalry, or what?"

"What type of joint is it?"

"Swank," Bruce said. "Five stars, easily."

John tutted. "Place like that is gonna have security cameras everywhere and who knows if the bad guys are friendly with the management. Did he see much of you before you knocked him out?"

"Enough to make a positive ID. We rode up in the elevator together and ended up having a tussle before I knocked him out. He's a bit bloody and I think his jaw might be broken, but he'll still be breathing when the chambermaid finds him."

"Right, in that case, I want you to make it look like a mugging. Take photographs for identification purposes, then steal his passport, money, documents, watch, jewelry, and anything else that looks like it's worth money. Put it all in one of his bags and walk out the front door."

"OK, boss. It's a big hotel, there was a line of taxi's out front when I came in. Shall I head back in one of those?"

"Sounds good," John said. "Don't head directly to the apartment. Ask the driver to take you to the Great Northern Hotel, and I'll meet you in the lobby."

"Who's staying there?"

"Nobody, but it's not far from where I am staying. Best to cover our tracks."

Bruce smiled, realizing he was being daft. "Yeah, of course."

"Call me when you get in the taxi."

Bruce ended the call and pocketed the phone. He crouched over the unconscious man, slid a hand inside his suit and found a wallet. He flipped it open and read the man's name off a credit card: Barry M. Cox.

It was gone ten o'clock when Bruce emerged from a cab outside the lobby of the Great Northern Hotel. John grabbed a smart leather bag as Bruce paid the driver.

"Keep the change."

"We'll head straight back to my hotel," John said as the cab pulled away. "It's only a few hundred meters. How do you feel?"

"No injuries," Bruce said. "But I'm knackered. Can we stop somewhere and get a Coke or something?"

"There's a mini bar in my room," John said as he set off briskly. "We're in a rush: Chloe and Kyle are waiting for us."

"Waiting for what?"

"Chloe's going to take all the documents and paper-work you stole from Cox back to the apartment. She's gonna scan them and e-mail the whole lot through to MI5 for analysis. You said you had a handheld computer?"

Bruce nodded. "Yeah, quite a flash one, it was in his jacket. I tried getting something out of it while I was in the cab, but it's got a password."

"That's no major surprise," John said. "I've got you booked on a BA fight leaving at one a.m. Last check-in for business class is at midnight, which gives you two hours to get yourself cleaned up, fed, and headed off to the airport. Chloe has brought your passport and a change of clothes over to my hotel room. It's a thirteen-hour flight. You land in London at seven a.m. GMT."

"Why am I leaving?"

"Help Earth always uses strong encryption. Any use-ful data on that PDA is going to take serious computer power to decode and that means I want that machine at MI5 headquarters in London ASAP. An intelligence officer will meet you at the gate when you get off the plane and take it off you.

"You'll be taking it because the sooner you're out of here the better. You've almost certainly been filmed by a security camera entering that hotel and then leaving with Barry Cox's bag. Hong Kong makes a lot of money out of foreign visitors and the police take crime against tourists seriously. They'll be on the lookout for a kid fitting your description."

"That's if it gets reported to the police. Cox might prefer to stay out of their way."

"The hotel management are bound to call in the cops when they find him trussed up. Whether Cox files a complaint or not is another matter."

"I cleaned up my fingerprints and I wore gloves during the search, but someone might still pick up traces of my DNA in that hotel room."

"We'll deal with it," John said. "Hong Kong was a British colony for a hundred and fifty years and MI5 still has deep roots around here. Once the heat dies down, we'll make sure any evidence linking you to that hotel robbery goes walkabout."

Bruce nodded. "Do you think there's any chance I could be picked up at the airport?"

John shook his head. "A hotel mugging isn't going to spark a full security alert."

The pair stopped at a crossing and waited for a walk sign.

"So what are you lot gonna be doing while I'm flying back?"

"We're discussing various options," John said. "I've given campus all the details we've got so far. Hopefully they'll come back with solid info in a few hours and we'll be able to start making some decisions."

CHAPTER 7

TIDYING

Kerry was woken by the doorbell at six forty-five the following morning. She rubbed her eyes as she wandered into the kitchen dressed in a gray vest and knickers. A motorcycle courier stood in the doorway and Chloe was signing for a small padded envelope.

"What's going on?" Kerry yawned as Chloe pushed up the door. "You look a state."

"Thank you, Kerry."

"Sorry," Kerry said. "I didn't mean to be rude. . . ."

"I know you didn't." Chloe smiled. "I'm sure I do look pretty rough. My head hasn't touched a pillow yet. Neither has John's."

"Why not?" Kerry asked.

Chloe walked to the cutlery drawer, grabbed a steak knife, and used it to slice open the envelope. "Fuses," Chloe answered cryptically, as Kerry poured out a glass of orange juice and sat herself at the dining table.

Chloe delved her hand into the envelope. She stripped out a layer of bubble wrap before removing four sticks of plastic explosive, identical to the ones Kerry had seen in Clyde's bedroom the afternoon before.

"At two a.m., we got information from CHERUB campus based upon the pictures you shot in Clyde's room," Chloe explained. "The fuses are a special design made in tiny quantities for the CIA. They've never fallen into the hands of terrorists before. The fuse is designed to trigger when air pressure drops below a certain level."

Kerry looked confused. "What good is that?"

"At high altitude, air pressure is lower than at ground level."

"Right," Kerry said. "So if you want to blow up a mountaineer . . ."

"*Or* an airplane," Chloe said.

"Oh," Kerry gasped, feeling like an idiot as she realized that American intelligence didn't go around blowing up mountaineers.

Chloe continued her explanation. "Viennese is a small Italian oil exploration company that just hit big with the discovery of a major oil field in the South China Sea. But they need the financial muscle and expertise of a larger company to develop it. The chairman and owner of the soon to be explosive overnight bag is a guy called Vincent Pielle. He's spent the last couple of days signing deals with executives from two major oil companies. He's chartered a jet out of a small airfield in the New Territories tomorrow morning and he's going to fly his new business partners and senior staff off to some plush Thai resort for a couple of days' rest and relaxation."

Kerry took over. "Except that Clyde Xu will have placed a bomb in his overnight bag that will blow a big hole in the airplane as soon as it reaches a certain height."

"You've got it, Kerry."

"How did we find all this out?"

"The mission support team on campus unearthed the information about the fuses. There's plenty about Viennese Oil's discovery on the Internet and the details that weren't public were easily picked up with a few calls to the right people inside the intelligence services. MI5 and the CIA have always kept a close watch on the oil industry; even more so these days with Help Earth around and the situation in the Middle East."

Kerry looked at the lump of plastic explosives sitting in the middle of the dining table. "I take it that isn't real and we're gonna go into the Xus' apartment and switch it over."

"Uh-huh." Chloe nodded.

"Where did it come from? It looks exactly the same."

"It's an expired batch of the same brand of C4 explosive that Clyde Xu has in his sock drawer. The manufacturers add a chemical to the compound that spoils the explosive after a couple of years. That way, terrorist groups can't stockpile it. Fortunately, the army keeps some old stock on hand to use in training exercises. There wasn't time to fly any in from the UK, so we got the Americans to deliver a few sticks in a diplomatic pouch from one of their bases in the Philippines."

"Couldn't we tip the Hong Kong police off about the bomb being in Pielle's bag?" Kerry asked.

"We could, but swapping the explosive while the Xus are all out shouldn't be hard. It's better if Help Earth think the bomb didn't go off because of a batch of dodgy explosives. If the Hong Kong police came charging in, they'd know someone was on their case."

"What about Barry Cox getting mugged at the hotel though?" Kerry asked. "It happened right after the meeting with Clyde, so it looks dodgy."

Chloe nodded. "They'll be suspicious, but they can't be certain. Anyhow, what really matters is that we've identified a senior member of Help Earth. Hopefully, there will be more information in the items Bruce stole from Cox's room. But even if there isn't, MI5 can start a detailed investigation into where Barry Cox has been over the past few years, what he's been up to, and who his associates are."

Kerry nodded, then looked up at the clock on the wall. "I suppose I'd better take a quick shower and start getting ready for school."

Chloe shook her head. "To quote Alice Cooper, *School's out forever*. Once we've swapped the explosive we're packing up and heading home. John's booked us on the three thirty flight to Manchester."

Kerry rang the doorbell of the Xus' apartment. Rebecca answered in her school uniform and was shocked to see her friend in tears.

"Kerry, my God! What's happened?"

"It's my dad," she sobbed. "He was in a huge car

accident back in London. It looks like he was hurt really bad."

"Oh, Kerry . . ."

Rebecca's mum was inside the kitchen. She overheard and came charging towards the door in a gray business suit and high heels. "Kerry, sweetheart. I'm so sorry."

"It's OK." Kerry sniffed, as Mrs. Xu gave her a sympathetic hug. "We're flying back to England later tonight."

"When will you be back here?" Rebecca asked.

Kerry shrugged. "We don't know. I mean, we only came out here because my dad's starting a new job. If he's badly hurt and he can't take the job, we might not be back at all."

That was enough to start Rebecca off crying too, and before long Mrs. Xu joined in as well, making it three women sobbing in the doorway. Clyde emerged briefly, took one look at the three howling females and promptly dived back into his bedroom.

Forty minutes after the mass hysteria, Kerry, Kyle, Bruce, and Chloe's stuff was lined up by the front door, packed into sports bags and backpacks. The cramped apartment felt sad as Kerry moved between the empty rooms, checking inside wardrobes and under beds to make sure nothing had been left behind.

When she came out of the bathroom, she found Chloe and Kyle in the kitchen watching the video feeds from the Xus' empty apartment on the laptop screen.

"OK, Kerry," Chloe said. "They're all either at school or work. Kyle and I are going in to switch the explosives and clean up shop. Keep an eye out on the camera in the corridor; we'll be wearing radio mics in case you need to speak to us urgently."

Kerry sat in front of the laptop and popped a mint on her tongue as she watched Kyle and Chloe walk down the hallway. They entered the Xus' apartment with an illicit copy of Rebecca's key. Chloe walked into Clyde's room first, unraveled the package in his drawer, and switched the four live sticks of C4 explosive with the expired ones. Once this was done, the pair moved quickly, clambering onto sofas and chairs as they removed the seven hidden cameras and microphones from light fittings. Kerry's five tiny windows into the Xus' apartment slowly turned black.

Finally, as the pair headed back to the apartment, Chloe unhooked the corridor camera that was built into the buzzer on their front door.

Kerry began unscrewing the two small satellite antennas on the balcony as Chloe and Kyle came back into the room, holding carriers stuffed with electronic surveillance equipment and the real explosive. Chloe unzipped the largest of the cases and tucked it all inside with a grin.

"I'll have to make sure I give that lot to John. He'll be traveling on a diplomatic passport."

Kerry put the two satellite aerials into her case and tucked the laptop into the backpack Chloe would carry on board as hand luggage.

"Where are we meeting John?" Kerry asked.

"At the airport," Kyle answered, checking his watch. "Four hours until takeoff, thirteen hours to London, then a couple more to pass through customs and ride the train to campus."

"OK," Chloe said, as she slung the largest of the backpacks over her shoulder and grabbed a suitcase. "Let's get moving. It's usually pretty easy to hail a cab out front."

"Famous last words." Kyle grinned.

Kerry took a glance back inside the apartment as she pulled open the door. She felt a little sad about never being able to see Rebecca again, and she certainly wasn't going to enjoy the nineteen-hour journey home, but she was looking forward to seeing the gang and catching up on six weeks of gossip.

CHAPTER 8

INTOXICATION

EIGHT DAYS LATER

James Adams staggered up the fire stairs to the eighth floor of the main building on CHERUB campus. He wore one sock, boxer shorts, a muddy tracksuit top, and an Arsenal bobble hat as he began pounding a fist on the door of his sister's bedroom.

"Yo, Lauren, let me in," James said, his voice slurring.

James banged again as Lauren emerged behind the door, dressed in a Scooby Doo nightshirt. She had her arms folded and a fearsome look on her face.

"What are you playing at, James?" she whispered angrily. "It's two in the bloody morning."

"I want you to come out and par-tay with me, sis."

"James, I'm not *partying* with anyone. You smell like a pub. How much have you had to drink?"

"Not partying, Lauren." James giggled. "Part*ay*ing."

"James, go down to your room and go to bed. If one of the night staff catches you stumbling around in that state, they'll murder you."

"But I want to have fun," James moaned. "It's Friday night, I got my Advanced Combat Certificate today. We've all been in town celebrating: shopping arcade, the dodgy off-licence, cinema."

"What happened to Gabrielle and the others?"

"Wusses," James sneered. "They all went to bed."

"James," Lauren said irritably. "You're gonna get in *so* much trouble. Then I'm gonna have to spend the next God knows how long listening to you moaning on about it. Go downstairs to your room and *go to bed*."

"Let me in for one minute," James begged, holding up a finger. "I just wanted to say that I love you."

Lauren dived out of the way, as her big brother stumbled forwards and tried giving her a hug.

"You know," James said, "I never get to tell you that I love you anymore. That stupid cow Bethany is always hanging around."

"James, when *exactly* did you and me ever go around saying that we loved each other?"

Lauren flicked on her light, and James noticed that her best friend was sitting up in the double bed scowling at him. There were three other girls lying in sleeping bags on the floor, as well as empty soft-drink cans and plates of half-eaten munchies scattered around.

"We're having a sleepover," Lauren explained.

"Then I'll join you." James grinned.

"Oh no you won't."

James gave Bethany a wave. "Hi, Bethany."

"Drop dead, James."

James giggled. "That's not nice."

"Nor's calling me a cow."

The other three girls were all sitting up in their sleeping bags, watching the drama in the doorway. They were whispering and shaking their heads. Lauren was totally embarrassed.

"Go to bed, James," Lauren repeated, shoving her brother back out of the room.

"OK, I will." James nodded. "Can I come in and have a quick pee first? I'm busting."

Lauren backed away from her door, "Go on, then. I suppose you're satisfied now that you've woken five people up? Make sure you lift up the seat for once, as well."

James stumbled over the legs inside the sleeping bags and walked into Lauren's bathroom. She bunched her fists and grimaced at her sleepy friends.

"Brothers," she huffed. "I'm really sorry about this."

Bethany smiled sympathetically. "You don't need to tell me about them."

"I like the bobble hat." One of the sleeping-bag girls giggled. The three others joined in the laughter, but Lauren wasn't in any mood to see the funny side.

James flushed the toilet and staggered back over the sleeping bags, but this time he managed to stick his foot in a plate of nachos, spewing crumbs and dip over the floor.

"Oh, crap," James gasped, crouching down and scooping up some of the dip with his bare hands.

"James, you're rubbing it all in," Lauren said furiously. "I'll do it, just get out of here."

"Sorry," James said as he opened Lauren's bedroom door to leave. "Good night."

Lauren stamped her foot as she shut the door behind her brother. "Idiot."

"Don't get upset about it, Lauren," Bethany said. "It's not your fault."

A couple of the girls had grabbed tissue from the bathroom and were using it to scoop crumbs and dip off the carpet.

"You know," Lauren said, holding her thumb and finger a few millimeters apart, "I was *that* close to giving him a slap."

"Good morning, James!" Meryl Spencer yelled cheerily as she leaned over James's bed.

Meryl was a retired Jamaican sprint champion who worked as an athletics coach on CHERUB campus. She was also James's handler, a role that was part form teacher and part guidance counselor.

"I've got a Post-it on my desk," Meryl said. "I read a glowing report about you from Miss Takada yesterday afternoon, so I wrote myself a little reminder. The Post-it says: *Make point to see James. Congrats on combat course!*"

James felt like there was a thousand-ton weight pressing down on his head as Meryl sat on the corner of his bed.

"But, judging by your demeanor and the smell of booze in this room, I'd say you took the celebrations a little too seriously, wouldn't you?"

James could hear Meryl's words, but his face was buried in a pillow and he kept remembering horrible stuff from the night before: falling over in the cinema, the popcorn fight, hitting on Gabrielle and failing miserably. And—worst of all—the 2 a.m. scene in Lauren's room. She was going to be furious.

"James, sit up," Meryl said stiffly. "I'm not prepared to conduct a conversation with the back of your head. You've missed first lesson already."

James turned over, not completely surprised that he'd managed to sleep through his alarm. As he moved, he felt his hand slide through something gooey.

I couldn't have.

"Miss, I think I'm sick," James gasped, as he sprung up in a state of shock.

"I'm not surprised, the amount of booze you must have downed last night."

"No," James said anxiously. "Really sick. I think I've done something nasty in my bed."

Meryl scrambled off the bed as James threw back his duvet and braved a look. He caught a waft of vinegar as he realized he was lying in a puddle of salsa.

"Oh my God," James said, scrambling out from under the covers with streaks of chili and onion goo soaked into his boxers and gliding down his legs.

Meryl couldn't help smiling. "I think someone's played a trick on you, James."

James knew it must have been a revenge attack from Lauren and Bethany, but he didn't want to grass them up. Meryl grabbed a large towel out of the bathroom and threw it at him.

"You'd better wipe that lot off before it goes all over the carpet, and get all the bedding down to the laundry as soon as you've showered."

"Yeah," James said as he rubbed his legs with the towel.

"Now, about last night. We're quite lenient about what you kids get up to in your own time. We know the off-licences in town do a roaring trade selling you lot booze and that some of you smoke. But we're prepared to turn a blind eye provided you're sensible about it."

"Yes, Miss," James said meekly.

"In my book, coming back to campus at one in the morning, urinating in the fountain, getting into pillow fights with Dana and Gabrielle, running up and down the fire stairs shouting *Up the Gunners,* and then waking up your sister and half the other kids on the eighth floor does not fit any standard definition of sensible. Would you agree?"

"Yes, Miss."

Meryl jiggled the note again. "Because of what Miss Takada said about your performance on the advanced combat course and because you had genuine reason to celebrate, I'm going to let you off with a warning. But I'm going to have zero tolerance for you consuming alcohol on or anywhere near campus for the next six months. Is that understood?"

James was pleasantly surprised. He was expecting Meryl to fine him pocket money and put him on a week of punishment laps.

"Yes, Miss."

"How's your head?" Meryl asked sympathetically as

James slumped on the edge of his bed trying to ignore the smell of salsa. The hangover made his stomach churn whenever he thought about it.

"Pretty rough."

"I'll write you a note excusing you from this morning's lessons."

"Are you OK?" James asked suspiciously.

"I'm fine, why?"

"You're being nice to me."

Meryl laughed. "Maybe I'm getting soft in my old age. If it bothers you, I can take you out to the athletics track and make you run fifty laps with a hangover."

"No, no, it's good." James grinned.

"Once you've showered, you can make your bed up with fresh sheets and rest until lunchtime. I'm told you've got an appointment with John Jones, and we don't want you turning up for that, feeling like death, do we?"

James looked surprised. "What's that in aid of?"

"I haven't heard all the details about the mission," Meryl said. "But it's a big one. Help Earth related, some-where Down Under."

CHAPTER 9

BRIEFING

James felt sluggish and ended up getting to the mission preparation building a few minutes late. John Jones liked to keep everything just so. All the papers in his spacious office were stacked neatly and everything down to the coffee mugs were tagged with electronically printed labels.

The man himself wasn't in. James was surprised to see Lauren and Dana Smith in the room too. Dana was a bit of a tomboy who preferred the distressed look; sauntering around in an oversize CHERUB T-shirt, trousers pushed down low, and muddy boots with the laces undone. She didn't look much different out of hours, when her uniform got swapped for baggy jeans and a pair of skateboarder shoes that were so tatty you could see her socks bursting out of tears along the sides.

"All right?" James said as he took a chair next to the other two in front of John's desk.

Dana nodded. "Slightly hung over, but not as bad as you I bet. You were *hammered*."

"Tell me about it," James said. "I've taken paracetamols, but I still feel like there's a bloke playing drum and bass inside my head."

"Did you sleep OK?" Lauren asked, grinning cheekily. "How did you feel when you woke up?"

"Slept fine," James said. "Thought I'd cacked myself when I woke up, thank you *very* much. I turned my mattress over when I put the fresh sheets on, but my bed still reeks of that stuff."

"What did you do to him?" Dana asked.

Lauren smiled. "Me and a couple of the girls sneaked in his room and tipped a catering-size tin of salsa on him while he was sleeping. We thought he'd wake up and chase after us, but he was so zonked he didn't even notice."

Dana shook her head. "That's *so* mean."

"Yeah, well *he* came into my room at two in the morning, made an idiot of himself, and woke all my mates up. I've never been so embarrassed."

James knew he was in the wrong and didn't want things to escalate.

"I'm big enough to raise my hands and admit it," he said. "I was wrong, you got me back and I deserved it. Let's not go into this mission with some feud going on between us."

"What are we feuding over?" John asked as he entered his office behind them.

"Nothing," James and Lauren said quickly as they turned around to see that John was with a tough-looking woman with red hair and a freckled complexion.

"Good," John said. "I'd like you all to meet Abigail Sanders."

The kids stood up and shook Abigail's hand. She said *hi* to each of them in an Australian accent.

"So these are my three kids," Abigail said. "They certainly look the part."

"Well, almost certainly your kids," John said as he sat at his desk. Abigail sat next to James on the opposite side as John continued speaking. "All CHERUB agents have the right to refuse a mission and these three haven't even been briefed yet. In practice though, they're usually pretty keen. I've worked here for eighteen months now and I've never known an agent turn a job down."

John explained for the benefit of the three youngsters. "Abigail is an ASIS officer, that's the Australian Secret Intelligence Service. We're hoping that you three will be prepared to work with her on an undercover mission based in Australia."

James and Lauren grinned at the prospect of going to Australia. Dana carried on staring at her boots; but she was the kind of person who probably would have carried on staring at her boots if an atomic bomb went off.

"Are the briefings written yet?" Lauren asked.

John nodded as he stood up and dialed the combination into a large wall safe. He opened the heavy door, removed an envelope, and distributed three copies of the mission briefing.

MISSION BACKGROUND—THE HONG KONG MISSION
In late 2005 the Echelon security network intercepted an e-mail message relating to a possible Help Earth attack in Hong Kong. The CIA contacted the British security service, who still have strong intelligence connections inside their former colony.

After identifying a young activist named Clyde Xu, MI5 decided to infiltrate Xu's family using three CHERUB agents. Their aim was to uncover a more senior member of Help Earth.

After six weeks, this mission proved successful. The CHERUB team foiled Clyde Xu's attempt to blow up a business jet with fifteen oil executives onboard and simultaneously tracked a senior member of Help Earth to his hotel room. After incapacitating the man—who goes by the name of Barry Cox—the CHERUB agent was able to steal his personal

possessions, including a passport,
diary, and handheld computer.

THE EVIDENCE
It took several days to decrypt
all the data on Cox's handheld
computer and analyze the accompanying
paperwork. Unfortunately, the
computer contained little except
saved games for an electronic chess
program. Paper documents gave details
of Cox's recent movements and
recorded expenses, but nothing could
be discerned from them, except that
he had made several flights between
Brisbane and Hong Kong over the
previous six months. The Australian
police could not match Cox's DNA or
fingerprints with any known criminals
in their database.

The MI5 analysts were in the final
stages of the investigation and had
almost given up hope when one of
them unraveled an old credit card
transaction slip in the back of Cox's
wallet. The credit card number on the
slip did not match any of Cox's cards.

The mysterious credit card was
traced to a company called Lomborg
Financial, based in Brisbane. The
transaction was for a lunch at a

Brisbane restaurant six days earlier. The Australian Secret Intelligence Service (ASIS) began a discreet investigation.

The restaurant still had CCTV footage of the afternoon in question. It showed Barry Cox meeting with Arnos Lomborg, chairman of Lomborg Financial. At the end of the meal, Lomborg paid with his credit card. Cox left a cash tip and accidentally pocketed the transaction slip.

With nothing else to go on, ASIS began looking into Lomborg Financial. The family-run company employs thirty people and has fewer than a dozen large clients. Lomborg's biggest client is a wealthy and secretive religious cult known as the Survivors.

When ASIS began investigating this business relationship, they noticed that Lomborg Financial was buying shares and futures through other stockbrokers in order to hide what they were doing. They also noticed that the Survivors' investment portfolio had risen more than 1,000 percent in just four years. These extraordinary profits suggested that the Survivors had some kind of illegal inside knowledge.

It soon became clear that the
Survivors investment strategy
coincided with attacks by Help Earth.
For instance, on October 27, 2004,
the Survivors purchased futures
contracts on four million barrels
of Venezuelan Crude oil. Three days
later, Help Earth destroyed an oil
pipeline between Venezuela and Brazil.
The price of Venezuelan oil rose by
6 percent and the Survivors' profits
exceeded $10 million on an investment
of less than $1 million. Evidence has
also been uncovered that the Survivors
have siphoned $300 million of their
profits into overseas bank accounts.
The most likely explanation for this
is that the Survivors are financing
Help Earth.

As in all intelligence work,
it is essential to gather as much
information as possible before making
the target aware that it is under
investigation. There is already
enough evidence to prosecute Lomborg
Financial and the Survivors with
fraud and money-laundering offenses.
However, ASIS and MI5 feel that
any fast move would involve turning
down an opportunity to probe deeper
and reach into the heart of Help

Earth, perhaps even destroying the organization entirely.

To this end, ASIS has devised a number of schemes to penetrate the Survivors' organization. They believe that a family unit, utilizing CHERUB agents, will stand the best chance of allaying suspicions and infiltrating the secretive cult.

A BRIEF HISTORY OF THE SURVIVORS
In 1961, Joel Regan quit a moderately successful career as a vending-machine salesman. He purchased a disused church building on the outskirts of Brisbane and began to preach his own brand of the gospel.

Regan claimed that he had received a message from God, telling him that nuclear war was imminent and to build an Ark in the Australian outback. Regan said that his true followers would emerge from the Ark as the only survivors of the war and rebuild civilization as a Christian paradise.

Most people expected the thirty-eight-year-old's kooky brand of homespun Christian values and predictions of an apocalypse to fizzle out, but they had not counted upon Regan's experience as a salesman, or his training as an intelligence officer in the Australian army.

Locals who attended Regan's meetings as a joke often found themselves surrounded by attractive members of the opposite sex imploring them to return and many did. Regan also opened his church to local community groups, including single and divorced mothers, war widows, and recovery groups.

Members of these groups were often lonely individuals who took up Regan's invitations to join his religious services and enjoyed the friendly atmosphere within the group, which Regan called the Ocean of Love.

But once a church member felt comfortable inside the Ocean of Love, the more sinister side of Regan's religion would come to the fore. Using a mixture of traditional salesmanship and sophisticated mind-control techniques he'd learned as an intelligence officer, Regan would invite his members to group therapy sessions where they would be asked to relive the most traumatic and upsetting times of their lives.

The sessions were designed to produce the effect commonly known as brainwashing. Regan would make stark contrast between the horrors of the outside world and the comfortable and friendly world of the people he called "Survivors." After as few as three or four intensive sessions, members who were susceptible to the mind-control techniques would begin to show radical changes in their thoughts and behavior. They would become distrustful of formerly close friends and family members and spend increasing amounts of time involved in group activities with the Survivors.

As sessions continued, Regan would begin to emphasize the more eccentric elements of his religion. In particular, the need to build an Ark in the Australian outback. The Ark would have to be completely self-sufficient and strong enough to withstand seven years of turmoil following a nuclear war.

Building the Ark would require vast sums of money. Once they had been successfully recruited, Regan's followers were asked to move into basic accommodations adjacent to his church, donate all their personal wealth to help build the Ark, and serve as a disciple of the church.

The work of Survivors varies. Some

work inside the church, preaching, counseling, and recruiting new members. Others are sent out to earn money, as cleaners, farm hands, construction workers, and even carrying on Regan's original business as a vending-machine salesman.

THE SURVIVORS TODAY
A two-hour flight into the outback from Brisbane will take you to one of the most spectacular and eccentric structures on the planet. Forty-four years after being founded, the Survivors Ark is a spectacular $5 billion construction, combining the high walls and dormitory-style accommodation of a prison, with a 150-meter-high temple, airport, modern offices, educational facilities, and a palatial sixty-room residence that is the official home of eighty-two-year-old Joel Regan. He is Australia's richest and most controversial man.

The Survivors have more than 13,500 full-time members living on twenty-three global survivor communes. Another seventeen thousand regularly attend Survivor meetings and self-help groups. A second Ark is under construction in Nevada and there are plans for a third in Japan.

The cult has sprawling business interests in farming, medical care, and information technology, and is the world's largest provider of vending machines and support services. If the Survivors were a corporation instead of a religious foundation, it would be Australia's tenth largest.

THE CHERUB—ASIS MISSION
The primary aim of the CHERUB—ASIS mission is to infiltrate the inner sanctum of the Ark and try to uncover the links between the Survivors and Help Earth. The mission is likely to take between two and six months to achieve success, and involves four complex phases.

(1) JOINING
Posing as a divorcée and her family, Abigail Sanders and three CHERUB agents will move into a wealthy Brisbane suburb that is known to be a hotbed for Survivor recruitment and activity. All four agents will make efforts to join the cult. This should be easy as the cult is always on the prowl for new recruits, particularly those with money.

(2) INTEGRATING

The four agents will be expected to undergo counseling and become full members of the cult by moving into a commune. It should be noted that once a person understands how mind-control techniques work, they are relatively easy to resist. There is no chance that a young agent who has adequately studied mind-control techniques before the mission will accidentally become brainwashed.

(3) ENTERING THE ARK

While the Survivors' Ark is primarily intended as a shelter in the event of an apocalypse, its day-to-day function is as a headquarters for the Survivors' business operations and a place of education. Unless they are employed as administrative staff, or are members of the cult's elite, adults are only likely to attend the Ark for short religious seminars and ceremonial events such as weddings and christenings.

Younger cult members stand a much better chance of becoming permanent residents inside the Ark. While most youngsters inside the Survivors attend regular state schools, or schools

within their commune, the brightest
10 percent of children aged 11+ are
creamed off and sent to one of five
Survivor boarding schools around the
world. Australian children are sent
to a boarding school within the Ark
itself.

These schools exist to train the
Survivors' Elite Corps, who Joel
Regan claims will run the world after
the apocalypse. Pupils are taught an
eccentric curriculum and graduates
can expect rapid promotion, often
attaining positions of authority
inside the cult by their early
twenties.

All CHERUB agents are intelligent
and it is expected that they will
meet the academic requirements for the
elite school.

(4) MAKING THE LINK TO HELP EARTH
ASIS are currently unsure how deeply
links run between Help Earth and
the Survivors. The arrangement could
be exclusively financial, with the
Survivors using their considerable
wealth to fund terrorist attacks,
or it could be that Help Earth is
effectively a branch of the Survivors,
with Survivors actively planning and

carrying out terrorist acts under the name Help Earth.

According to former members of the Survivors cult who have lived inside the Ark, there can be anywhere up to a thousand Survivors in residence at any given time attending courses and ceremonies. However, the permanent community consists of Joel Regan and a few close members of his family, 120 senior cult officials and support staff, plus about 150 pupils who attend the boarding school.

The community is close-knit and the adults closest to Joel Regan are notorious for their petty jealousies, one-upmanship, and gossip. The children attending the boarding school are expected to do chores inside the Ark and many of the older pupils do part-time administrative jobs.

Although ASIS and CHERUB have had less than a week to prepare this mission briefing, preliminary assessments suggest that CHERUB agents who get accepted into the boarding school and make good use of their espionage training will have an excellent chance of uncovering information about the link between the Survivors and Help Earth.

THE CHERUB ETHICS COMMITTEE
UNANIMOUSLY ACCEPTED THIS MISSION
BRIEFING BUT REQUESTED THAT ALL
POTENTIAL MISSION CANDIDATES CAREFULLY
CONSIDER THE FOLLOWING:

(1) This mission has been classified
HIGH RISK. Agents may be expected
to work in a remote location
without close support from mission
controllers.

(2) The Survivors cult espouses
"traditional" values, including the
physical punishment of children.

(3) Because of the remote location
of the Survivors Ark, agents may find
it difficult to withdraw from the
mission at short notice.

(4) The length of the mission means
you will be separated from siblings
and friends for a significant amount
of time.

CHAPTER 10

AIRBORNE

Dana had been born in Australia and recruited from a Melbourne children's home, but for James and Lauren the trip to Australia was set to be the longest of their lives. The first stint to Singapore was thirteen hours, then they had a six-hour layover before an eight-hour flight to Brisbane.

They flew out on a Sunday morning with John, his assistant Chloe, and Abigail Sanders from ASIS. Once word got around that James and Lauren were going away for up to six months, a few friends decided to make the journey to Heathrow and say good-bye: Kyle, Bruce, Kerry, Callum, Connor, Bethany, and four of Lauren's other girlfriends. While they babbled on the minibus ride to the airport, Dana stuck her iPod headphones in her ears and started reading a battered copy of *Lord of the Rings*. She didn't have any close friends, and while James felt bad for her, Dana didn't seem to care one jot.

Mercifully, the economy section of the plane was booked out and CHERUB had to stump up for business class tickets. After a short wait at the check-in counter, the six passengers headed upstairs and joined the gang in the self-service restaurant.

James got a cooked breakfast with orange juice and went to join the others, but he noticed Kerry was on her own at the next table across and she waved him over.

"Hey," James said. "What are you doing over here?"

Kerry looked down at her mug of tea. "I kept thinking about you when I was in Hong Kong. I was gonna say something when I got back, but I never found the right moment."

James smiled uneasily. "Say what?"

"You know, we've ended up snogging quite a few times since we broke up last September and neither of us has really been with anyone else . . ."

James grinned. "I've struck out *enough* times."

"So Gabrielle tells me." Kerry smirked.

"Yeah, well . . . that one didn't really mean much, 'cos I was so wasted."

"Should I relay that information?" Kerry grinned.

"*No*, she'll kick my arse. So what exactly are we having a conversation about here?"

"When you get back—whenever you get back—I'd like us to give it another go."

James smiled. It was something he'd wanted to hear

Kerry say for five months; just a pity the timing was so awful.

"That's if you're around," James said. "You might be off on a mission yourself."

"I know," Kerry said, stirring her drink sadly. "And I'm not gonna start turning down juicy missions, even for you."

"You're not a cherub for very long when you think about it," James said, shaking his head slowly. "I was talking to Kyle about this before you went to Hong Kong. He's sixteen now. Another year or eighteen months and he's not going to be around."

Kerry smiled. "Mind you, Kyle's such a titch. It's only a couple of tufts of bum fluff that makes him look any older than you."

Kerry looked up with a needy little expression that James recognized as her *I want you to kiss me* face. There were more than a dozen cherubs and staff sitting at the next table, so it wasn't exactly discreet, but James realized it might be his only opportunity in months.

They both leaned forward. It started off with a standard kiss, but they got quite excited and James ended up with his hands around the back of Kerry's head and his T-shirt dragging through the runny yolk of a fried egg.

It took a barrage of bread rolls and butter pats to break them apart.

"Get a room!" Kyle shouted.

Lauren deepened her voice, mocking James. "I don't know why you keep going on about me fancying Kerry. We're just good friends now."

James and Kerry both smiled guiltily at their mates before looking back at each other.

"So, I'll try and keep in touch," James said. "You know, e-mail and that."

Kerry held her mug of tea up to her face, looking sad. "Yeah."

Six weeks of getting up early for ACC training with a full day of school afterwards had left James bruised, aching, and run down. He usually struggled to sleep on airplanes, but this one had sleeper seats that reclined into flat beds and the attentive staff fetched you pillows and a duvet as soon as you showed any sign of nodding off.

When he was awake, James played on his PSP, ate junk food, chatted to Abigail about the Australian lifestyle, and skimmed some books John had got hold of on cults and mind control. The books looked stuffy, but James was amazed by some of the facts and got quite interested.

He'd never devoted any thought to cults, but had always assumed you had to be a whack job to join one. According to the books, the truth was different.

People recruited into cults tended to be thoughtful and intelligent. Their backgrounds were normal, although they were usually recruited at a time in their lives when they were lonely and ill at ease with everyday life. Typical cult joiners were people who had recently divorced, or lost their jobs, university students living away from home for the first time, and older people who'd recently been widowed.

According to one of the books there were seven thousand known cults with more than five million members around the world. They ranged from dirt-poor groups of a few dozen people who lived in tents and ate out of Dumpsters, to billion-dollar corporations with their own TV networks and branded products.

Lauren was in the seat next to James. She'd got interested in the books too, and they kept reading bits to each other, especially the more lurid stuff about cults that had assassinated politicians and kidnapped judges, and especially about mass suicides.

"Here," Lauren said, "listen to this: *There have been more than seventy recorded incidences of mass cult suicide. The largest was the People's Temple, where leader Jim Jones ordered his followers to commit suicide, resulting in nine hundred deaths. Babies and small children who were unable to take their own lives were given bottles laced with cyanide.* Then further down it says, *Cults based around an apocalyptic vision are usually the most destructive.*"

James smirked. "Well, that's reassuring."

February is high summer Down Under, and Australia greeted James with a thirty-eight-degree blast of heat; the muggy kind that makes your shirt stick to your back three steps out of an air-conditioned building.

John and Chloe headed off to check into a hotel in the city. Abigail and the three youngsters took a yellow Toyota taxi. Brisbane was clean and modern, but there were road works on the way out of the airport and they spent three-quarters of an hour tangled in traffic.

While they crawled, the sky darkened and giant globs of rain began drumming the metal roof, while lightning exploded behind the tall buildings in the city center.

Once they got past the jam, they hit 120 kph around the outskirts of the city and ended up in a suburban area ten kilometers from the center.

They pulled into an upscale development of houses. The cropped lawns, recently planted trees, and rain-washed tarmac had the orderliness of a town made from Lego. By the time the taxi pulled onto a sloping brick driveway at the front of an imposing house, the sun was back and the afternoon rain was evaporating into a shimmering heat haze.

James lugged his backpack and a couple of cases inside with him. He dumped them in a large wooden-floored hallway and looked up at two curved staircases and a gigantic concrete dome with a chandelier hanging off it.

"Holy crap." James grinned. "We're loaded."

Abigail smiled as she waddled in behind him and dumped two cases. "Of course were loaded, James. If there's one thing that'll really get the Survivors salivating, it'll be the prospect of recruiting Abigail Prince: wealthy divorcée, settling back in her native Queensland after a gory divorce from her millionaire husband."

"With her three delightful kids in tow," James added.

Lauren and Dana followed in, and they all stood looking up at the fancy hallway for a moment. Even Dana allowed herself to look impressed.

"I haven't seen this place before," Abigail said. "Everything was arranged while I was in Britain. The rooms are supposed to be set up for us, but I don't know whose is whose."

James and Lauren bounded up the staircase to check the upstairs. There were six main rooms on the upper floor and James found his bedroom at the second attempt. Usually, all you have on a mission is a few bits you've packed up and carried with you, but because this mission was so long and because the plan called for the Prince family to eventually move in with the Survivors, James needed all the stuff a wealthy Australian boy was likely to own.

ASIS had gone to great lengths creating the material history of James Prince. He had drawers and wardrobes full of clothes—most of them chemically treated to look lightly worn—and everything else you'd expect, from stationery to a surfboard, a computer, and even a few tatty board games and soft toys that his alter-ego must have grown out of.

James flipped on the air-conditioning and started going through his new clothes to work out what he was going to wear when he came out of the shower.

CHAPTER 11

settle

Thirty-five hours trapped inside airports and airplanes combined with a ten-hour time shift had left James with his worst ever jet lag. He spent the night tangling up his sheets and gave up trying to sleep altogether for a while, spending the first hours of Monday morning wide awake playing on his PSP.

When the sun came up, he had a headache and felt groggy. He found some shorts and swam a few laps of the fifteen-meter pool to wake himself up.

The morning got taken up with the routine details of settling into a new home. James cut an acre of shaggy lawn with a ride-on mower, while Dana called up local tradesmen to arrange for someone to come in regularly and clean out the pool and for a plumber to come and fix a broken tap in one of the en suite bathrooms. Abigail and Lauren drove to Big Fresh and did the grocery shopping.

After lunch they all went out together and visited their high school, which was about three kilometers from home. It was set in a large expanse of grassland. The four long lines of classrooms were at ground level, exiting on to a covered walkway that looped the entire school. They had a quick introductory meeting with their new deputy headmaster and Abigail shelled out five hundred dollars in the uniform shop.

On the way home they stopped at Target and bought a bike for Lauren—something ASIS seemed to have over-looked—before heading back out for dinner at a fancy restaurant on the Brisbane River.

The food was Mexican, and they ate in a private function room overlooking a harbor full of flash yachts, powerboats, and motor launches. John and Chloe were there, along with a psychology professor from Brisbane University called Miriam Longford. James immediately recognized her name from one of the books he'd skimmed through on the flight over.

Longford had counseled hundreds of ex-Survivors who'd been traumatized during their involvement with the cult. Recently, she'd been involved in a legal wrangle with the Survivors over a book she'd written about them.

Although Longford had done criminal profiling work for ASIS and the Queensland police, she'd only been sworn to secrecy and informed about the existence of CHERUB a few hours earlier. She was fascinated by the psychology behind using children in undercover operations.

As the meal stretched through dessert, coffee, and three extra rounds of drinks, Longford answered dozens of questions from the kids and threw dozens back. By the time they left, the three cherubs felt they had a much deeper understanding of the Survivors than ever could have been gleaned from books.

It was dark by the time Abigail drove them home in their smart E-class Mercedes wagon. James was relieved to find himself feeling sleepy at the right end of the day, but he was depressed at the prospect of having to sit through school in the morning.

At least the uniform wasn't bad: polo shirt with the school logo on the breast, navy cargo shorts, and you were allowed to wear trainers and whatever socks you liked. Before joining ASIS, Abigail had worked her way through university in the kitchen of a top hotel. She set the three youngsters up for the day with a blinding cooked breakfast plus a fruit garnish and French toast on the side. Their packed lunches had fancy-looking rolls, with fresh fruit salad and handmade cake from a bakery Lauren had spotted on the drive back from the supermarket.

The three kids set off on bikes at 8:40 a.m. As they got closer to the school, the population of bikes grew, until they pulled into a noisy mass of youngsters jumping off and walking their bikes under a covered shed, before locking them to the metal railings spaced every few meters.

"Later," James said to his real and pretend sisters as he headed off to a formroom that had been pointed out by the deputy headmaster the afternoon before.

James moved slowly, anxious not to make the wrong impression on his new classmates. Until now, James's missions had required him to get in with a bunch of boys with a similarly lax attitude to work and class discipline to his own. On this mission, James had to override his natural instincts to muck around and be one of the lads. He had to appear shy and troubled, a kid who'd been upset by his parents splitting up and being forced to move into a new neighborhood.

Even the youngest Survivors were asked to prowl for potential recruits and the idea behind James acting this way was to pique the interest of the seventy-odd pupils of North Park High School who lived in the nearby Survivors' commune. That meant, on average, there were two Survivor children in each class. Unfortunately, ASIS had planned the mission at short notice and hadn't been able to identify whether there were any Survivor students in James, Lauren, and Dana's tutor groups.

As James stepped out of the bright sunlight into a classroom, he deliberately found a lonely seat in the back corner where he could study his classmates. Every kid wore school uniform, but James had learned that Joel Regan didn't splash out on designer gear for the children who lived in his communes around the world. He scanned along the rows of kids. Nike Air trainers, expensive backpacks, flash watches or jewelry were all signs that you didn't live at the commune.

It took a couple of minutes for James to spot something he liked the look of: at the front of the classroom in the good-kid zone, a boy and girl sat together. The girl had a fit body and a nice face, but her long hair was tied back into a severe bun, her uniform looked like a hand-me-down, and she wore basic canvas plimsolls, with bright pink socks. The boy sitting next to her was heavy-set, with dark sweat patches on his polo shirt, brutally short hair with the acne in his scalp showing through, and a pair of no-brand running shoes with chunks of the sole drooping off at the back.

First lesson was history, and James managed to sit beside the sweaty boy. The teacher was a youngish woman with a square jaw and manly shoulders. She hadn't quite mastered class control and a group of boys took full advantage, talking about a fight that had happened before school that morning and some stuff that had gone down at the beach the previous Friday night. Before long, a couple of boys were out of their seats facing towards their friends and the teacher lost her rag.

"You boys *sit* down."

James could tell the cool kids didn't have much respect from the way they sauntered back to their seats. Five seconds after the teacher went back to writing on the blackboard, one of the boys chucked a massive chewed-up paper spitball, and it splatted against the rolled-up projector screen.

"Right!" the teacher shouted. "Who threw that?"

A girl sitting directly behind James put her hand up and tried to keep a straight face. "Miss, I think it came in through the window."

"Don't be ridiculous," the teacher said.

All the kids at the back of the classroom were laughing and acting rowdy, and James couldn't stand not being able to join in and have a laugh. He wanted to know about the fight, he wanted to chat up the smirking girl with incredible legs sitting behind him, but he had to shrivel into himself and be James Prince, the lonely kid. It was agony: like living in a sweet shop and only being allowed to eat sprouts.

The sweaty patches on the dude in the next seat got bigger as the lesson wore on, but he didn't say a word. When class ended, James tapped him on the back and spoke politely.

"Excuse me."

He'd tapped the boy, but it was the girl who answered. "What is it?" she said, breaking into a slight smile and tilting her head to one side. The mannerism made her seem motherly, and a lot older than fourteen.

"Um, next lesson," James said, sounding confused. "It says room W-sixteen on my timetable. Do you know where that is?"

"W means the west block," the girl explained. "Along the path to the end of the row and turn left. I've got a different class, but it's on my way if you want to walk with us."

James grinned, not a confident James Adams grin, but an uneasy James Prince grin.

"I'm Ruth and this is my brother Adam," the girl said as they walked along the sunny path between classrooms. "Where are you from?"

"Sydney originally," James said. "But the last couple of years I've lived in London."

"Oh, that must have been great. You've really picked up their accent."

"Explains why he's so pale," Adam said, stuttering on the *P*.

James didn't think of himself as pale, but he did look pasty among kids who'd grown up in year-round sunshine.

As James walked alongside his two new pals, one of the lads from the back of the history class walked past and nudged him in the back.

"Mind the freaks, new kid," he said.

Another simultaneously passed Ruth on the opposite side and coughed loudly. *"Loooooonies,"* he chanted.

The boys jogged away, looking pleased with themselves.

"What was that about?" James asked innocently.

"They mock us because of our beliefs," Ruth answered stiffly. "But we never rise to words of devils."

CHAPTER 12

PACING

The faster the mission progressed, the greater the chance that something could be done about Help Earth before their next major attack, but things couldn't be forced. Rushing might create suspicion and slow every subsequent stage of the mission, or even destroy their chances of getting inside the Ark and penetrating the Survivors' inner circle.

Over the following two days of school, James had a few conversations with Ruth and Adam. One time he asked a couple of questions about the commune. Ruth was happy to share knowledge and even gave him an introductory pamphlet from her backpack: *Ten myths and ten facts about The Survivors and their Christian lifestyle*. James took the pamphlet and studied it, but made no comment.

• • •

James was average height for his age, but he was naturally stocky and CHERUB's physical training programs had built him into a person who was obviously better not messed with. Even though he acted withdrawn, nobody had the stomach to give him any stick.

Dana got a few hassles from boys hitting on her, but she'd had years of experience at telling them where they could stick their idea of a night on the beach.

Lauren had a tougher time. There had been a mix-up about her age between CHERUB and ASIS, which had left the eleven-year-old in a first-year class with twelve- and thirteen-year-olds. By the time the mistake had been recognized, the paperwork for the Prince family's identity had all been sorted and putting things right would have delayed the start of the mission by up to a week.

Lauren was easily clever enough to cope with the schoolwork, but having pale skin and an English accent, combined with being smaller than most of her classmates, made her a target for constant verbal bullying and earned her the name *Pommy Girl*.

The two main bullies were called Melanie and Chrissie. They both looked older than thirteen, with bums and breasts eager to escape their uniforms. On Friday morning, the two of them started on Lauren as she walked between the bicycle racks and her formroom. They walked behind and kept slapping her backpack, knocking her off-stride.

"Leave off," Lauren said furiously.

"Leave off," they mocked.

They sat in a different part of the classroom during registration, but first lesson was math and they sat at the next table to Lauren. As the teacher handed out marked textbooks, Lauren set out her pencil case with her math stuff in it and put a chewy sweet in her mouth.

"Can I have one please?" Melanie asked, acting as if butter wouldn't melt.

Lauren reluctantly held out the packet of sweets, but instead of taking one, Melanie snatched the lot. She took one for herself, before passing the packet on to Chrissie.

"Hey," Lauren said angrily.

As Melanie gave Lauren a look as if to say, *what you gonna do, titch?* Chrissie held the sweets out to a group of boys.

"Pommy Girl's giving away her lollies."

The boys grabbed the packet and passed them around until there were none left. The teacher noticed as he got back to the front of the classroom.

"Excuse *me*, who gave you lot permission to eat in class?"

"They're Lauren's, sir," Melanie said.

The teacher tutted. "Lauren, I know you're new here, but kindly remember that we don't allow eating in class."

As soon as the teacher turned back to face the blackboard, Melanie grinned and gave Lauren the finger.

"Bitch," Lauren snarled.

"Why don't you cry, Pommy Girl?"

"Do you want me to punch your face in?"

Melanie laughed. "You're too little. You're not even tall enough to punch me in the tits."

Lauren was bursting with anger. She knew she was a trained CHERUB agent and that her character, Lauren Prince, was supposed to be quiet and withdrawn, but she found it unbelievably hard putting up with this kind of abuse for hours at a time.

She tried thinking positive thoughts, like how this mission could make her one of the youngest ever black shirts if they pulled it off and how she'd be able to laugh about it with Bethany and her other mates when this was all over.

"Earth to Lauren, can you hear me?" the teacher asked sarcastically. "Stop staring at your desk and start copying this diagram off the board, *please*."

Lauren grabbed her pencil and began writing the title on a clean page in her textbook. As she was halfway through drawing up pie charts from statistics written on the board, she felt a sharp pain in her upper arm. She was too shocked to make any noise as a drip of blood welled up on her skin. Melanie had stabbed her with the point of a compass.

Up to now it had just been verbals and the odd shove, but the stabbing was clearly a major escalation. Lauren contained the urge to lash out as she dabbed her blood on to a tissue.

"Wanna make something of it, Pommy Girl?"

Lauren grinned uneasily. Her arm hurt, but she bit her lip and looked back at her textbook.

Concentrate on the mission.

"Pooooommy girl," Melanie whispered as she menacingly twirled the compass in her hand.

Melanie lunged forward with the compass again, but this time Lauren was ready. She sprang up, knocking her chair backwards, and grabbed Melanie's wrist. She jerked Melanie forward, and swung a punch with her free arm.

The fist landed square on Melanie's lips with enough force to knock her sideways out of her chair and into Chrissie's lap.

"Satisfied now?" Lauren said as she bunched her fists and defied Chrissie to stand up and get a taste for herself.

Melanie's mouth was bleeding and there were gasps and a few *holy shits* from her classmates. She started bawling as the teacher came charging between the desks towards them. Lauren let him push her backwards into her seat.

"What in the name of *God* is going on?" the teacher shouted.

"I'm sick of her winding me up!" Lauren screamed. "She's been doing it since I got here, and I'm not having it anymore."

Lauren sat back down in her plastic seat and started to sob. Part of it was put on, because you'd expect a girl in her first week at a new school to be upset when she got herself in serious trouble, but part of it was real. She'd acted out of character and was worried it might have harmed the mission.

The deputy headmaster looked across his desk at Lauren.

"So, you say Melanie stabbed you with a compass and that she was bullying you, but why didn't you come and speak to your form tutor? A violent response was entirely inappropriate."

"I know, sir," Lauren said sheepishly.

"Melanie needed four stitches in her bottom lip. Under normal circumstances, your behavior would have resulted in immediate suspension. However, I can see

from the blood on your shirt that you were clearly pro-
voked and I believe Melanie and Chrissie had a history
of exactly this sort of unpleasantness at their previous
school. I think you'll benefit from speaking to one of our
student counselors."

Lauren nodded.

"OK," the deputy head smiled. "Why don't we try
to write this difficult first week off and you can make a
fresh start on Monday?"

Lauren nodded. "Thank you, sir."

"And, just out of curiosity, where did you learn to
throw a punch like that?"

"My dad," Lauren lied. "He was a karate champion
when he was at uni. He taught all three of us from when
we were little."

CHAPTER 13

INVITATIONS

Lauren had to spend the remainder of the day sitting at a desk in a corridor outside the senior teachers' offices. She worried what Abigail and John would say when they found out what she'd done, but the more thought she put into it, the more she suspected that it probably hadn't caused the mission any lasting damage.

When it got to lunchtime, Lauren was allowed to go off and meet James and Dana in their usual secluded spot. She bumped into a half-dozen of her classmates, who were on her side all of a sudden.

"That big lump totally deserved it, Lauren."

"Maybe you could teach me some of your moves."

"Little tiger." One of the boys grinned. "Come and rough me up anytime, Lauren."

The group laughed and Lauren smiled at them, but she was pretty disgusted. Not one of them had helped her when she was just the titchy new kid, but now the balance of power had shifted they wanted to suck up. She couldn't resist eyeballing the lad who'd called her *little tiger*.

"Didn't you eat one of my sweets earlier?"

The kid looked worried. He knew an encounter with a smaller girl who packed a serious punch wasn't going to lead anyplace good.

"It was a joke, Lauren. . . . You know . . . ? I never realized how bad those two were riding you."

"I tell you what, son," Lauren said, playing up her London accent. "You bring me a packet of sweets on Monday and I won't say anything more about it, OK?"

"Yeah." The kid nodded. "Don't worry. I'll get them."

As Lauren walked away, his mates were teasing him. "Man, I hope you forget. I want to see that little girl batter you."

She headed for the spot where she always met James and Dana. They sat in the grass eating one of Abigail's killer sandwiches.

"Oh dear, oh dear, oh dear." James grinned. "I heard what happened. I thought I was supposed to be the violent one in the family."

Lauren pointed fiercely at him. "Shut it, James, I'm not in the mood."

"What did you get?" Dana asked.

"Nothing," Lauren said. "Except I've got to write an apology and stay after school to see some dumbass student counselor."

The counselor was sixteen years old, with shoulder-length blond hair, a little on the dumpy side but you wouldn't have called her fat. After four days at North Park, Lauren had got so that she could recognize a member of the Survivors with a glance.

There were lots of clues. Not just the shabby uniform and no-brand accessories, there was something distinctive about their body language: a bounce in their step and the appearance of being slightly happier than a kid wandering a school corridor has any right to be.

"Hi," the girl said, reaching out to shake Lauren's hand. "You must be Lauren Prince. I'm Mary."

Lauren had spent most of the day stuck at the desk outside the senior teachers' offices, so she was glad to get away.

"So, how's this work?" Lauren asked as they headed towards an empty classroom.

"I've been assigned as your student counselor," Mary explained. "If you have any problems at school or home that you want to discuss in confidence, I'm always ready to listen."

"So, in confidence means you can't tell teachers what I say?"

"Absolutely not," Mary said, smiling as usual.

"So, what if I told you I'd killed someone?"

Mary laughed. "It's confidential. Have you killed anyone, by the way?"

Lauren smirked. "Not that I can remember."

"That's a good start."

Mary stopped by a classroom door. She unlocked it and led Lauren inside.

"Plant your bum," Mary said. "I've got some tins of drink and a few biscuits if you'd like something."

Mary got Lauren a Sprite and a Pepsi for herself, before the two girls sat at a desk and turned their chairs to face each other.

"I'm afraid the drinks are warm," Mary said. "No fridge in here."

Lauren took the can and broke it open.

"OK, let's start," Mary said. "How did you end up at North Park High?"

The school wasn't air-conditioned, so the kids always headed straight for the shower when they got home. By the time Lauren arrived from her student counseling, James and Dana were sitting on the living room carpet with wet hair, watching twenty-four-hour news. The pictures were helicopter shots of a 170,000-ton oil tanker breaking apart in the Indian Ocean.

"What's this?" Lauren asked, a touch breathless from her ride home in the sun.

James looked backwards at his sister. "It was a brand-new tanker out of a shipyard in Japan. Looks like it got rammed by a powerboat packed with explosives."

"No oil on board," Dana added. "The crew all got off in lifeboats and they seem to think that the powerboat was under remote control."

Lauren looked stunned. "Help Earth?"

"Nobody's admitted responsibility, but who else is it gonna be?" James asked.

"Anyway," Lauren said, struggling to take her eyes off the TV, "I've got to go and speak to Abigail."

"I already sweet-talked her about what happened at school," James said. "She says it's OK to stick up for yourself, as long as you don't make a habit out of it."

Lauren shook her head. "It's not that. The student counselor I had to see was one of *them*."

Dana looked surprised. "Eh? That's outrageous. How can the school allow a bunch of religious nutter kids to counsel the ordinary ones?"

James shouted into the kitchen, "Abigail, you'd better come listen to this!"

Abigail came through wearing an apron with flour marks on it. "I hope you all like veal meatballs." She smiled.

James slapped his tummy and grinned. "You're gonna make us fat, Abigail."

"What did you call me in for?"

Lauren explained about her counselor.

Abigail wasn't surprised. "It's a statewide thing. I've read about it in the newspapers. The counseling encourages younger and older kids to interact and helps them deal with bullying and other issues."

James nodded. "Some schools in Britain do it as well. But you wouldn't think they'd let Survivors become counselors and go round recruiting kids into their cult."

"They've got no choice," Abigail said. "If Survivor kids weren't allowed to become counselors, the group would kick up some big legal stink about religious discrimination and start sending in the lawyers."

James looked at Lauren. "So, did this Mary chick try and recruit you?"

"A bit." Lauren nodded. "It wasn't the main thing. But she asked me all about my background and about you lot, and our dad leaving and living in England. Then she asked me if I had any friends around, so I go, 'No,' and she goes, 'Well, we've got this group that meets up at our commune on a Saturday.' So I acted like I was just a tiny bit interested, and she told me that it was just a fun group. You know, I'd make some friends and stuff, play games, sing songs. She made it sound like girl guides or something."

Abigail nodded. "Did you say you'd go?"

"No, 'cos I thought you might have said it was too soon and not wanted me to. So I just said I'd think about it. She wrote the phone number and address down for me. She said to call ahead and say how many of us were coming."

"She invited all of us?" James asked.

"Yeah." Lauren nodded. "Including Abigail."

James looked at Abigail. "So, do we go or not?"

Abigail rubbed a floury hand against her chin. "Well, we weren't looking to make first contact with the group until we'd been in the area for a little bit longer, but this is such an unforced opportunity. I'll run it past John for a second opinion, but I don't think it would do any harm to show our faces up there."

CHAPTER 14

TOGETHER

Abigail dropped the kids into the center of Brisbane on Saturday morning and left them to spend the day shopping and exploring their new hometown. She picked them up late afternoon and fed them another bang-up meal before the trip to the commune in the evening. Dana stayed home, so that it didn't look as if they were trying too hard.

The Survivors' original Brisbane church and ramshackle commune was now known as the Survivors' Museum. The current commune was a conversion of a failed shopping mall. The illuminated store signs had been replaced with wooden crosses and Christian slogans.

There were less than a hundred cars on a stretch of tarmac designed for thousands. Abigail pulled up by what had once been the main entrance to the mall.

James grinned at Lauren as they got out the back of the car. "Today's special mall offer, crazy mind-bending religion, just twelve ninety-nine."

Lauren grinned, but Abigail shushed him. "James, keep in character and remember to call me mum."

"OK, *Mommy*."

Three Survivors emerged through the automatic doors at the main entrance. James recognized Ruth, Lauren recognized Mary, but they were led out by a grinning middle-aged man with rectangular glasses, beard, and a corduroy jacket.

"Hello, I'm Elliot Moss," the man said, grinning at Abigail. "It's *fantastic* that you all took time to come out here and meet us this evening."

Abigail grinned. "Well, actually, I was going to drop the kids off at the youth group."

"Oh," Elliot said sadly. "Couldn't you just spare us a few moments? We've got coffee and excellent cake inside. How do you like your coffee?"

"Strong and black," Abigail said.

"You'll love ours, then; it's grown on Survivor plantations in Nicaragua. We sell it to gourmet delis and coffee shops all over the world and make sure that the growers earn a decent living out of it."

Abigail glanced at her watch, before tapping the plipper to lock her car. "I'll just pop in for a little while, then."

"Great." Elliot beamed as he turned around and led them towards the ex-mall.

Ruth paired off with James and Lauren with Mary. They

were led through the automatic doors, beneath a sign that read, EVERY HONEST SOUL IS WELCOME HERE. The main hallway was run down and had lots of tasteless 1970s touches: lurid orange floor tiles, dark wood paneling, and colored panes in the windows. There was a musty smell, caused by too much floor polish and bad air-con.

Elliot whisked them into a medium-size ex-shop that now contained a reception area and a multimedia exhibition about the Survivors. The displays focused upon Christian beliefs, charity work, and the humble beginnings of the Survivors, rather than the $5 billion Ark and Joel Regan's predictions of a nuclear apocalypse.

At one end of the room, a narrator with a sturdy voice was telling the story of Regan and his rise from humble farm boy to a religious leader of global stature, while a giant video screen showed archive footage of Regan shaking hands with Bill Clinton, Elvis Presley, and the pope. These shots were followed by pictures of contented African women carrying sacks of grain with the Survivors logo on and the interior of a vending-machine repair shop staffed entirely by disabled people.

"Every year the Survivors raise more than two hundred million dollars for some of the world's neediest people. . . ."

Mary handed James and Lauren clipboards with forms to fill in and asked them to look up as she snapped their photograph with a digital camera.

"It's just a formality," Mary said. "In case you're in one of our groups and you have an accident or something."

The form asked James for basic personal information, such as name, date of birth, home phone number, and address. James had read that the combination of friendliness and a desire to get hold of personal information were classic first steps in a cult's recruitment process.

Elliott handed Abigail a much longer form and she returned a look of surprise.

"What's all this?" she asked, flipping through six pages of questions.

"We like to have your contact details in case of an emergency involving a child at one of our youth groups," Elliott explained. "The rest of the form is a survey. We're trying to get a better idea of who is using our center here. You don't have to fill it in, but we'd really appreciate it if you could help us out."

"Well . . . ," Abigail said.

"I tell you what, Abigail." Elliot grinned. "While you're doing that, why don't I indulge you with a cup of our *amazing* coffee and a piece of cake?"

Abigail smiled. "That's really nice of you, Elliot."

As Elliot headed off to get the cake he took the forms from James and Lauren and looked at Ruth. "Why don't you take your young friends through to the community room?"

They headed out through the shop front and halfway along the mall corridor, passing disused shops that had been turned into offices and storage areas. The community room was a giant open space that had once been the ground floor of a department store. It had been turned into a gymnasium, with green rubber flooring. There was basic sports equipment spread around, like goal posts, basketball hoops, and cricket stumps. A hand-painted banner hung along the far wall: *Welcome to the Ocean of Love.*

There were about fifty kids spread over the gym, and based upon the amount of unfashionable footwear,

three-quarters were Survivors. Some kids were playing volleyball, others soccer, or cricket in practice nets.
A bunch of the youngest kids played a leapfrog game,
supervised by older teenagers. The orderliness surprised
James, given that there was no obvious adult supervision.

"Is there anything you'd like to try?" Ruth asked.

Lauren had her eye on a giant trampoline and headed
off with Mary. James spotted a miserable-looking kid in
the corner and pointed him out to Ruth.

"Isn't that Terry, from our class? I didn't think he was
one of you lot."

Ruth smiled. "Terry's father goes to one of our therapy
groups."

"He doesn't exactly look happy to be here."

"He's a devil," Ruth said.

James looked confused. "Why do you lot call people
devils all the time?"

Ruth smiled again; in fact, Ruth seemed to be smiling
permanently. "We Survivors believe that the world is
divided into a battle between angels and devils. Survivors
are angels. Anyone who isn't is a devil."

"So, am I'm a devil?"

"Not for as long as you have potential to become an angel."

James shrugged. "To be honest, I don't think I even
believe in God."

"Then I feel sorry for you," Ruth said curtly.

"Does that make me a devil?"

Ruth shook her head slowly. She was fourteen, the
same as James, but she had an authority about her that
made her seem far older.

"James, if you're interested in our beliefs I can give

you a book to read. Maybe you could even speak to one of our counselors if your mum will let you. But right now, it's Saturday night, and on Saturday night we invite all of our friends into the community room to play games and have fun. There's only one rule: Everyone has to join in."

"What about Terry?"

"He's a devil. As far as we're concerned, he's not here. So what do you want to play?"

James looked around the gym and spotted Lauren bouncing several meters into the air on a giant trampoline. A group of barefoot girls playing volleyball caught his eye. There were a few mingers, but most of them were fit.

Ruth worked out what he was looking at. "Volleyball, that's a really good idea, James."

They walked over to the girls.

"This is James, everyone!" Ruth shouted excitably. "This is his first visit to our community."

All but one of the girls on the court were Survivors and they stopped playing and smiled while they queued up to shake his hand.

"Have you played volleyball before?" a pretty redhead called Eve asked.

"A couple of times," James said. "Not seriously though."

"That's good," Eve said. "We're not serious and you're only allowed to say positive things on the court."

"Eh?"

"Just follow our lead," Eve said, handing James the ball to serve.

James rested the ball in his palm before batting it away. It skimmed limply over the net, making an easy return for the other team.

"Nice try," Eve said, as she backed up and pounded the ball back over the net.

"Crap," James said as his clumsy swipe missed the ball entirely.

Before he knew it there were three girls in front of him with Survivors' smiles on their faces.

"James," Eve said sweetly, wagging a finger under his nose. "You're doing great, but remember you're only allowed to say positive things."

Ruth had joined the other team to even up the numbers and was grinning through the net. "She's right, James. Negative thoughts are for devils."

James couldn't help smiling back at them. "You girls are weird." He grinned. "Wonderfully, positively, weird."

Eve laughed and gave him a friendly rub on the back. "That's the spirit, James. Do you want to serve again?"

James hung out in the community hall for two hours, following the girls between volleyball, soccer, and the trampoline. When it got to nine o'clock, a couple of adult Survivors came in and switched off most of the lights. Everyone in the hall formed two circles, tired little kids in the inner circle and older kids and teenagers outside. Lauren's counselor Mary stepped into the center of the circle holding a guitar.

James's instincts told him that sitting in a big circle with a bunch of guitar-playing religious nuts was lame, but the Survivor girls who'd all been smiling, chatting, rubbing his back, and hugging him for the past two hours dragged him into the circle and James couldn't help laughing and smiling back. He felt really good as he sat cross-legged on the floor. Eve grinned, held his hand, and sat so close that her toes were touching his knee.

Mary strummed the guitar. James was expecting her to start singing some dreary hymn, but she played a few bars and then chanted.

"Boogie, woogie, woogie, woo!"

Everyone chanted back noisily. "Boogie, woogie, woogie, woo!"

The next line was, "La de, la de, la de, la!"

And everyone chanted back. This chanting went on for ten minutes and James couldn't help getting into the stupidity of it all, with the two girls sitting on either side of him grinning and putting their arms around him. He looked over at Lauren and noticed she seemed to be having a ball too.

At the end of it, Mary played a longer and much more dramatic version of the chanting song, getting faster and faster until all the lights got switched back on. She screamed out, "Are you angels?"

And the kids, especially the little ones in the inner circle, jumped up and answered, "Yes, we're angels."

Mary shouted back, "Little angels go to bed!"

All the little kids began running happily out of the room. A few of them split off and joined parents who'd filed into the gym while the lights had been dimmed, but most were commune members and they headed up a disused escalator to the living quarters.

James couldn't help laughing as Mary called him and Lauren across to the center.

"Did you enjoy yourselves?" she asked. "Are you glad you came?"

It was half nine and James was sweaty and tired after all the exercise, but he felt jubilant.

"Yeah." James nodded. "It was a good laugh."

Lauren was smiling too. Abigail wandered out from the group of adults at the back of the hall.

"Hi, kids," she said.

"Hey, Mum," James said. "Where have you been?"

"I ended up staying here and talking to Elliot," Abigail said. "I'm thinking about enrolling in one of the counseling sessions for single parents."

"Well, I certainly hope you all come back," Mary said. "You seem like such a nice family."

Elliot joined them again. He was holding a carrier bag stuffed with goodies. "I'll walk you to your car," he said as he handed Abigail the carrier. "Those are the books and CDs I spoke to you about, and I put in a bag of our Nicaraguan Roast and a few slices of cake for the kids."

Abigail looked at all the stuff inside the bag. "I must owe you money for some of this."

"I wouldn't hear of it," Elliot said. "Just promise that you'll give me a call if there's anything you want to talk about."

As James, Lauren, and Abigail headed down the mall corridor towards the main entrance, Elliot, Eve, Ruth, Mary, and a couple of younger girls Lauren had befriended walked with them. They followed through the automatic doors and stood around the car.

Even though it was dark, it was still extremely hot and Abigail reached inside the stifling car and turned on the air-conditioning. They waited outside for a minute while the interior cooled down.

Eve smiled at James. "You'll be coming back to see us again, won't you?"

"Sure." James nodded enthusiastically. "Next Saturday."

"Maybe even sooner," Elliot said. "You could come by with your mother when she attends our single parents' group on Wednesday."

"I guess." Lauren smiled. "Maybe my big sister can come too."

The Survivors headed back indoors, waving as Abigail switched on the engine, while James and Lauren belted up in the back.

"That was fun," Lauren said.

"I think the mission's going well," Abigail said.

James realized that he'd been playing sport and chanting with the Survivors all night and hadn't considered the mission for over an hour.

He looked anxiously at his sister. "I think we might have enjoyed ourselves a bit too much in there."

"Eh?" Lauren said as she wiped her shining forehead on the sleeve of her T-shirt.

"I actually want to go back in there and do that again," James explained. "With the grinning girls, and everyone touching me and paying me heaps of attention. It felt *really* nice."

Lauren realized what her brother was getting at. "We knew how it worked. We read all the books and that, but we still fell for it."

Abigail looked between the front seats at her two passengers. "Are you kids saying what I think you're saying?"

James rubbed his eyes and looked ashamed of himself. "It was like falling under a spell."

CHAPTER 15

CONTEXT

Abigail was concerned at the way the kids had lost their objectivity and been lured by the Survivors within hours of entering the commune. She'd also enjoyed her evening with the charming Elliot.

She phoned John first thing Sunday morning and he called the psychologist Miriam Longford for advice. Miriam was arranging a family lunch, but she agreed to speak with Abigail and the kids provided they drove out to her home near the university campus on the opposite side of the city.

A red setter greeted them on the driveway. James's hand got a warm lick as he clambered out of the car. Miriam's young nieces and nephews chased around and splashed in her pool, as she led Abigail and the three cherubs to a muggy double garage. The cars had been pulled out and she'd set some stackable picnic chairs into a circle. It wasn't ideal, but it was private and the rest of her home crawled with relatives.

Abigail explained what had happened over the previous forty-eight hours, from Lauren lashing out in class and getting sent to the student counselor, to their visit to the Survivor commune the night before.

"OK." Miriam smiled. "It's understandable that you're worried by the rush of positive feeling you experienced last night, but I think it will turn out to be a good thing, because it's given you a warning about the power mind-control techniques can have over people who let down their guard."

"It's all to do with the power of context. Have any of you ever heard of something called the *Elevator Door Experiment*?"

Everyone shook their heads, so Miriam began to explain. "A person getting into an elevator will always stand facing the door, so that they can see what is going on and know when it's time to get out. However, what happens if a person gets in and finds that there are several other people already in the elevator facing away from the door?"

"Oh, I've seen this now that you've said it," Abigail said. "If the other people in the elevator are all facing away from the door, then the person getting into the elevator will usually do the same."

"That's it," Miriam nodded. "People think they have free will, but there is actually a strong tendency for individuals to behave in the same way as those around them."

"Like peer pressure at school," Lauren said.

Miriam nodded. "That's a very good example, Lauren.

If you're at school and all your friends smoke cigarettes, the chances are that you'll start smoking cigarettes too. I've been inside that gymnasium you were at last night. Do you remember the big banner along the back of the hall?"

"Welcome to the Ocean of Love," James said.

"That's right, and I'm afraid you and Lauren accidentally dipped your toes into the ocean. I take it the Survivors asked you to call ahead and say you were coming?"

Abigail nodded. "Uh-huh."

"That's so they can set up a welcoming committee. As soon as you arrive there's a friendly face to greet every one of you. Then they take you inside, split you up, and everyone starts acting warm and friendly. They asked you to play sport, because it tires you out physically. But the whole time you were being worn out physically, the compliments and touching built you up emotionally."

"We weren't supposed to say anything negative when we were playing games," James said.

Miriam nodded. "That's a technique called *thought stopping*. By encouraging you to think and say positive things, you inevitably start feeling good. And because you only hear positive things from other people, you start feeling guilty and shut out your own negative thoughts. The good vibe is reinforced with lots of touching, hugging, and even the occasional kiss. Within a couple of hours, you two found yourselves exhausted, but happy and uninhibited. That's exactly the state you want a person to be in if you're trying to sell them something, whether it's a secondhand car or a lifelong commitment to a religious cult."

James and Lauren both nodded.

"It makes sense now you say it," James said. "But at the

time I didn't feel like anything special was happening to me."

"You wouldn't have," Miriam said. "When people hear phrases like *brainwashing* or *mind control*, they imagine that it involves being stuck in a room with a gun to your head, or being tied up and made to watch videos while your eyelids are propped open with matchsticks. In reality, harsh methods like that only create fear and resentment. The techniques used by groups like the Survivors are extremely subtle and all the more powerful because of it."

Abigail looked stressed. "The thing is, can we safely send these kids undercover into that environment? They'd read about mind control in books and you'd spoken to us, but James and Lauren still came out of there like a couple of grinning zombies."

Miriam furrowed her brow and looked thoughtful for a second. "Research has consistently shown that people who understand how mind control works are not susceptible to it."

"But we *did* understand it," James said anxiously.

"No," Miriam said. "You read about it in books and you listened to me speak, but you didn't respect what you'd learned. You went into the commune with your defenses down and you let yourself get drawn in by a few pretty girls telling you what a great guy you are."

James looked sheepishly at the barc concrete between his Nikes.

"Sorry," Lauren said, "we didn't mean to mess up."

"Don't be daft, sweetheart." Miriam smiled. "Older and more experienced heads than yours have thought themselves too clever to fall into the lure of a cult. Hopefully, this has taught all of you an important lesson.

"As long as you immerse yourselves in cult life slowly and

consider the motivations behind the things people do and say at the commune, the danger of becoming brainwashed is virtually nil. If you come by my office on the university campus after school tomorrow, I'll teach you a few basic concentration techniques that will prevent you from being hypnotized or ending up in a state where you're easily manipulated."

Elliot called Abigail on Monday evening and kept her talking about life and religion for over an hour. On Tuesday, Abigail phoned the commune to confirm that she was bringing the whole family the following night when she attended her first session with the single parents' group.

They were greeted in the parking lot by Elliot, Mary, Eve, and a younger girl called Natasha, who had made friends with Lauren on Saturday. James hugged Eve and they kissed each other on the cheek, but this time he reminded himself that Eve's affection was put on to encourage him and his family to become Survivors.

Lauren, James, and Dana were immediately taken in separate directions by their chaperones. The community room was being used by a group of elderly ladies for a music and movement class, so Eve took James upstairs to a shop with an elaborate glass frontage. It had clearly been a jeweler's before the mall went bust.

The inside was filled up with bean bags and foam blocks and a group of teenagers were sprawled over the cushions. There was a TV hanging on the wall, and it was showing a program about the building of the Survivors' second Ark in Nevada.

James smiled. "You've even got your own TV station."

"The programs get flown in once a week from the

Ark on videotape." Eve nodded. "It's a mixture of films, shows from normal TV, and documentaries and news programs that we make ourselves."

"Looks a bit dull," James said. "Can't you flip to something else?"

"No," Eve said, looking thoroughly offended. "We don't want to bring the influence of devils into our home. Besides, it'll be switched off in a minute when our service starts."

As James strode uneasily over stacks of bouncy cushions and trailing legs, he was greeted with smiles and handshakes. A few minutes later, a forty-something women dressed in a white robe came in. She introduced herself to James as Lydia, before sitting in the center of the room.

"Welcome, James," Lydia gushed, as if she'd been waiting her whole life to meet him.

As soon as she said it, the two-dozen teenagers started clapping, before repeating her welcome. When it quieted down, Lydia stared directly into James's eyes and smiled at him.

"James," she said. "You visited us here for the first time on Saturday. Did you have fun?"

James nodded. "Yeah, it was cool."

"You saw the exhibits in the hall downstairs. You saw the good work we do for the environment and for poor people around the world?"

He nodded again, though he hadn't actually paid much attention.

"But I'm told you don't believe in God."

James was surprised to find that his casual remark to Ruth had been reported. He wondered if anything else he'd said would come back to haunt him.

"Well . . . ," he said weakly.

"That's OK, James." Lydia smiled. "Maybe one day you'll feel differently. We can tell that you're a kind and considerate person. We understand that you've moved to a new town where you don't know very many people. But hopefully you've found friends among us here?"

James nodded. "You're all really nice. In fact, you're *amazingly* nice."

James felt cold inside, because he knew Lydia was trying to manipulate him. But he was still disturbed by how easily he'd bonded with the group four nights earlier. If this had been his real life instead of a mission, he'd still be sucking up the warm feelings while the Survivors took control of his life.

"Does everyone here think James could become an angel?" Lydia asked.

"Yes!" every teenager in the room shouted, before breaking out in cheers, whoops, and clapping.

James smiled, but as soon as he found himself feeling genuinely flattered, he used one of the techniques Miriam had taught him. She'd explained that thinking of something you found physically repulsive stops you from becoming overwhelmed by strong positive feelings. In James's case, he'd trained himself to think of a soggy cheese and mayonnaise sandwich that he'd encountered in Arizona ten months earlier. Just imagining the smell of it made him gag.

"James, would you like to learn about the Survivors and the work we do for the planet?" Lydia asked.

He nodded uncertainly.

"We'd very much like you to become our friend and learn about us, James. We don't want to force you into doing anything you don't want to do. But we would like to offer you this necklace as a token of our friendship."

Lydia stood and pulled a leather strap necklace out of a pouch on the front of her robe.

She stood above James. "James Prince, do you take this necklace from us as a symbol of our friendship?"

"Sure," James said, making a point of grinning and nodding as if he was really flattered.

He raised himself up on his kneecaps and allowed Lydia to loop the necklace over his head. Once it was on, she urged James to stand, before giving him a hug. While they embraced, a line of clapping kids had formed behind Lydia and they started hugging him in turn.

They all repeated the same phrase: "Welcome to the Ocean of Love."

After the formal greetings, James found himself surrounded by smiling teenage boys and girls, inviting him to barbecues, ceremonies, and a fund-raising trip at the weekend. When their enthusiasm died down and most of them had wandered out of the room, James found himself back in the company of Eve.

"Wasn't that exciting?" She grinned. "I'm so pleased you chose to take the necklace. It's the first step towards becoming an angel."

"I dunno." James smiled wryly. "You're a nice bunch, but this is all a bit odd if you don't mind me saying so."

Eve ignored the remark. "I visit an old folks' home after school most days," she said. "Maybe you'd like to come along with me tomorrow?"

"Why?" James asked.

Eve tilted her head to one side and gave him an extra special smile. "It's entirely up to you, of course. But I'd really like to give you a taste of the charity work the Survivors do."

CHAPTER '16

ELDERLY

Lauren got her leather necklace that evening in a ceremony identical to her brother's, except that the surrounding kids were her own age. Abigail emerged from her meeting, holding Elliot's hand, looking happy and carrying more Survivors literature and a $229 set of CDs and DVDs in a glossy orange folder entitled *Survive Life!—Revolutionize your lifestyle through the teachings of Joel Regan and his Ocean of Love.*

To make their recruitment as Survivors more realistic, Dana had been asked to take a more skeptical approach. She spent the evening with a seventeen-year-old male chaperone, grilling him ruthlessly about every aspect of Survivor lifestyle, from the negative aspects of living in a commune to questions about how a supposed Christian like Joel Regan had famously sired thirty children with more than a dozen young women. Dana rather enjoyed making her young companion squirm.

It was gone midnight when the Prince family got home from the commune. James scratched and yawned his way through Thursday's lessons. At the end of school, he unlocked his bike and walked it across the playing fields to meet Eve at the rear entrance.

They rode ten kilometers in the blistering afternoon heat. Their destination was a sprawling facility called North Park Elder Care Community. Elliot was waiting for them in the driver's seat of a white van.

"James," Elliot said enthusiastically, as he stepped out. He grabbed the soggy collar of James's school shirt, making sure he still wore the leather necklace, before pulling him into an enthusiastic hug. Elliot stepped back and reached into his shorts, pulling out a painted wooden bead.

"Each bead symbolizes a positive step," Elliot said. "And this afternoon represents your first contribution to our community."

"I thought you were just going to show me around," James said, thinking it best to sound a touch suspicious.

"I'm sure you and Eve will enjoy yourselves," Elliot said, deliberately ignoring James's comment.

James took the necklace off, but he didn't have the fingernails to undo the knot in the leather and slide on the bead. While Eve took care of his necklace, Elliot walked James around to the back of the van. Refrigerated air wafted out as James peered inside at stacks of large plastic trays. Each one was identical; set out with local newspapers, confectionery, cigarettes, small bunches of flowers, drinks, and lottery tickets.

Elliott placed two trays on the tarmac, before stepping inside the van and taking out two collapsible trolleys. The double-handled trolleys unfolded and the trays slotted on top.

"What's all this about?" James asked.

Elliot smiled and rubbed James's shoulder. "I've got to get to six more retirement homes. Eve will tell you what to do."

As Elliot drove away, Eve looped the necklace, complete with bead, over James's head.

"What's this trolley business?" James said. "I thought you were showing me around?"

"Oh," Eve said, sounding wounded. "I told Elliot you wanted to help us with our charity work. He'll be really cross with me."

James acted confused. "Why? It's just a misunderstanding."

"Yes, but the Survivors have had some bad publicity about us taking people and making them do stuff they don't want to," Eve explained. "Of course, it's not like that and we *always* give you a choice, but Elliot's very sensitive about it. He'll go bananas at me if he thinks I pushed you into this."

James realized it was a setup: the way Elliot gave him the bead and ignored his question, followed by Eve saying she'd get in trouble if he didn't do what they wanted.

"I can go inside and call Elliot," Eve continued, sounding worried. "Oh dear, I'm really in for it now."

James smiled and said what he knew Eve wanted to hear. "OK, I'll do it. . . . It was a surprise, that's all."

Eve made a little squealing noise and pulled him into a hug. "Thank you, James. You're fantastic."

"Don't mention it," James said, catching a sneaky downward glance at Eve's cleavage as she squeezed him. "What exactly is it we're supposed to do with this stuff?"

"All we do is take it around to the rooms, knock on the old folks' doors, and ask if there's anything they want to buy."

The home was built on a single floor and the mostly female residents lived in rooms with balconies and private bathrooms. The building was modern and it wasn't horrid, but it seemed lifeless and the squeaky-floored corridors reminded James of a hospital.

After the receptionist buzzed them through a locked door, James followed Eve into the first few rooms to watch her sales technique. Eve spent at least three minutes talking to each resident, most of whom were in the final stages of life and were either bedridden or barely mobile. Eve traded banal news about school and the commune for information about each resident.

Almost everyone bought something. It was usually a small item, like a chocolate bar or newspaper, but there were also requests for Elliot—who visited each resident weekly—to put something on the van. These items ranged from an old gent who wanted a monthly fishing magazine to a brash old lady who requested a particular brand of toilet paper because, *The stuff they give you in here leaves your arsehole as red as a radish.*

After the first few rooms, Eve sent James off to work

a different section of the home. He spent nearly an hour passing from room to room, having more or less the same conversation, which always started with, *Where's Eve today?* and ended with the purchase of a couple of dollars' worth of goodies. James noticed that the prices were double what you'd pay in an ordinary store.

James met a newly arrived resident on his last call. The name on the door said Emily Wildman, and he found her sitting on the corner of her bed looking bewildered. Some of her belongings were still in packing crates, the curtains were closed, and she'd clearly been crying.

"Hello," James said, trying to sound friendly as he pushed his trolley into the room.

"What are you; a bloody boy scout?" she said abruptly.

James did a little spiel that Eve had taught him, explaining that he'd volunteered to wheel the stuff around the home and that the profits went to help development projects in the third world. Eve hadn't been especially clear about what the development projects were, but Miriam Longford's book claimed that most of the money raised by Survivor charities went on administrative expenses and ended up in the organization's own coffers.

"Have you got a mother?" Emily asked sharply.

James thought of Abigail and nodded, but it pricked him when he remembered that his real mother was dead.

"When she's old and she goes dotty, are you gonna sell her home and make her live in a place like this?"

James smiled. "You've got a great big patio and a garden outside. All the people I've met here seem really nice."

"It smells like old people and piss," Emily said bluntly.

James laughed. "It doesn't smell *that* bad."

"If they can make you better, they send you to a hospital. If they can't, they send you here to die."

Emily was thin and barely looked strong enough to stand up, but James still felt intimidated as he backed his trolley up towards the door. "Well, I hope you settle in. I bet you'll get used to it."

"Hang on," Emily said. "I'll take one of the Cadbury Turkish bars. I don't eat a lot these days, but I expect I'll nibble a few squares."

"That's three dollars."

Emily looked a bit shocked at the price.

"Blow it." She grinned, swiping her hand in front of her face. "I'd rather a bunch of Africans got it than my prat of a son."

James smiled as Emily handed him three one-dollar coins, but he felt awful as he backed his trolley out and stepped up to knock on the final door. Everything about the place reminded James that he was going to get old and die.

CHAPTER 17

INTEGRATION

Ten days after their first evening with the Survivors, Abigail and the three cherubs had begun spending most of their free time either visiting the commune or involved in Survivor activities.

Abigail began what Elliot described as "A personal journey into the Ocean of Love." She listened to Survivor CDs and watched videos during the day. In the evenings she drove out to the commune and attended either the single parents' group, or one-to-one counseling sessions with Elliot. She also began doing volunteer fund-raising work, canvassing for money in the city center. On the occasional evenings when Abigail wasn't attending the commune, Elliot would usually phone her for a prolonged conversation and once even dropped by the house for a surprise visit.

Dana kept up her role as the difficult recruit. The unfortunate seventeen-year-old chaperone whom Dana questioned mercilessly got replaced by a middle-aged woman made of sterner stuff. Elliot suggested that Dana undergo an intensive counseling program, to deal with "emotional and hostility issues." Abigail agreed and wrote a check for $780 worth of therapy.

The sessions were designed to make Dana feel good about herself, while subtly introducing ideas about the Survivors' beliefs and the supposed benefits of their lifestyle. Her skepticism was a ploy to make the Prince family's integration into the cult more credible. But it wasn't meant to seriously hinder the mission, so Dana allowed the counselor to win her over and received her leather necklace a week after the others.

Lauren made plenty of friends of her own age within the commune. These preteen cultists had yet to master the manipulative recruitment skills possessed by older members and Lauren had a relatively easy time. While Abigail and Dana attended counseling sessions, Lauren roamed around the disused mall.

On a typical visit, she would meet her friends in the gymnasium or communal living quarters and tag along with whatever they were doing. Activities ranged from playing games to doing homework, or attending one of the many small religious services that took place every night. Lauren found many of the activities enjoyable, especially games in the gym and the happy clappy services, with their chanting and dancing. But after the overpowering effect of her first visit, she carefully applied Miriam's thought-control techniques: a few seconds thinking about the smell of James's laundry basket was enough to stop her from being overcome with euphoria.

Because James seemed to be integrating nicely, he wasn't asked to attend one-on-one counseling like Abigail and Dana, but Eve and Ruth kept him under close supervision, even waiting outside the door when he used the toilet. They encouraged him to attend religious services and lectures about the teachings and life of Joel Regan. He visited the retirement home after school every day and often rode back to the commune with Eve instead of going home afterwards.

CHERUB mission controllers John Jones and Chloe Blake were staying at a hotel in the center of Brisbane. Their role was going to be minimal until Abigail and the cherubs were fully integrated into cult life, but they'd done some background research and one of the facts they turned up was that the North Park Elder Care Community was owned and run by Survivors.

James gradually got used to the oldies on his daily trolley route. He was often asked to read out letters for residents with poor eyesight. He listened to them moaning about their ailments and the staff who looked after them. Many residents complained that they were being charged for therapies and outings that they hadn't taken and that bed linens weren't being changed. The plumbing was noisy, the water was never hot, and the air-conditioning didn't work. James couldn't tell how much was genuine cause for complaint and how much was to do with the fact that the residents had little to do other than watch TV and find stuff to gripe about.

Eve encouraged James to spend time with the residents. He came to realize that they looked forward to his brief visit every afternoon and they'd often set aside something they wanted to talk about: an article trimmed from a newspaper, their husbands' war medals, or a photograph from their past. He found it disturbing, seeing pictures of residents who could barely shuffle across their rooms as teenage brides and bare-chested soldiers.

James always spent more time with Emily than any of the others, usually ten or fifteen minutes. It was partly because she reminded James of his Nan, but mostly because she was livelier than the other residents and often hilariously drunk.

As Emily slugged back endless cups of milk mixed with vodka, she relayed a wonderful line in anecdotes about her son, whom she referred to as either *the Dolt* or *Nugget Head*. He'd apparently squandered a significant family fortune by setting up and bankrupting a discount airline, followed by a chain of DIY superstores. Emily said she was down to her last "few million bucks." James particularly enjoyed the story of how Nugget Head had managed to nail himself to a sheet of plaster-board while demonstrating power tools inside one of his stores. Humiliated, he then chose to lash out at a laughing man who unfortunately turned out to be the Australian fly-weight boxing champion.

On the Friday thirteen days after his first visit to the commune, James stepped into Emily's room and found her listening to the words of Joel Regan through the speakers of a brand-new mini hi-fi.

"Elliot gave it to me when he brought in my new towels and bathmats," Emily explained, anticipating James's question. "I hope I'm not offending you, James. I know you're in with that lot, but it all sounds like a load of tosh to me."

It was six when James got in from the care home. He went straight in the shower and came down to find Lauren setting the table in the dining room. Dinner was almost ready and James was visibly disappointed when Abigail came through with trays of overbaked supermarket cannelloni.

"Man." James grinned. "The standard of cooking sure isn't what it was around here."

Abigail smiled. "I've not got time these days. I spent most of the morning with Elliot and three hours this afternoon stuffing promotional coupons into envelopes."

"What for?" James asked as Dana came in and sat next to him.

Abigail shrugged. "It's one of Joel Regan's businesses, producing customized marketing materials for big companies. Elliot said they were shorthanded and begged me to go over there and help out."

Lauren shuddered. "I've really gotten to hate Elliot. He's *such* a greaseball."

Dana nodded as James helped Abigail dish up the food. "Have you ever noticed that he seems to be in three places at once?"

"Mary told me that Elliot only sleeps four hours a night," Abigail explained. "Apparently he was one of the top men at the Ark until he had a row with The Spider. Now he's trying to get back on her good side by making the Brisbane commune the most profitable in the world."

James looked confused. "The Spider?"

Dana and Lauren spoke contemptuously and in unison, "Regan's eldest daughter."

"Oh," James said.

"Don't you know anything?" Lauren sneered. "She's like the wicked witch of the west. Joel Regan is eighty-two years old. Everyone says it's The Spider who calls the shots nowadays."

As James pushed his fork down into his chicken cannelloni, Abigail noisily cleared her throat.

"James, how many times have I asked you wear something over your chest at the dinner table?"

James tutted. "I'm *perfectly* clean. I just showered and squirted myself with deodorant."

"I don't care," Abigail said sharply. "I'm not sitting at the dinner table with you in your underwear. Go and put some clothes on."

James wasn't in the mood for Abigail's obsession with table manners. "Fine," he said, holding up his hands. "I don't know what your problem is."

Abigail snapped back, "If you don't like it, James, make your own dinner."

"All right, *Mum*. Keep your tampon in; I'll go and get a T-shirt."

James stormed up to his room to get dressed. Three weeks in, the combination of school, homework, the care home, and the ever increasing amount of time spent at the commune was wearing him out.

He got back down and slumped into a dining chair, scowling at Abigail.

Lauren tutted, unable to resist a dig at her brother. "You're so immature, James."

"Lauren, I really don't give a shit what you think," James answered back.

"Language," Abigail gasped.

"God," Dana moaned. "Will you shut up? I can't sit through another meal listening to James and Lauren pecking at each other."

Abigail started to snigger as James took his first mouthful of pasta.

"What?" Lauren asked.

Abigail snorted. "It's funny, the way we've started bickering like a real family."

The three youngsters smiled.

"Sorry everyone," James said. "I didn't mean to start biting people's heads off. I'm just stressed out."

"Apology accepted." Abigail nodded. "Unfortunately, I think things will be getting worse before they get better: Elliot paid me a visit here this morning. He told me he thought we were making a valuable contribution to the Survivors, and he invited us to move into the commune on a trial basis."

James and Lauren grinned at each other and even Dana managed a contented nod.

"I take it you accepted?" James said.

"Grudgingly," Abigail said sarcastically. "I said I thought it was too soon and that I wasn't sure I wanted to make that sort of commitment, but somehow he managed to talk me into it."

Lauren laughed. "I bet he was looking around at this house trying to work out how much money it's worth if we donated it to his commune."

"I know." Abigail nodded. "He won't be happy when he finds out we're renting."

CHAPTER 18

REMOVAL

Moving into the commune was good for the mission, but James wasn't happy. Up to now, he'd been able to take some time for himself, even if it was just a long shower and an hour on his PSP when he got back from the nursing home. Once he moved in with the Survivors, he'd be trapped inside their mind games 24/7.

Two white vans descended on the house early Saturday morning. A middle-aged Survivor got out of each one and began carrying out bags of clothes and belongings they'd packed up the night before. They also took a computer and big-screen TV that Abigail had agreed to donate to the exhibition space at the mall.

There was no traffic on the roads as the Prince family

set off, following the vans in their Mercedes. James was surprised to find that Eve wasn't there to meet him at the entrance. Instead, he was greeted by Paul, a boy he'd seen at school and on the commune but had never spoken to before.

Paul was thirteen, with rounded features that made him seem younger. He grabbed one of the bags containing James's belongings before leading him inside. They walked up two static escalators to the second floor of the mall. James had never been up this far before. It was a compact area, with glass sides and a courtyard that had originally been a rooftop bar and restaurant.

The stuffy room had mattresses lined up along the walls on either side and smelled like the sweat and farts of the twenty boys who slept there every night. Paul pointed out a row of cupboards behind a bar.

"All our stuff goes in there."

Most of the cupboard doors hung open, with strands of boys' clothing dangling over the edges of shelves. As James approached, he realized the space was communal, with each section containing a different sort of garment.

"How do you know whose is whose?"

Paul shrugged. "There's no personal property here, James. We share everything, except things like trainers and toothbrushes where it isn't hygienic."

James was gutted at the prospect of mixing his designer gear and three-week-old school uniform with the faded tat in the cupboards. But he didn't have much choice and at least he'd had the sense not to bring his good watch or his PSP.

"I forgot your welcome present," Paul said, reaching

around to the back pocket of his shorts and sliding out a slim paperback entitled *The Survivors' Manual*. There was a cellophane packet containing a white bead stuck to the cover.

James did his best to sound happy. "Thanks, man."

"Congratulations," Paul said cheerily. "You're an angel now, mate."

James had already read *The Survivors' Manual*. The book sets out the major ideas behind Joel Regan's cult. The first edition appeared in 1963 and over the years it has been revised a dozen times, with the date and cause of the apocalypse getting vaguer in each new edition.

The manual sets out Regan's theory on angels, devils, and the impending nuclear holocaust that will wipe out humanity. He claims this will be the work of the Devil, and that God gave him a message, commanding him to build an Ark and save a small section of humanity by turning them into angels. The Devil loathes Survivors, because God has chosen them to defy his plot to wipe out humanity.

The book claims that Survivors can only stay safe by living and worshiping in communes where God can watch them closely. They must avoid excessive exposure to the outside world, in particular to media such as television, radio, and newspapers. Idleness and negativity encourage devils to enter the communes and anyone who leaves the Survivors will have turned their back on God, having already angered the Devil. To leave the Survivors, or make contact with a member who has already left, is to invite a torturous death followed by eternity in the lowest depths of hell.

In her book on the Survivors, Miriam Longford notes that Regan's ideas are designed to frighten cult members, while leaving them with little time to think for themselves and reconsider their devotion to the group:

Survivors living inside communes are tightly scheduled to ensure that they are deprived of sleep and remain constantly active while awake. They eat a diet high in sugar and other stimulants such as caffeine. In combination, these factors create a buzz that one former Survivor described as, "Living in a cheerful fog." Unfortunately, lack of sleep, poor diet, and high activity levels can have a disastrous impact on a person's long-term health. The most common reason given for leaving the Survivors by ex-members is that they burned out with exhaustion.

To avoid idleness and the lowest depths of hell, James was given a detailed timetable mapping out his entire life. By the time he'd thrown his possessions into the cupboards and slipped the white bead on to his necklace, it was 8:30 a.m. James quickly studied the Saturday timetable, as Paul urged him to run for morning service:

SATURDAY
6:45 Rise
7:00 Morning Run/Physical Activity
7:45 Shower and personal care time
8:10 Breakfast
8:35 Morning Service
9:00 Work Assignment
13:00 Lunch
13:30 Afternoon Service

14:00 Fund-raising Activity
17:40 Dinner
18:20 Evening Service
18:50 Sporting Activity
20:30 Shower and personal care time
20:50 Late Service
21:15 Retire to dormitory
23:00 Lights out

The Survivors kept their services small, upbeat, and fast. James sat beside Paul in the outer circle. The all-male congregation joined hands to form a barrier against the Devil, while a gray-haired woman known as Ween strode into the center of the circle. She sat and placed a set of tom-toms on the floor between her legs. She called everyone to silence, then began energetically thumping her little drums.

"We thank you, God, for choosing us to Survive. We thank you for our shelter. We thank you for protecting us from devils. The circle starts here."

Ween pointed out someone at random, who thanked God for forsaking his son, Jesus Christ. Everyone chanted *Thank you, Our Lord*. Then the next person thanked God for his beautiful children and everyone chanted, *Thank you, Our Lord* again. Ween drummed madly as each person in turn gave thanks.

James couldn't think of what to say, and finally blurted, "We thank you God for making me an angel."

Everyone appreciated this, and James received the loudest *Thank you, Our Lord* of the whole ceremony. After going around the two circles and thanking God for thirty different things, Ween put aside her drums and told everyone to stand up and jiggle their hands and feet.

"Breathe deep," Ween said softly. Then immediately afterwards, "Exhale."

James had read about breathing exercises, but this was his first encounter: The simple act of taking forced deep breaths for a few minutes raises the level of oxygen in the blood and produces a slight feeling of elation. Miriam had taught him to defeat the forced breathing technique by taking normal breaths, while making dramatic gestures to make it seem as if you are doing the same as everyone else. However, the technique was harmless in small doses, so James decided to see what it was like.

The group breathed and exhaled rapidly for three minutes, while Ween soothed her congregation, urging them to relax their muscles and imagine God's love warming their hearts.

"Now," Ween said, returning to her normal voice, "find somebody to hug."

James turned to Paul and the two boys wrapped their arms around each other.

"You're a beautiful human being and God loves you," Paul said, with complete sincerity.

James couldn't help smiling. "You're pretty amazing yourself, dude. I'm sure God loves you too."

Ween picked her drums off the floor, stepped between the pairs of hugging men, and left the room. James and Paul were two of the last out. James felt happy. It reminded him of the sensation you get after you've rocked out to a good tune, or pulled off some amazing feat in a PlayStation game.

As they headed along the mall corridor, James reflected upon how easily a skilled cult member like Ween could take a roomful of people and manipulate their emotions.

"Do you like services?" James asked.

Paul smiled. "Yeah, they really make you feel alive, don't they?"

James nodded, before looking down at his timetable. "So," he said, "what's Work Assignment?"

A little of the postservice glow dropped out of Paul's expression. "That's the one thing I don't like about weekends."

"What do we do exactly?"

Paul smiled. "Let's just say that after four hours as a picker, you'll never want to see another Survivors book or DVD."

CHAPTER 10

PICKING

The Survivor warehouse was directly across the road from the mall. It was a giant, single-story box built from corrugated aluminum. James and Paul headed out of the blistering sunlight, through a set of double doors, and into a reception area that seemed dark until their eyes adjusted. A foreman with soggy patches under his arms sat behind a chipboard counter.

"Hey, Joe," Paul said. "This is James, the new kid. I need a couple of stations next to each other so I can show him the ropes."

Joe reached under the counter and took out two plastic discs with numbers on them, like the ones you get when you try on clothes in a shop.

"You'll want some water, James," Paul said, pointing to a wire rack stacked with clear plastic bottles.

Both boys grabbed a bottle, before heading through another set of double doors and into the warehouse proper.

The first thing that hit James was the heat; there was no air-conditioning. It was thirty-five degrees outside and hotter in. The lines of shelving were stacked five meters high with videotapes, CDs, DVDs, and books. Some were on their own, others bundled into elaborate packages like the one James had seen in Emily's room the afternoon before.

After passing between a hundred meters of shelving, the boys reached a line of twenty workstations at the front of the warehouse. They found stations eighteen and nineteen and Paul showed James what to do. Each station had a computer, which printed off orders for Survivor tapes and merchandise. The front sheet was a label and invoice for the customer; the back sheet was for the picker. The picker's job was to head into the lines of numbered shelving and grab the correct items.

Once you'd rounded the order up, you took an appro-priately sized box from the flattened stacks alongside each station, placed the items inside, and lined it up under a fat plastic tube that led up to the ceiling. There was a foot pedal on the floor, which unleashed a torrent of Styrofoam packaging chips to fill the box and stop the items getting damaged in transit. Once the goods were packed tight, you stuck on the address label, tucked the invoice inside, and sealed it with either brown parcel tape or binding strips.

After watching Paul complete his first order, followed by a couple of overenthusiastic stabs on the foot
pedal that caused Styrofoam spillages, James had the job
mastered. The computer timed each job and a red light
flashed above your workstation if you were moving too
slowly.

For the next four hours, James moved frantically
around the warehouse picking out orders for Joel Regan's
businesses. The items ranged from the $19.95 CD *Surviving
Work—The Motivational Speeches of Joel Regan*, through
vending-machine service manuals to the heavyweight
$399 tome *Building the Ark*. Each copy of this glossy slab
included a vial of sacred earth taken from around the Ark
and blessed by Joel Regan.

The biggest seller was employee motivation courses
sold to big companies by a Survivors front company.
According to the cover blurb they had been used by
"hundreds of America's largest corporations." These giant
orders caused James's heart to sink when they spewed out
of his printer, because they involved sending out hundreds of chunky coursework folders, booklets, tapes, and
videos at a time.

By the end of his shift, James had drunk two liters of
water. Paul's last order was gigantic and filling it took up
the first third of the boys' forty-five-minute lunch break.
They rushed back to the mall, cooled off quickly in a set
of shabby communal showers, and sprinted up to their
bedroom wrapped in towels, with soggy trainers hooked
over their fingers.

James opened up the clothes cupboard and realized

that his stuff was already gone. He didn't make a fuss, but it was depressing rummaging through crummy-looking piles of laundered clothes trying to find something that fit and didn't look too disgusting. He ended up with a tight yellow T-shirt, boxers that were better not thought about, gray trainer socks, and a pair of cutoff jeans so battered and ripped that they actually looked cool.

Once dressed, the boys—who'd already missed breakfast—had to bolt downstairs in time for lunch. The food was clearly made on a budget and smelled like the kind of stuff James had been eating in children's homes and schools his whole life. He got macaroni and cheese, with a jug of orange juice and chocolate ice cream with sprinkles on it. At the end of the meal, Paul led him to take his dishes back to be washed up. James spotted Abigail and Dana on the other side of the counter. They wore hair nets and aprons and both looked stressed out as they unloaded crockery from a steaming dishwasher.

They exchanged nods, but James and Paul were already late for their lunchtime service, where they found that the circles had already formed and the service was underway. It was being conducted by Mary, who stopped playing her guitar and smiled.

"Join the circle," Mary urged, as a bunch of people in the outer circle shuffled backwards to make a space big enough for two bums to squeeze in.

James sat on the floor and caught his breath as the service resumed. Mary clapped and everybody clapped back. Then she began a nonsense chant and everybody joined in. James was exhausted from the shift in the warehouse and high on the sugar from the orange juice and ice cream. He came out of the service feeling happy and had to remind himself not to get carried away.

The boys faced another run out to the parking lot when the service ended. James had never visited the commune in the daytime before and was surprised by the way everyone rushed around. Even adults routinely jogged in the mall corridors and a brisk walk seemed to be as laid back as things ever got.

James and Paul piled into a white minibus and sat next to each other. It was already half full and within a couple of minutes another eight kids, including Eve and Lauren, had joined them. Elliot came bounding out of the mall and slid the door shut before getting in the driver's seat and pulling out.

"How's our new recruit doing?" Elliot asked as he pulled the van out of the parking lot.

"Not bad." James nodded. "Can't say I exactly enjoyed four hours in the warehouse sweating my guts out."

The chatting kids suddenly went quiet and Paul dug James in the ribs.

"What?" James said, mystified.

Paul didn't answer, but Elliot did once he had the van up to speed.

"That's an exceptionally negative comment, James," Elliot said. "You learned how to work your station and how to package your products properly, didn't you?"

James nodded.

"How many loads did you dispatch?"

"It was a hundred and something," James said.

Paul rattled off the statistic. "One hundred and twenty-six, only a few less than me."

"That's excellent work, James," Elliot said. "The warehouse is very important. Every one of those products makes us money that goes towards building and maintaining the Ark. In a way, James, what you do in that warehouse is your contribution to building the Ark. Do you understand?"

"Yes."

"OK," Elliot said. "So, next time you work a shift in the warehouse, try and imagine that each book and each DVD you carry is a brick for the Ark. And set yourself a target. Make it your goal to dispatch one hundred and fifty items next time. Some of our best people average more than fifty dispatches an hour."

James really hated Elliot and his upbeat attitude, but he was supposed to be fitting in with the cult and all its gobbledegook.

"I'm glad I'm an angel," James said. "I'll try not to be negative."

"Good stuff." Elliot smiled. "That's what I like to hear."

They headed to an arts and leisure complex on the Brisbane River known as South Bank. The area had galleries, a market, restaurants, parks, playgrounds, and a manmade beach. The kids piled out of the minibus and Elliot began handing out plastic tubs with coin slots in the top.

"OK!" he yelled. "Good luck. There's a lot of people around, so get out there and start earning. Lets see if the twelve of you can raise a thousand dollars this afternoon. I'll be picking up from here at quarter to six. Do *not* be late. I'm on an exceptionally tight schedule today."

James strolled over to say hello to Lauren, Eve, and a couple of the other girls.

James looked at Eve. "I was expecting to see you this morning."

"I'm glad you became an angel," Eve said flatly.

James spoke to a couple of other girls, but they all seemed reluctant to answer. Eve organized the twelve kids into four teams of three and sent them off to cover different areas of the South Bank complex. Lauren got the nod when she asked to fund-raise with James and Paul.

"So what's the cause?" one of Lauren's pals asked.

Eve smiled. "Cancer research. That's a good money-maker and we haven't used it for a while."

Paul headed off with Lauren and James in tow. Whenever James passed someone, he'd smile and shake his coin box. "Australian Cancer Research."

About every third person found some coins to stick in the box.

"I thought we were raising money to build the Ark," Lauren said, when nobody was nearby.

"We are," Paul said. "But there's a lot of prejudice against the Survivors. If we say it's for the Ark, we don't make a cent and get a load of abuse to boot."

Lauren's mouth dropped open. "But that's *lying* . . ."

Paul shook his head confidently. "You can lie to devils, Lauren; they don't really count."

They ended up in a park a kilometer from where the van had dropped them off. Paul stood by a gate and told James and Lauren to head for the other entrance.

James shook his box at a passing family. "Australian Cancer Research." He grinned.

The man handed a bunch of dollar coins to his toddler son, who reached up and put them in the box.

"Thank you," James said enthusiastically.

Lauren shuddered and looked back over her shoulder to make sure Paul was out of earshot. "This is so nasty," she whispered. "It's the lowest thing ever by about a *million* percent."

"Australian Cancer Research," James said to a passing pensioner, who ignored him. He turned and looked at Lauren. "I know, sis. Just grit your teeth and remember that it's for the mission."

"And this cult is totally sexist: Girls get all the domestic stuff. If you think four hours filling up boxes is bad, you should see what I've got. I spent this morning polishing floors. Tomorrow I've got four hours in the laundry."

James shrugged. "What can I say, Lauren? We knew this mission was going to be tough. At least we know the evenings are a bit mellower and there's school Monday to Friday."

"I know," Lauren said, shaking her head slowly. "I'm just having a little rant to get it out of my system." She rattled her tin at a passerby. "Australian Cancer Research," and got a few cents for her trouble.

James grinned, trying to cheer Lauren up. "When I've got a few more dollars, I'm gonna crack this baby open and buy an ice cream. You want one?"

CHAPTER 20

HORROR

Following an afternoon walking around fund-raising and an enjoyable evening playing soccer with the lads, James was exhausted. When the late service ended at quarter past nine he walked up the escalators to the second floor and found a couple of pillows and some frayed sheets to cover his mattress. Twenty-six boys lived in the room, their ages evenly spread between eight and eighteen.

As the tired lads stripped off and crashed onto their mattresses, two of the oldest—Sam and Ed—switched on a large but decrepit TV and put on a DVD. James was expecting worthy Christian entertainment and was pleasantly surprised when the title music of *The Exorcist* came on. He'd seen the movie during a horror marathon at the CHERUB summer hostel and realized why it was being shown as soon as he remembered the plot: What better way to influence the minds of young Survivors than by sending them off to sleep on a movie about a girl possessed by the Devil?

James's mattress was next to Paul's, almost touching. Twenty minutes into the movie a younger boy crept into the space between them and Paul slid an arm around his back.

"This is my brother, Rick," Paul explained in a whisper.

James gave the youngster a smile. Within a few minutes Rick's eyes were sagging and he'd started drifting off to sleep. Paul gently flicked his ear to wake him up.

"Keep your eyes open," Paul said firmly. "Do you want to get the test?"

James didn't ask, but he could tell from the look on Rick's face that the test was something worth being woken up to avoid.

By the end of the movie, even the older boys were struggling to stay awake. When the closing titles began scrolling, Sam and Ed flicked on the lights. They were the biggest dudes in the room and they looked full of themselves as they glanced around at the kids lying on the mattresses. Staying awake had been too much for a couple of the younger boys.

"I think we'll take Martin," Sam said.

The pair closed on a scrawny nine-year-old a few mattresses along from James. He was curled up on his pillow, wearing nothing but red underpants.

"Test time!" the lads shouted as they shook him awake.

Martin woke with a start and scrambled up his bed, away from grabbing hands. "*Noooooo*, please."

"Why did you fall asleep?" Ed asked, as he dragged the unfortunate kid off his bed. "You know you have to watch the movie."

Sam smiled wickedly. "Now you've got to go out on your own and face the Devil."

"Are you really an angel? Only an angel can survive the night out there alone."

"If the Devil sniffs weakness, he'll get you; you'll spend the whole night in agony."

"Don't make me." Martin bawled desperately.

Sam slid open a glass door, while his partner dragged the gangly youngster across the floor and shoved him outside onto the roof terrace. Martin screamed as he clambered to his feet and banged on the glass door, begging to get back inside.

"Sleep tight," the lads said in unison as they laughed.

As Martin gave up banging on the glass and slumped into the gravel with his bare back pressed against the glass, Sam noticed a glistening streak across the floor.

"Oh, man." Sam giggled, before kicking the glass behind his sobbing victim. "You pissed your pants, you dirty boy."

Ed grabbed the pillow off Martin's bed and used it as a foot rag. "Don't worry, mate, we've found something to wipe up with."

Most of the older lads in the room were smiling, but the little guys looked scared. Sam and Ed were nothing special and James reckoned he could easily have battered them, but getting in a fight now might ruin his chances of being accepted into the Survivor boarding school.

James felt bad as he looked at Rick's tense fingers

digging into Paul's shoulder. The Survivors closely controlled everyone's lives and James didn't see how this bullying ritual could have become established without people in high places turning a blind eye.

Once the lights went out, Rick scrambled back to his own mattress. James pulled his duvet over his head and tried to block out the muffled sobs of the petrified boy sitting out on the balcony.

Martin was allowed inside at sunup. His skin was puckered from a night curled up on gravel, but the Devil seemed to have left him alone.

James's Sunday started with five brisk laps around the mall parking lot and a cool shower. Breakfast was honey puff cereal and orange juice, which set up a little sugar rush for the twenty minutes of chanting and singing that followed. At the end of this carefully designed emotional tune-up, James found that he'd shaken off his tiredness and was feeling alert and fairly happy.

But he didn't need any of Miriam's thought-control techniques to douse his spirits. The prospect of another four-hour shift as a picker was enough. He smiled at Paul as they crossed the road between the mall and the warehouse.

"Each book is a brick for the Ark."

Paul smiled halfheartedly. "Elliot would be proud of you."

As soon as they entered the warehouse, the foreman looked at James. "Are you Prince?"

James nodded. "Yeah."

"I just got a call. You're due over at administration for an induction test."

James smiled at Paul, well pleased to get out of the warehouse. He headed back to the mall and an open-plan office inside a shop unit on the ground floor. There were a dozen paper-strewn desks, but nobody was working at them.

James spent a couple of seconds thinking he'd come to the wrong place, until a head bobbed up behind one of the cloth-covered partitions. It was Judith, a fit-looking woman in her early twenties who worked as Elliot's assistant. As he walked to the back of the room James passed by Lauren and Dana, who both sat at desks scribbling away on a photocopied question paper.

"I didn't realize there were three of you," Judith explained as she handed James a paper: *Survivor Aptitude Test—Ages 13–15.* "I should have called you at breakfast. You've got two hours, starting as soon as you sit down."

Judith pointed him to a desk near the front of the room, a good ten meters from Lauren and Dana. The space was already set up with a couple of sharpened pencils and an eraser. James sat in an office chair and flicked through the pages. It looked like a reassuringly straightforward mixture of math, spelling, a short creative story, and an IQ test.

CHAPTER 21

PASSION

James Prince was supposed to be withdrawn and decently behaved, but James Adams hadn't found any time for homework during his hectic weekend and got ratty when his geography teacher demanded it on Monday morning. He earned a thirty-minute detention for his trouble.

After detention he headed to the deserted bike shed and rode to the North Park Elder Care Community at breakneck speed, nearly getting on the wrong end of a Mazda when he charged an amber light.

Slightly shaken, James moodily wheeled his bike through the care home's reception, exchanging nods with the cute-looking nurse at the counter, before pushing the bike into a storage cupboard. He was surprised to see two bikes beside Eve's. He changed his sweaty school top for a fresh T-shirt and hurried back to reception.

"Have you seen Eve, or noticed where Elliot left my trolley?" he asked.

The nurse pointed down a corridor into the section of the home where the residents Eve visited lived. "I didn't think you were coming when I saw the other two lads."

"What other two?" James asked.

The receptionist shrugged. "I don't know who they are, but they're all down there."

James jogged along a hundred meters of corridor, passing by his trolley on the way. He could have just grabbed it and got on with visiting his residents, but he wanted to ask Eve why she'd been blanking him all weekend and find out who the others were.

Part of the answer came when Paul stepped out of a room. Eve followed him with her trolley and last came Terry—the boy in James's class whom he'd seen sitting reluctantly in the corner of the Survivor gymnasium a couple of times.

"Ah, you made it," Eve said brightly. "You know Terry, don't you? He's volunteered to help out with our charitable work."

"Cool," James said. "So what's the score with these two being here?"

Eve smiled. "I'm introducing Paul to my patients. He'll be taking over my job here from tomorrow. Terry and I will be going off to start doing rounds at another care facility. The Survivors have never worked there before and we're all *terrifically* excited about the opportunity."

"Oh," James said, unable to cover his disappointment.

"Is there a problem?" Eve asked.

"S'pose not." He shrugged.

Eve smiled sweetly at Paul and Terry. "You boys have seen me go through the patter a few times. Why don't the two of you take the trolley into the next room, while I have a word with James?"

Paul nodded as Terry turned around and knocked on a door.

Eve's expression stiffened as Paul and Terry stepped into the adjacent room. "What's the matter, James?"

James rested his palm against the wall and shrugged. "I dunno. I just expected you to be there when I arrived on Saturday. Then when you spoke to me in the afternoon you made me feel like I was the shit on your shoe. Now you're not gonna be coming here anymore. What did I do that's made you mad?"

"You haven't made me mad." Eve smiled. "I wanted to help make you an angel, James. Now Terry has been through some difficult one-to-one counseling sessions, and I'm trying to help *him*."

"But you can still say hello to me, can't you? We can still speak to each other?"

"James, now you're an angel it's not really appropriate for us to be close."

"Why not?"

"Because we're old enough to be attracted to each other, but we're not old enough to be married. It's a combination that only leads to trouble."

James shook his head. "I'm not asking to *marry* you, Eve. I'd just like the odd conversation."

"The survivors keep teenagers separate until they're old enough to marry."

"But we spent hours playing volleyball and stuff."

Eve smiled. "You weren't an angel then, James. I was helping you, the same as I'm now helping Terry."

James was hurt. He knew Eve had been stringing him along to get him to join the cult, but at the same time he'd imagined that there was a bedrock of real friendship between them. James couldn't make a move himself because of the mission, but he'd harbored hopes that they'd end up snogging or something.

"Maybe I should speak to Elliot about this," Eve said. "Perhaps you should talk to one of our counselors about our beliefs on the sanctity of marriage."

"No," James gasped, letting his anger show. "Can't we have a normal conversation without you reporting every detail to Elliot?"

"Ruth and I saw you and Lauren eating ice cream in the park on Saturday and your collection tins were *very* light," Eve said acidly. "We didn't report that. You would have been in serious trouble with Elliot if we had."

James couldn't believe that Eve had spied on them. He'd had a stressful day. He felt used; he was jealous of Terry and would have loved to wipe the grin off Eve's manipulative little face. But Terry and Paul were coming out of the room. Eve started smiling again and James remembered that the important thing was the mission, not his crumpled ego.

"Try and be extra nice to Terry," Eve said quietly to James. "He really needs our love and support right now."

James smothered his emotions and nodded curtly. "I'm

sorry, Eve. I was confused. I've still got so much to learn."

"So." Eve beamed, raising her voice and looking at Terry. "How did it go?"

"Great." Terry smiled. "She only bought peppermints, but she was really friendly."

Eve hooked her arms around Terry and rubbed his back as she hugged him. "You're going to be *so* great at this, Terry. I can always tell."

"Yeah," Paul added. "Congratulations on your first sale."

It looked daft from James's detached viewpoint, but the once reticent Terry smiled and gobbled up the compliments.

As Eve knocked on the door of the next room, James headed off to get his trolley and start his round. He began at the far end of the corridor, which made Emily his second call. James held up a large bottle of vodka as he entered her room.

"Hi there. This comes as a freebie, compliments of Elliot."

"Cheers, handsome," Emily said. She was in bed and didn't have her usual color. "Could you prop up my pillows please?"

"What's the matter?" James asked as he stepped up to the bed. Emily leaned forwards and James plumped her pillows before setting them straight behind her back.

"Just my usual tummy trouble." Emily smiled. "Back and forth to the loo all day. I know it sounds daft, but when you get to my age that's enough to sap your strength."

James put the vodka on Emily's bedside table, where he noticed another bunch of Survivor leaflets and tapes.

"Is there anything you'd like me to do? I can have a word with the nurse if you want something for your stomach."

Emily smiled. "No point; nothing ever works. Can you mix the vodka for me? My hands are shaking."

James grabbed the bottle and twisted off the metal cap, then grabbed a tall plastic jug that held a liter of fluid.

"Say when," James said as the vodka glugged into the jug.

Emily usually spoke when it was about a third full, but James was nearly at the halfway mark when he stopped.

"Did I say when?" Emily asked. Her voice was sharp, but James didn't take offense because that was just her way.

"Are you sure you want it mixed this strong when your stomach is playing up?"

Emily smiled. "Don't be lily-livered, handsome. Vodka's good for the stomach."

"Is that a fact?" James grinned as he reluctantly splashed a drop more into the jug.

Emily had a tiny fridge in her room. James grabbed a rack of ice cubes and cracked them into the jug before topping it off with milk and brown sugar. He stirred the mixture with a long plastic spoon before pouring the first glass into a tumbler.

"You make them so good," Emily said as she downed two-thirds of the tumbler in one smooth gulp. "Top me up."

The ice in the jug rattled as James refilled the tumbler. He stepped back to his trolley. "I'd better be going, Emily. I copped a detention and I'm running *so* late."

"I know you're busy," the old lady said, "but can I please ask you one thing?"

James glanced at his watch. "I guess."

"Elliot was here today."

"He's here a lot," James said.

Emily smiled, "He's after my money."

James acted surprised, though he'd already guessed that this was the motive behind Elliot's interest in the elderly residents.

"No offense, handsome. I know you're a Survivor, but I've listened to some of the CDs and I'm not buying Mr. Regan and his angels and devils."

James wanted to say *good for you*, but there'd be trouble if it got back to Elliot, so he kept his trap shut.

"I'm not as wealthy as I was, but there's still going to be a few bucks sloshing around when I go toes up. All I've got is my son, and money only brings out the worst in him. I'd really like everything to go to a good cause when I die."

"Haven't you got grandkids?" James asked.

Emily shook her head sadly. "Though to be honest, I don't reckon my Ronnie would have made much of a father. He's got a ferocious temper on him."

"That's a shame."

"So I was thinking about the Survivor charities," Emily said. "I don't want them wasting it building that daft Ark in the outback, but Elliot was talking about the Survivor Development Foundation. He says it helps the people in third-world countries. I could change my will and leave my money to them. Do you think that's a good idea?"

James would have liked to tell Emily that there were far more worthy and efficient charities that helped out the world's poor, but he had to think about the mission.

"The Survivor charities do really great work." James smiled. "I'm sure hundreds, maybe even thousands, of people would benefit from your money—not that you'll be dying anytime soon, of course."

"Oh, I don't think I'll be hanging around much longer." Emily smiled as she reached out to touch James's hand. "He's a smooth talker that Elliot, but there's a bit of a con man beneath that corduroy jacket. That's why I wanted to ask you, James. I reckon I can trust you."

James managed a guilty smile. "How do you figure that?"

"Because you're a nice boy. You've got an honest face."

"Right . . . ," James said as he backed his trolley out into the corridor. "I'll catch up with you tomorrow. Hopefully you'll feel better, provided you don't go too mad with the booze."

James felt like absolute slime. As her door clunked shut, he slumped backwards against the wall and bunched his fists tight with frustration. James knew he wasn't a perfect human being. He was impulsive, usually in some kind of trouble, and prone to lashing out, but he didn't think he'd ever be able to sit in a room and rip off a fragile old woman the way Elliot had done.

CHAPTER 22

RONNIE

FOUR WEEKS LATER

From: John Jones
[johnjones@cherubcampus.com]
Sent: Mar 23, 2006 08:51
To: Dr. Terence McAfferty
Copy: Zara Asker, Dennis King
Subject: Survivors Mission

Dear all,
With regard to your recent e-mails, I'm afraid
there continues to be little progress in our mission to
infiltrate the Survivors' Ark. It has now been nearly a

month since James, Dana, and Lauren moved into the commune and took the aptitude test.

The extremely strict rules on personal property inside the commune make it difficult to contact Abigail and the three cherubs on a regular basis. Mobile phones would easily be spotted, though ASIS technical support teams are looking into providing small radio transmitters that can be hidden under the inner sole of a training shoe when not in use. We hope to have these devices in place within days.

I have mainly been communicating through James Adams, meeting him inside a nursing home where he plies a confectionary route after school. Although he tries to put a brave face on things, I get the impression that James is depressed and worn down. He often seems listless and his concentration wanders during our conversations.

I have also met Abigail on a number of occasions and her behavior is similar. All four agents have managed to avoid being lured by the cult's mental-control techniques, but the mixture of high activity levels and limited opportunities for sleep are taking their toll.

Chloe and I met with ASIS officials yesterday. Miriam Longford attended and made a useful contribution. She has been in contact with ex-Survivors whom she has counseled, to ask questions about admission to the boarding school inside the Ark.

Acceptance of high ability pupils into the Survivors' boarding school usually happens within one or two weeks of them taking an admissions test. This is because bright youngsters have a tendency to ask probing questions, combined with a natural taste for rebellion. It is therefore in the cult's interests to quickly move these youngsters to a remote location where they can take absolute control of their lives.

Unfortunately—for reasons we do not understand—this has not happened to James, Dana, and Lauren. After consultation with the ASIS team, we have decided to leave our agents in place for a further two weeks, but we feel that the mission's chances of succeeding are shrinking rapidly. ASIS has already begun considering alternative strategies, including the risky possibility of a large-scale police/military raid on the Survivors' Ark.

I hope to be able to come back to you soon with better news.

Yours,

John Jones

P.S. Zara, thank you so much for organizing my daughter's birthday present!

*** THIS E-MAIL CONTAINS SENSITIVE DATA. DO NOT ATTACH OR RESEND WITHOUT USING RANDOM BIT ENCRYPTION ***

James had PE on Thursday afternoons and needed two sweltering hours playing touch football like a hole in the head. To make things worse, the school didn't have showers, so he arrived at the care home stinking of grass and BO. Fortunately, he'd sweet-talked one of the care assistants into letting him use the shower in an unoccupied room.

As he stripped off, James caught himself in the mirror and wasn't impressed. His clothes were ragged, the man who'd clipped his hair at the commune was a butcher, and something about the Survivors' lifestyle was playing havoc with his skin. James had broken out in spots, especially on the back of his neck where he currently sported three giant whiteheads.

He was surprised by a knock at the door as he sat on a bare metal bedframe pulling on a clean sock.

"Hiya," Elliot said brightly as he stepped in. "What's occurring?"

James shrugged as he wriggled his foot into his trainer. "I can't go round stinking the joint up."

"I like that," Elliot said, wagging his finger. "Initiative."

But James could tell that Elliot didn't like it. It wasn't that he objected to James taking a shower; he just didn't like any Survivor deviating from his plans. Elliot took every tiny breach of the timetable as a threat to his authority.

"But next time, run it by me first, OK?" he added.

"What are you doing here?" James asked.

"I'm afraid we have a situation," Elliot said.

"What situation?"

"I got a call from a Mr. Wildman, Emily's son. I tried to arrange her new will through a friendly solicitor, but there was confusion over some property Emily owns and the idiot went and contacted her family solicitor, who turns out to be a friend of Emily's son. So the son finds out and—cut to the chase—half an hour ago I get a call from Emily. She's all upset. Her son is here and he's refusing to leave until he's talked to me."

"Is he angry?" James asked, secretly delighted that the Survivors might not get their hands on the old girl's money.

"I don't suppose finding out that his mother has left two million bucks to charity will have him dancing a jig," Elliot said. "I'm going to see if I can talk him around, but I wanted you alongside me. Emily seems terrifically fond of you, and people tend to behave more reasonably in front of a larger audience."

James grinned as he pulled his clean shirt over his head and began rolling a deodorant stick under his pits. "Anything I can do to help, boss."

"Those are truly words of an angel," Elliot said, giving James a pat on the head that made him feel like a dog.

Emily's room was fifty meters down a corridor. They found her sitting out on the patio with her son. There was a jug of milk and vodka and a couple of half-eaten fish-and-chip lunches on the table between them.

"Ronnie Wildman," the son said, introducing himself as he shook Elliot's hand. He was a short fellow, but well built, with half a head of hair.

James shook his hand too. "Nice to meet you."

Ronnie nodded. "My mother's taken a shine to you, young fella."

"So," Elliot said as he and James took up chairs around the table, "I understand you wanted to speak with me."

"Oh, I *did*," Ronnie said ominously, his eyes lighting up as he slid a folded document out of a leather organizer. "This is a copy of my mother's new will. Miraculously, she seems to have revised the terms so that instead of leaving everything to me, 90 percent of her money goes to something called the Survivors Development Foundation."

Emily interrupted, "It's my money, son. You've already squandered your share. I sold off the house to cover your last disastrous scheme."

Ronnie snatched an angry look at his mother. "Well, I don't think that's what Dad would have wanted. But if you want to donate a few bucks to charity, let's talk about Oxfam or the Red Cross, not these Survivor lunatics."

Elliot smiled and spoke smoothly, "Mr. Wildman, the Survivors' religious activities and our fund-raising efforts for the world's poor are totally separate operations. We work in conjunction with all the other major development agencies around the world. Last year we opened up more than four hundred hospital beds in some of—"

James jolted with fright as Ronnie cut Elliot off by smashing his fist against the table. "Cut the bullshit, you smooth-talking son of a—"

"Ronnie," Emily snapped. "I told you to keep the leash on that temper of yours. Elliot, would you like something to drink?"

Elliot nodded. "A strong black coffee would be nice."

Emily smiled at James. "Would you be a dear? Take whatever you want for yourself, there's Coke in the fridge."

James was relieved to step out from the tense atmosphere around the table. He filled the kettle up to boil and opened a can of Sprite for himself.

The conversation outside got louder as he sprinkled Survivor brand coffee granules into a cup. By the time the water boiled, Elliot and Ronnie were standing up, facing each other off across the table.

"I'll make you sorry you did this!" Ronnie shouted.

"Mr. Wildman, if we can just talk this through in a civilized fashion. I'm sure we'll be able to reach some sort of compromise."

"*Civilized!* The Survivors are the biggest bunch of money-grabbing freaks going. Joel Regan will only get his mitts on my money over my dead body."

"It's not *your* money, Ronnie," his mother reminded him.

As far as James was concerned, the two men could kill each other, but Emily looked stressed out and he felt really sorry for her. He didn't want to carry out the boiling hot coffee when it looked like World War Three was about to erupt, so he stood inside the doorway holding the steaming cup and saucer.

"It's all mind games with you people," Ronnie growled, tapping his finger against his temple. "You've messed up her head. She's in no fit state to make decisions like these anymore."

"From what your mother tells me, you've squandered plenty already," Elliot snarled back, losing his slippery cool for the first time James could remember.

"I bet you've got all your big-shot lawyers backing you up as well," Ronnie said.

Elliot smiled. "If you choose to call the legality of your mother's will into question, I'm confident that—"

Ronnie's posture tightened. He snatched a fish knife off the table and screamed as he lunged at Elliot. "Don't you grin at me like that."

Elliot tried to back away, but got his foot tangled around the leg of his chair. Ronnie plunged the knife into Elliot's stomach. Emily howled out as Elliot crashed backwards into the glass patio doors.

"Spend it now!" Ronnie shouted, as he pulled out the knife.

"Ronnie!" Emily screamed desperately.

"Spend it," Ronnie repeated, as he lunged again. "Spend it."

As James saw the second stab, he put down the coffee mug and backed into Emily's room. Ronnie had a big knife and a murderous rage; this wasn't a time for half measures. He grabbed Emily's plastic kettle jug, which was still half-full of boiling water. He unplugged the cord and ripped off the lid.

The second stab had been aimed at Elliot's chest, but he'd turned away and the only damage was to the shoulder pad of his jacket. As Ronnie lunged a third time, James scrambled onto the patio and threw the boiling water at his head.

It hit from close range, making the stocky man howl as he stumbled backwards, clutching his face. But anger can overcome a great deal of pain and James knew he'd only have an instant while his opponent was stunned to take him down easily. As Ronnie staggered, James clenched the handle of the plastic jug and battered him in the face with it. The plastic splintered in a dozen shards, and Ronnie was unconscious even before his head hit the patio with a hollow thunk.

James snatched the bloody knife from Ronnie's limp hand, before turning and studying the growing red stain on Elliot's shirt. Emily had hauled herself out of her chair and was making her way inside.

Elliot waved his hand, indicating that he wanted James to move close so he could say something. "Call Judith," he gasped. "Keep the cops out of this."

James nodded uncertainly as he reached into Elliot's jacket and pocketed his mobile phone. He tore open the bloody shirt, making buttons fly in all directions. The wound was too messy to see the extent of the cut, but James knew the number one priority was to stop the blood loss. He pulled his T-shirt over his head, folded it into a square, and pressed it against Elliot's stomach.

"Listen," James said as he placed Elliot's hand on the cloth. "Hold it in place as tight as you can."

"It was an accident," Elliot repeated. "Call Judith. Don't speak to the police."

"All *right*," James said angrily. "Maybe I should try and stop you bleeding to death first, eh?"

Emily had hit the emergency alarm beside her bed. James stepped back from Elliot, greatly relieved as a male and female nurse scrambled onto the patio and took control.

"Sweet *Jesus*," the male nurse said when he saw Elliot. He looked up at James holding the mobile. "Call an ambulance. We can't deal with this here."

The female nurse crouched over Ronnie and inspected the blistered skin on his face, while James dialed for an ambulance. As the call rang in his ear, he noticed Emily collapse to the floor beside her bed.

CHAPTER 29

MEDICAL

James feared a heart attack, but Emily had only collapsed from shock. He rode in the back of her squalling ambulance, holding her hand while another vehicle dealt with Elliot and Ronnie. Ronnie remained unconscious. Elliot's blood loss looked dramatic, but the ambulance crew said the wound was unlikely to be fatal.

When they arrived at a modern casualty unit, all three patients got wheeled away. James found himself abandoned in a busy waiting room, with a bare chest and Elliot's dried-out blood staining his fingers. He felt OK, but he was shaken up and the skin on his arms stung in a couple of spots where the boiling water had splashed him.

He called Judith, who arrived within ten minutes, accompanied by Ween. While Judith dashed off to find Elliot, Ween stayed with James and started an interrogation. He'd not previously realized that the gray-haired woman was one of the Survivors' lawyers. After telling Ween the whole truth, she immediately began reinventing it.

"Did anyone call the police?" Ween asked.

James shook his head. "Elliot said not to. I told the emergency operator there'd been an accident."

"Excellent stuff." Ween nodded. "If the cops do get involved, you say you were in the bathroom and that you saw *nothing*. We run that nursing home. I'll make sure none of the staff speak out of turn. Elliot will say it was a bizarre accident. He was carrying out the kettle and slipped into Ronnie, who was holding the knife. Ronnie's unlikely to complain about us covering things up when the truth would put him on trial for attempted murder— and the old girl won't want to see her son locked away."

James was confused. "Why are we doing this?"

"*Why?*" Ween smiled. "Can you imagine what the press would do if they got hold of a story like this? Survivors make an eighty-seven-year-old woman change her will. Jealous son turns up and stabs commune director. It could turn into a national scandal and cost us millions in lost revenue."

"But . . . ," James gasped, totally aghast.

Ween cut him dead and spoke strictly. "Understand this, James: if the devils get their hooks into our organization they'll rip us to shreds. This is an attack on the Survivors, straight from the lowest depths of Hell."

James remembered he was on a mission and tried to think what an angel should say under the circumstances. "Maybe I should pray."

Ween nodded. "That's a good idea. What's Emily's room number?"

"Eighty-six."

She ripped out her mobile, phoned the commune, and began barking orders. "I want two people over to the North Park Elder Care Community, room eighty-six. I want the whole room scrubbed with bleach and hot water, including the garden furniture and the patio. Make sure you find the kettle and collect all the pieces of plastic— No, Lyle, not in half an hour. *Do it now.* I'm heading back with James. If you hear a sniff of anything from the police or the media you know nothing, understood?"

The commune always crawled with gossip. Lauren heard that something had happened to Elliot during dinner, then she bumped into Dana who'd heard that James was involved. By the time she'd got upstairs to her first-floor dorm for homework hour, everyone was talking about it, but apparently the only solid fact was that Elliot had been taken to hospital.

Lauren was taking an outdoor shortcut to the gym when she spotted Paul and cornered him in a sunlit alleyway.

"Where's my brother?" Lauren asked. "Why didn't he come back from the care home with you?"

Paul shook his head and made a gesture, like he was zipping up his mouth. "Sorry, Lauren. I've been sworn to secrecy."

Paul moved to walk off, but Lauren blocked his path. "Is my brother OK, Paul? I *have* to know."

"He's not hurt; I can tell you that much."

Lauren still wanted the whole story. "But what actually happened over there?"

"I can't tell you. Ween swore me to silence. They'll probably make an official announcement later."

Paul stepped forwards, but Lauren blocked his path again.

"Quit doing that," Paul said sharply.

Lauren was desperate to know what was going on. She took a quick glance around to make sure nobody was about, then grabbed Paul's wrist. She twisted his arm up behind his back and shoved him against the wall. Paul had a couple of years on Lauren, but couldn't break the expertly held arm lock. Paul seemed like a nice kid and she didn't want to hurt him, but she had to know if James was in any danger.

"I've sworn an oath," Paul gasped. "You can hurt me all you like; the Devil will do a billion times worse to me if I break my oath."

Lauren tightened the hold, making Paul gasp in pain. She was worried that he might be so strongly under the Survivors' influence that he'd rather suffer a broken arm than break an oath.

"Please," Paul begged, almost crying. "Please don't make me break my oath."

Lauren didn't have the stomach, either to break Paul's arm or for the trouble it would cause. She let him go and backed off.

"What's your problem?" Paul screamed, humiliated

and trying not to sob. "I told you he's not hurt. What more do you want?"

"Everything," Lauren said, with a sense of desperation that was exaggerated, but not entirely false. "You've got a brother. Wouldn't you want to know if something happened to Rick?"

The emotional tug had more of an effect on Paul than the arm lock, making Lauren wish she'd used this tactic first.

"Okay . . . ," Paul said, thinking hard. "Ween made me swear not to say anything about what happened, but I guess I can tell you where James is. Then you can find out for yourself. But you've *got* to swear not to say it was me that told you."

Lauren nodded. "I swear as an angel on pain of eternity in a fiery Hell."

Paul seemed reassured by this oath, which was as strong as they come in Survivor speak.

"James is over in Elliot's office."

"Is Elliot there?"

"No, but Ween's around."

Lauren smiled. "Right, I'll go and see him."

"You'd be better off leaving it," Paul said. "Ween's going crazy. You'll get punished if you stick your nose in."

Lauren lied to reassure Paul. "OK, I'll leave it for a while and see if they make an announcement. You're a good guy, Paul. I'm sorry I hurt you."

"It didn't hurt much," Paul lied. "But I'll report you if you pull a stunt like that again."

Lauren thought everything through as Paul headed off to play basketball on one of the outdoor courts. She would have liked to ask Dana or Abigail for advice, but they were both on washing-up duty and she knew there was no chance of a private conversation in the commune's chaotic kitchen. Besides, if she got caught she could just say that she overheard someone who'd seen James going into Elliot's office.

Lauren headed inside the mall and towards the offices at the far end of the ground floor. The corridors were busy, and she'd learned that you had to move purposefully around the commune unless you wanted a bunch of overhelpful angels asking what you were up to.

She passed through the open-plan offices where she'd taken her aptitude test a few weeks earlier and found them deserted. The trouble was, she'd never gone past this point and didn't know what to expect beyond the double doors that led to the senior staff's private offices.

After poking her head through the door for a cautious glance, Lauren stepped into a reassuringly empty corridor containing a water cooler and piles of stationery. There was a glass-fronted office on either side of her, with Venetian blinds blocking off the view inside. She crept between a photocopier and a stack of boxed paper and peeked between the slats into the office on her left. She felt a rush of nerves and ducked down when she saw Ween, sitting at her desk having a highly animated telephone conversation.

It took Lauren a couple of seconds to get her nerve back. She popped her head above the copier paper and took a longer look. There was no sign of James, so she stepped across the corridor and looked into the other office.

James was on a sofa, with the back of his head touching the glass. Lauren was tempted to rap on the glass and make him jump, but these were hardly the right circumstances. She crept around and stepped into the office. James looked well scrubbed. His hair was wet and he wore nothing but trainers and his favorite pair of ragged denim shorts.

"What's going on?" Lauren whispered, as her brother turned and smiled at her.

James explained briefly, keeping to the essential details. He told Lauren to find Dana and Abigail and tell them everything, but Ween came into the room before she got a chance to leave.

"*What* are you doing here?" Ween said, so fiercely that her opening word sounded like a whip cracking.

Lauren played the innocent little sister, making herself sound scared and whiney. "I was frightened that the devils had got my brother. I came to make sure he was OK."

Ween huffed, but then her mood changed abruptly. "Oh well, I was about to call your mother up here anyway."

"What for?" James asked.

"Remember the aptitude test you sat the day after you arrived?"

"Now you mention it, yeah."

"Well, I'm pleased to say that your test results were outstanding. Your mark was easily high enough for you to ascend to our elite boarding school inside the Ark. Unfortunately, the Ark is undergoing a lot of rebuilding work and the school isn't currently accepting new pupils. However, present circumstances dictate that it would be a sensible precaution if you were taken out of this area until the incident with Elliot blows over. I've explained the situation to Eleanor Regan, and she's agreed to accept you into the Survivors' boarding school as a special case."

James's mind raced. He was well pleased to get into the boarding school, but the mission plan had been based upon two, or even all three, agents being accepted.

"Wow," James gasped. "I've heard about the school. It's like a massive honor, only . . ."

Ween screwed up her face. "Only *what*?"

"I don't know." James shrugged. "My dad buggered off, then we moved out here, then we moved to the commune. Now you want me to go off into the outback."

"James," Ween said reassuringly, "your family isn't Lauren, Dana, and Abigail anymore. You have a family of angels, ten thousand strong."

"I know." James shrugged sullenly, looking down at the carpet. "It's not that I don't want to go; I just think I'd be scared going all that way on my own."

Lauren realized what James was trying to do and butted in. "Did I pass the test?" she asked enthusiastically. "I'd *love* to go to the Ark, and I could keep James company."

Ween looked stressed out. She clearly didn't relish the prospect of having to call Eleanor Regan and ask her to accept another pupil, but on the other hand she desperately wanted to hush up the whole thing with Elliot. James being hundreds of kilometers away in the middle of the outback greatly reduced the chances of him opening his mouth to someone he shouldn't.

Ween looked at James and spoke firmly. "If I call the Ark and try getting them to accept Lauren too, will you both definitely agree to go?"

"What about Dana too?" Lauren asked.

"*No,*" Ween said, with surprising firmness. "There's no prospect of Dana going. She's been chosen for another path within our movement."

James and Lauren exchanged a quick glance, hardly able to avoid grinning at each other.

"Well, I guess I'll go with Lauren," James said. "As long as it's OK with our mum."

CHAPTER 24

ARK

Abigail acted like you'd expect from a mother facing the prospect of her children being sent to boarding school seven hundred kilometers away. Of course, she eventually let Ween talk her into letting James and Lauren leave.

The Survivors owned a small aircraft that spent its life shuttling provisions, mail, and people between a small airfield twenty kilometers outside of Brisbane and the Ark. The evening flight was due out at 10 p.m. Ween pulled rank and bumped two other passengers so that James and Lauren could skip town.

All the two kids owned now were the clothes they stood up in and a few personal items like toothbrushes and deodorants. This lack of money and possessions was deliberate, because it left Survivor families dependent on their commune for everything and made it extremely difficult for them to leave the cult and resume a normal life.

Abigail volunteered to drive out to the airport. Dana abandoned her precious Survivors timetable to come along and say good-bye. She rode in the back of the Mercedes wagon beside James, while Lauren was up front with a map spread over her legs.

Although Abigail hadn't officially donated the car to the Survivors, she'd allowed members to use it for errands over the previous month. The interior was now grubby, the smell of baby puke lurked in the air, and there were even a couple of punctures in the leather upholstery.

James looked back at the commune as they pulled out of the parking lot, knowing he wouldn't be back. Everywhere else he'd been on a mission—even prison— there'd been something or someone that he'd miss. But none of the Survivors he'd met gave him that feeling. They were all dedicated to cult life and so obsessed with devils and the Ark that he didn't care for any of them. It had been impossible to make an emotional connection with a bunch of people who only smiled when they were supposed to.

Dana looked miserable at the way things had panned out.

"You OK?" James asked.

"What do you think?" Dana asked bitterly. "I *never* get any of the breaks on my missions. I'm gonna retire in a gray shirt."

Abigail spoke. "That's the wrong attitude, Dana. We're all part of a team."

Dana bit her head off. "Spare me the patronizing crap, Abigail."

Lauren looked back over her shoulder. "Me and James *did* ask, but Ween acted really strict. She said they've chosen a different path for you, or something."

"Whatever," Dana said miserably. "I expect they've got me marked down for an epic career in dishwashing."

"You never know," James said. "It might be something good."

"Can you just stop going on about it, *please*?"

James turned away and looked out of the window at the setting sun.

Once they'd driven about five kilometers towards the airfield, Abigail pulled up at a Hungry Jack's burger joint. She called John Jones from a pay phone. After getting an update, John asked to speak with James.

"You nervous?" John asked.

"A bit," James admitted. "They're a bunch of loonies, and we're gonna be totally isolated up there."

"I know," John said. "But remember, if you're ever in any danger the number one priority is always your safety. Just grab the keys to the first vehicle you can find and head the hell out of there. Chloe and I have already been up there to stake the Ark out. We've got the lease on a disused ranch house twenty kilometers away. Chloe and I will need cars to get around, so I expect we'll set off by road first thing tomorrow. We should be there by the evening.

"What about communications?" James asked.

"I was just coming to that. The miniature receivers are on a flight up from Melbourne as we speak. The ASIS engineers have done a lot of testing to make sure that they're robust enough to survive the pounding and moisture of life hidden inside a shoe and the boffins reckon they've cracked it."

"How will you get them to us?"

"There's no way we can get them to you tonight. The Ark itself is sealed off tight, but the kids run around it every morning, like you've been doing around the outside of the mall. Try staying behind the pack and keep your eyes and ears open for a signal or hidden package."

"What kind of signal?"

"We haven't thought it out yet."

"That's not exactly encouraging, John."

"I know, James. I'm sorry. Everything about this mission has been done at short notice. One other thing. Don't attempt to use any of the telephones inside the Ark if you're talking about the mission. Several of Miriam's patients told her that Eleanor Regan has the switchboard bugged. There are also rumors that the offices and bedrooms of some senior staff are bugged too, so if you're talking about the mission, keep your voices down and try to do it outdoors or in public areas."

"Gotcha," James said. "I'll pass all this info on to Lauren."

"Great," John said. "Good luck."

James shook his head. "Sounds like we'll need it."

The propeller-driven aircraft carried six passengers. James and Lauren sat in the cramped third row of seats, with aluminum cargo pallets strapped into position behind their heads. It was dark by the time they took off and the two-and-a-half-hour flight passed over seven hundred kilometers of nothing: black desert, with no artificial lights and just the occasional rocky outline illuminated by the half moon.

The sense of distance and isolation combined with the aircraft's brutal ventilation kept sending chills down James's back. There were a million things he wanted to say to Lauren, but with four Survivors lined up in front of them they had to keep quiet. The seats were upright and too cramped to attempt sleep, so James had to content himself by flipping through the in-flight reading: a well-thumbed catalog of tacky Ark souvenirs and DVDs of Joel Regan's finest speeches with his day-glow white grin on the cover.

As he flipped through the pages, James found his sister's head on his shoulder, then her hand sliding under the armrest and resting on his bare knee. James put his own hand on top, with his fingers spread between Lauren's, and they stayed that way for ages.

An orange glow lit up the horizon for the last 150 kilometers of the flight. It grew ever bigger, until you could make out three gigantic spires, painted gold and basking in yellow light, with one of the world's largest domes set between them. There were six turrets, one at each corner of the hexagonal perimeter, topped off with a thirty-meter-high cross designed to ward off devils.

James had seen photographs of the Ark, but nothing had prepared him for its outrageous scale. It was part fortress, part Las Vegas glitz, and 100 percent the last thing you expected to see in the middle of the Australian outback. James didn't think much of Joel Regan and the way he'd made his fortune through brainwashing and deceit, but he couldn't help being impressed by the spectacle.

Lauren whispered in James's ear as the plane took a sharp turn to line up with the runway. "That has got to be the *maddest* thing I've ever seen."

The small aircraft had taken off from a landing strip edged with grass, but touched down on a runway big enough to handle jumbo jets. There was a two-story terminal building alongside the control tower, with an illuminated sign above its glass frontage: *Welcome to Joel Regan International Airport*. The airport was built in the 1980s, at a time when Regan had planned on turning the Ark into a money-spinning tourist attraction, with thousands of hotel rooms, golf courses, and a Disneyland-style theme park.

Regan later changed his mind and declared that the Ark was a sacred place that devils were unfit to enter. Critics of Regan say this simply hid the fact that very few tourists wanted to spend their vacations as guests of a religious cult in the oppressive heat of the Australian outback.

As a result of Regan's failed ambition, James, Lauren, and the other passengers faced a lengthy walk from the aircraft to the Ark itself. It took them through several hundred meters of eerily deserted corridors and into a silent arrivals lounge, where most of the lights were burned out and the dust-covered baggage carousels hadn't moved in a decade. Finally, they headed outdoors and along a wide ramp that led towards the Ark itself.

James and Lauren didn't know where they were going, so they walked behind the four other passengers. As they passed through a reinforced steel gate, each passenger bowed reverently at a spindly woman with straight dark hair. James and Lauren had seen photographs and knew it was Joel Regan's eldest daughter Eleanor, the one they all called The Spider.

James thought there was something wonderfully appropriate about the nickname, as The Spider stepped forwards to introduce herself. She wore a tight black polo-neck sweater and had long fingers as slender as pencils. Her voice ought to have been a witchlike cackle, but she opened with a smile and an ordinary Australian accent.

"Hi." Eleanor smiled. "You must be James and Lauren. Congratulations on ascending to the Ark."

The kids both smiled back as they shook The Spider's hand. She led them through the turret and outside onto a broad path. The Ark had six pedestrianized roads inside its walls. Each one ran from a turret towards a giant square in the center of the Ark, which contained the Holy Church of The Survivors, with its gigantic dome and three golden spires.

While the church itself was impressive, the rest of the buildings were surprisingly ordinary. They were mostly one or two stories high and constructed in the most basic utilitarian style, with corrugated metal roofs and white plastic windows. It smacked of cheapness. James felt as if he'd arrived at the swankiest restaurant in town and found Big Mac and fries on the menu.

CHAPTER 25

RISE

"Wakey, wakey!" a great slab of a woman called Georgie shouted as she burst into James's bedroom.

It was better than the makeshift facilities at the Brisbane mall, with eight metal-framed beds, personal lockers, plus a purpose-built shower and laundry area at the end of the room.

James was bleary-eyed as he rolled out of bed. He'd arrived at one in the morning and stripped off without waking the room's seven other residents. These boys were now scrambling into a uniform that looked like a PE kit: white rugby shirt, blue shorts, and blue football socks. James took longer than the others, because he had to grab new clothes from inside his locker and remove a mass of plastic bags, tags, and stickers.

Once dressed, James joined the back of a line, queuing up to pee into the single stall or the urinal. He was the last to go, and even though he skipped washing his hands, James couldn't catch up in time to see where everyone had legged it to.

Georgie came in from another bedroom. She screwed up her eyes as if she couldn't believe what she was seeing and bellowed in James's ear. "Why the *hell* are you still here?"

"I haven't got a timetable," James explained. "I don't know where I'm going."

"All pupils are on the same timetable!" she shouted, spraying James with spit. "Follow the others."

"But they've gone."

"You'd better learn to keep up with them if you don't want a punishment. Down the stairs, through the doors, and on to the quadrant for morning exercises."

James sprinted down the corridor, through a door, and into a face-full of sunlight. A set of steps on the outside of the building took him down to a dusty patch at the rear of the accommodation block. The hundred and fifty pupils ranged between ten and seventeen years old and stood in four long lines. Everyone wore the same white shirts, but each line wore different color shorts and socks signifying the building they lived in.

As he joined the end of the blue line, James spotted Lauren standing two rows ahead in yellow kit. Georgie and a couple of other teachers stood up front and started the kids off with some old-school warm-up exercises. They did stretching and toe touching, working their way up to thrusts, push-ups, crunches, and star jumps. They had to chant a short sentence between each movement:

"Good morning, Lord. We are your angels. Here to serve you. Make us strong. Please protect us. Our souls are honest. Our thoughts are pure. We are leaders. We will take humanity. Through the darkness."

The ten-sentence chant matched the ten repetitions of each exercise. After fifteen minutes of springing up and down in the dirt, James was breathless. His skin was covered in a layer of reddish grit and the lines of the chant were the only things in his head.

After getting two minutes to catch their breath, the four lines were led out through one of the turrets for their run around the perimeter. James estimated that each lap was about a kilometer and a half. They ran a lap in formation at a modest pace, keeping up the chant. At the end of this, the instructors shouted *break* and the kids were expected to run two more laps as fast as they could. James spotted Lauren and ran alongside her.

"You OK?" James puffed.

"Could have done with more sleep," Lauren said, her words jerking as her trainers pounded the tarmac path around the perimeter. "And I've got grit all down my shorts."

James scratched his belly. "Tell me about it. It's driving me nuts."

"What's your name?" a kid asked as the line of dusty boys staggered back across the dirt towards the Blue accommodation block. The kid looked twelve, but was actually a year younger. He had a rugged build and a squished-up nose.

"James."

"I'm Rat."

James didn't quite believe what he'd heard. "Did you say *Rat*?"

"Well, my name's Rathbone. But if you ever call me that, I'll kick you in the bollocks."

James smiled, but he was also surprised: Survivors didn't swear.

"Cat got your tongue?" Rat asked, apparently pleased to have shocked James.

"I'm just knackered," James said, shrugging listlessly.

Rat nodded. "You did good. I've seen plenty of new arrivals keel over from the heat when they first get here."

"How long have you been here?" James asked, when they reached the bottom of the metal staircase.

"Just my whole life," Rat said.

He pulled the leather necklace from under his shirt. It had half a dozen beads on it, but he pointed to a gold one.

"What's that for?" James asked.

Rat smiled. "It means I'm part of the royal family."

"Eh?"

"Joel Regan saved the best 'til last: I'm his thirty-third and final kid."

"Cool."

Rat shook his head, like James was an idiot. "What's cool about it?"

James found himself lost for words again as they reached the entrance of the boys' dorm. The lads were stripping off for a shower, but Rat stopped walking in the doorway.

"Are you queer?" Rat asked bluntly.

James shook his head. "No way."

"So you like girls?"

James smiled. "Yeah."

"Naked girls?"

"They're my favorite kind."

"Come on, then." Rat grinned, tugging at James's shirt.

James looked uncertain. "What are you doing?"

Rat tutted. "Don't be a pussy. It'll only take a minute, and I swear, this will *blow* your tiny mind."

James tried to work out what he should do. There was part of him that wanted to behave until he knew the lie of the land, but on the other hand Rat clearly wasn't your average brainwashed Survivor brat. He might make a useful ally.

"Go on, then," James said. "We're not gonna get in trouble, are we?"

"Don't be an idiot all your life, James. I'm gonna be standing right alongside you. I've done this a million times."

James let Rat take him a few meters back along the corridor. He opened a door into a wiltingly hot room, which contained a huge water heater, with pipes and gauges running in all directions.

Rat whispered as he headed towards a table in the far corner, "Keep your voice down."

He clambered onto a table and signaled James to follow. James stepped up and turned to the wall. There was a metal grille in front of his face, which Rat was already staring through. James put his eyes up to the holes and gasped.

"Isn't that awesome?" Rat whispered.

James was looking into a steaming shower room,

packed with the girls who lived in the dorm across the hall. They were laughing, shampooing their hair, and rubbing soapy hands over themselves.

"Oh." James grinned, as his mouth dropped open.

"Told you it was worth it," Rat whispered.

"Totally worth it, dude. I want to stay here for the rest of my life."

There was so much female flesh on display, James couldn't keep his eyeballs fixed in one place.

Suddenly, Rat smashed his hand against the grille and shouted out, *"Perv alert!"*

Before James knew what was going on, Rat had jumped off the table and was heading for the door. He'd unscrewed the grille in anticipation of the prank and it clattered down inside the shower, causing a flurry of screams and a mass exodus of girls.

James jumped off the table and lunged for the door. Rat had pulled it shut and as James grabbed the handle he heard the unmistakable sound of a key turning in the lock.

"You butthole!" James shouted, kicking the door hard. "Let me out of here. I'll smash every bone in your body."

James panicked as he looked around and realized that escape was impossible. A bunch of girls were shouting abuse from inside the shower room, "You're gonna get punished for this, pervert!"

Thirty seconds later, someone was banging on the door. He recognized Georgie's voice.

"Open up this instant."

She pounded again and James tutted at Georgie's apparent lack of brainpower. "Do you think I'd lock *myself* in here?"

This triggered a pause in the noises coming through the door, before Georgie erupted into a bellow.

"Rathbone Regan, get out here."

When there was no reply, she shouted again. "Don't make me come into that shower and drag you out!"

James heard a kerfuffle through the door. It sounded like Rat had been bundled out into the corridor by some of the other boys.

"Was it him?" Georgie demanded.

Normal kids wouldn't have grassed, but Survivors are taught that the Devil will get them if they lie to a superior.

"We saw Rat with the new kid, Miss."

"He came running into the shower half a minute ago."

Rat started screaming at his roommates, "You snitch-assed motherf—"

"*Rathbone!*" Georgie shouted. "You're in enough trouble. Do you want me to soap your tongue as well? Where is the key?"

Rat's response to this demand was a giant raspberry, blown into the palms of both hands. "I don't care what you do to me, fat-ass. You don't *own* me."

"Miss, we've got the key," another boy said. "It was under Rat's dirty shorts."

The key turned. Georgie grabbed James by the collar of his shirt and shoved him up against the corridor wall. The floor was covered in puddles, where various dripping boys had scrambled in and out, but Rat was the only one left. His hair was foamed up with shampoo, and he wore nothing except a towel around his waist.

James shot Rat an angry look, before speaking to Georgie. "Miss, he tricked me into it."

"I know he tricked you." Georgie nodded. "I know he locked you in there, but look at the size of him. He didn't put his arms around your waist and stand you on the table, did he?"

"No, Miss," James said weakly.

"I want you both to shower and wait downstairs for the service. You can expect to be *severely* punished."

"What about breakfast?" Rat asked.

"Tough."

James stepped into the bedroom, which was muggy from the steam escaping the showers. The other boys were either in the final stages of getting dressed, or they'd already headed downstairs for breakfast.

"Thanks for sticking up for me, guys!" Rat shouted to nobody in particular as he threw off the towel and stormed back into the shower to rinse his hair.

James ripped off his sweaty kit, before following Rat into the steaming shower area. They were the only lads left and Rat backed up to the far wall, looking scared.

"I ought to slap the piss out of you," James said, pointing angrily as he grabbed a bottle of shampoo from a ledge.

"I'm not scared of you," Rat said, but he looked less sure as James closed him down. He ended up with his back against the tiles and James's chest a few centimeters from his face.

"Go on, batter me," Rat said defiantly. "I don't care. That cow wants you to and you won't be the first."

After lashing out and landing himself in trouble more times than he cared to count, James had recently become a master of turning the other cheek.

"Why'd you play such a stupid, *pointless* trick on me?"

Rat tutted. "Beat me up and get it over with, but don't expect me to squirm in front of you."

James didn't know what to make of this kid. Was Rat some kind of Survivor rebel, or did he just have a screw loose?

"What's our punishment gonna be?" James asked.

"Oh, you'll love it." Rat grinned, turning around and showing James his bum.

James recoiled as he looked at a mass of scabs and bruises, some of them still pretty fresh.

"Are you *kidding*?" James gasped, suddenly a lot more worried about the trouble he was in.

Rat shrugged. "They can paddle me all they like. I'm not gonna tow the line. Come to think of it, you're not one either, are you?"

"One what?"

Rat smiled. "You don't *really* believe."

"How do you figure that?" James asked nervously, as he lathered up his pit hair. "I took the oath. I've got the necklace."

"You might wear a necklace," Rat said, "but if you really believed, you never would have come into that boiler room to look at naked girls. And right now, you'd be telling me to repent and accept our punishment."

"Maybe I'm just easily led," James said.

Rat shook his head. "If you were dumb, I'd be sitting on the floor with a bloody nose right now."

"Don't get too full of yourself, Rat. It might still happen."

"So how come you ended up here?"

James explained about Elliot getting stabbed and

Ween covering it up as they stepped through to the bedroom and started toweling off.

"I know him." Rat nodded. "We used to call him Elliot the Eel, 'cos he's so slippery. Do you realize, you and your sister are the first new faces to come inside the Ark in three months?"

"Yeah, the people in Brisbane said there's a lot of construction work going on, or something."

Rat smiled. "Have you seen any?"

James realized he hadn't. "So what *is* going on?"

"Joel Regan's dying," Rat explained. "The Spider doesn't want people outside the Ark finding out, because when my dad dies several billion tons of crap are gonna hit the fan."

"Why?" James asked.

Rat was clearly getting a kick out of finding someone who wanted to hear what he had to say. "The whole Survivor religion is based on the idea that God asked Joel Regan to build an Ark and save humanity. But how can he save us when he's dead?"

"Yeah." James nodded thoughtfully. "I can see that's tricky."

"On top of that, there's a war raging over who takes control when he dies."

"Between who?"

"My dad's fourth wife, Susie, and my eldest sister, Eleanor—The Spider. Susie is sane, she doesn't even wear a Survivor necklace. Eleanor's lot are the opposite; they believe every word in the manual. They say that if my dad dies before the apocalypse, it's a sign that the Devil is winning. When he dies, they're gonna freak."

"Like how?"

"They think the Devil is going to rise up from Hell and try to kill them when my dad dies, and they live in a fortress with a guns, explosives, and ammunition stashed in the basement. It's not a healthy combination."

James remembered that he was supposed to have fallen into the cult's belief system. "But how can this be true? *The Survivors' Manual* says . . ."

Rat burst out laughing. "Yeah right, James. Your Survivor beliefs are somewhere between paper thin and nonexistent."

"That's *not* true," James insisted unconvincingly as he pulled on a pair of boxers.

He was worried. If an eleven-year-old could see through him, who else was going to?

"Do you know, when my dad joined the Australian army, they gave him an IQ test and he scored one hundred and ninety-six. That basically means he's a certified genius. They tested me and guess what I got?"

"Low thirties?" James grinned.

"One-nine-seven," Rat said. "I'm the smartest kid you're ever likely to meet, so don't even *try* pulling the wool over my eyes."

James couldn't help smiling at the irony of this situation. "If you're so clever, how come your butt looks like a rugby team used it for kicking practice?"

Rat shrugged. "People are always telling me I'm too smart for my own good."

CHAPTER 26

OUCH

Except when nonmembers were present, Survivors' services were always single-sex affairs. James and Rat were taken into a large hall and made to lie facedown on the wooden floor at the center of the two circles, which contained all the girls in the boarding school. James didn't know what to expect, but it was reassuring having Rat alongside him, because the smaller boy had been through this before and didn't look too scared.

The service was taken by Georgie, whose instruments of choice were a harmonica and a twangy steel guitar. After the standard fifteen minutes of clapping, singing, and chanting, Georgie's voice took on a somber tone:

"The Ark is a place of godly purity. But to sin within

the Ark is to invite devils into the holiest place on earth. Before we can forgive, such sin must be severely punished. The Devil must be beaten from the souls of the miscreants."

Georgie gleefully slipped a wooden paddle out of her shorts and snapped her fingers. Two girls carried a school desk into the center of the circles. James caught an awkward glance at Lauren as he was made to stand up.

A padded belt that fastened with Velcro was wrapped around James's waist, to protect the base of his spine from injury, then the back off his shorts were tugged down, exposing his bum. A plastic bit was placed in the boys' mouths to stop them biting their tongues and they were made to lean over the table.

"It is the duty of those whose dignity was undermined by these perverted and *lustful* boys to step forward and offer punishment," Georgie said, bouncing on the balls of her bare feet.

James was alarmed as a dozen blue-socked girls stood up and formed a queue. There had only been seven or eight in the shower, but James was in no position to complain with a chunk of rubber jammed in his mouth.

"The older boy is new to this Ark, one stroke each," Georgie said. "Rathbone is a persistent menace, give him three. *Commence.*"

James had his head dangling over the edge of the table, so he could only see an upside-down view of the girls' trainers through the underside of the table. The first one stepped up and took the small paddle from Georgie. There was a sharp crack and the table rocked forwards onto its front legs as Rat took his first lick.

By the time he'd taken three, James could see tears in the corner of Rat's eyes.

"I forgive you, Rathbone," the blue-socked girl said as she stepped across to James.

James quaked with fear as he braced for the first lick. The force of the paddle made him jolt violently, but it hurt less than he'd feared.

"I forgive you, James," the girl said tautly as she stepped back and handed the paddle down the line.

James's relief didn't last long. The second hit hurt more than the first and each one after that grew more painful.

After the thirteenth girl took the final swing at James's bare buttocks, Georgie hauled him off the table and snatched the bit from his mouth. As the girls filed out of the room to start morning lessons, James ripped off the padded belt and hitched up his shorts. He noticed that the wooden paddle on the ground beside him was spattered with blood, but James felt his bum and found nothing but one slightly bloody graze.

Then he stepped back and looked at Rat. The eleven-year-old had taken thirty-nine paddle strokes. He was struggling to find the strength to pull himself off the table and had streaks of blood trickling down his legs.

"Stand up then, lad," Georgie said, sounding extremely pleased with herself. "We'll beat the devils out of you yet, young Rathbone."

Rat used the table to push himself up, and James grabbed his arm to steady him. He wiped tears off his face and scowled defiantly at Georgie.

"Didn't hurt a bit," he said.

Georgie ignored him and stepped across to eyeball James.

"So, new boy," she said as she picked up the bloody paddle and waved it in James's face. "That was a taste of what you can expect if you tempt devils into the Ark. I will demand *absolute* obedience from now on. Is that clear?"

"Yes, Miss," James said, hardly able to conceal his sense of outrage.

A further glance at Rat's bloody legs gave James an urge to pick up the paddle and give Georgie a taste of her own medicine. He had the strength, but he'd known there was a risk of physical punishment when he'd signed up for the mission and he wasn't going to blow six weeks of work in one crazy outburst.

"*Riiiiight,*" Georgie said, twisting her face into an evil smirk. "Let's have the pair of you off to the sweatbox."

James guessed that something called a sweatbox wasn't going to be an air-conditioned space filled with fluffy cushions, and he was spot on. Georgie frogmarched the two boys to a metal shed near the Ark's concrete perimeter. The inside was three paces across, with a sand floor and two buckets. The one containing drinking water had a plastic beaker bobbing in it, while the other served as an emergency toilet.

James and Rat reluctantly stepped inside. There was no window, but the brilliant sunlight escaping through gaps in the metal was enough to see by.

"Contemplate your sins," Georgie said severely.

The metal door clattered shut before it was secured with two sliding bolts. James panicked as the searingly hot air reached into his lungs.

Rat saw James was struggling and spoke firmly, "Calm down."

"I can't breathe."

"Take little breaths until your lungs adjust to the heat," Rat said as he rubbed James's shoulder to reassure him. "You'll be OK. Just don't get too close to the metal: It'll fry your skin."

While James steadily took deeper breaths, Rat used his shoe to turn over the baking sand so that part of the floor was cool enough to sit on.

"How long are we in here for?" James asked.

"Until school ends at one."

"That's five hours," James gasped.

James copied Rat, turning over the baking dirt, before lying on his side so that his throbbing bum didn't touch the floor. He remembered the tortures he'd been through in basic training and began thinking of the slogans they chanted:

This is tough, but cherubs are tougher. This is tough, but cherubs are tougher.

He smiled at the irony as he realized that this was part of CHERUB's own brand of thought control. But the similarities between the tough regime on CHERUB campus and life inside the Survivors' Ark were only skin-deep: Everyone who joined CHERUB knew what they were signing up for and if you wanted to leave, it was as simple as asking.

Within a few minutes, James had got his breathing back to normal and he'd rehydrated himself from the morning run with three beakers of water.

"You know," Rat said, speaking slowly because of the

heat, "this is all my fault. I reckon I owe you a favor. Anything you like."

James smirked. "What *exactly* does a kid with a sore butt and attitude problems have to offer me?"

"More than you think," Rat said indignantly. "Being one of Regan's kids counts for quite a bit and feeding gossip into the right ears can earn you plenty of favors around here."

James tried thinking of something that would be good for the mission, without making his goals seem obvious.

"OK, Mr. Big Shot," James said. "I take it we get work assignments here, the same as in Brisbane?"

"Sure, school lasts until one, then we work until dinner."

"Could you fix me and my little sister up with something cushy? Like, a nice desk job, instead of cleaning toilets, or laundry."

"No sweat," Rat said, surprising James with his air of confidence. "I'll have a word with my stepmum, Susie. That's my dad's fourth wife. She's the second most powerful person in the Ark after The Spider."

"What about your mum?" James asked.

Rat made a gesture like there was a noose around his neck, followed by a gagging sound. "My mum couldn't handle all the other women my dad was carrying on with. She ended up going ga-ga and hanging herself."

"*Christ,*" James gasped. "I'm sorry."

"Not as sorry as me," Rat said. "You've got a family outside of this nuthouse. If you're enough of a pain in the arse, they'll kick you out to go and live with your dad or something. I'm stuck here 'til I'm eighteen."

"Doesn't your dad care what's happening to you?"

"He's eighty-two years old, he needs an oxygen cylinder to breathe, he's got thirty-three kids, and I remind him of the nutty wife who topped herself."

"Bummer," James said.

"It was cool back when my mum was alive. We'd visit other communes all over the world with my dad. I was like five or six, and everywhere we went we were treated like royalty. Cameras flashed when we arrived at airports. I remember one commune in Japan, I wanted to be normal and play, but none of the other kids would go near me because they were scared of who I was. They'd hand me toys, do a little bow, and then scarper."

"Quite a fall from grace," James said.

"More like a plummet. Now I'm just in the way. I'm not a Survivor and I'm too smart to buy their brain games, but there's nowhere else I can go."

CHAPTER 27

SUSIE

The metal shed got more unbearable as the sun rose. James tried all sorts of positions to get comfortable: sideways, on his belly, crouching, standing up, clothes on, clothes off. The only relief came from pouring water on his shirt and slapping it over his face.

Mercifully, the bucket got refilled every hour by a round-faced girl who'd perfected all the standard Survivor nods, head tilts, and smiles. Each water delivery came with a syrupy blessing:

"Sweat out the devils. The lord shall forgive you both."

Neither boy had a watch, but Rat had spent enough of his life in the sweatbox to gauge time by the position of the sun. When he sensed it was close to 1 p.m., he told

James to clean himself as well as he could using the limited water available, then put on his trainers and clothes and get ready to run.

"This heat has done me in," James gasped. "I'm not sure I'll even be able to walk."

"You'd better get it together if you want that cushy work assignment," Rat said. "I nicked some papers out of the office for my stepmum and she owes me a favor, but we're talking about Joel Regan's wife. She's a bit of a psycho. You can't just knock on her office door and say *hi* anytime you want. We'll have to catch her while she's at lunch in the restaurant around the back of the Holy Church."

James nodded. "I'll try, but I'm dying here."

Rat practically barged the girl out of his way when she released the bolts to let them out. James was impressed by how tough Rat was, disregarding dehydration and the pain from the savage paddling as he sprinted towards a single-story building fifty meters away. The dazzling sunlight made James's eyelids scrunch up as he struggled to keep pace.

Rat cut around the side of the building and clanked down a metal staircase cut into the ground. He grabbed a rubber handle and levered open a metal door with a yellow and black radiation symbol on it: *Emergency Decontamination Area*. The door was fifteen centimeters thick and Rat had to drive with both legs to shift it.

"I know every tunnel in this joint," Rat said as James followed him into a gloomy, low-ceilinged room. There was a line of radiological protection suits hanging from a rail and shower heads jutting out of the wall.

A second thick door took the boys into a corridor, with lines of strip lighting glaring off the shiny floor. The air was chilly, which gave James a boost as he ran past rooms filled with dated-looking electronics, provisions, and ventilation equipment.

"What is this?" James shouted as their running and breathing echoed.

Rat looked back over his shoulder. "There's more to the Ark than meets the eye. It goes four levels below ground in places. There's enough canned food to keep us underground for years."

The Ark was starting to freak James out. The Survivors in Brisbane were manipulative and eccentric, but they didn't have underground bunkers, radiological protection suits or guns, and they didn't beat kids into a bloody mess before baking them in metal sheds.

A four-minute run wouldn't normally have taken much out of James, but by the time he reached the line of elevator doors at the end of the corridor he was shattered. The sweatbox had sapped his strength, leaving his muscles tight and his head thumping.

"OK," Rat said as they stepped into a giant cargo elevator with a paint-spattered floor. "When we step out, you'd better be on your best behavior. This is the temple restaurant."

"What's that?"

"It's where the high-ups inside the Ark go to eat proper grub, instead of the tinned slop we get at the boarding school. So behave yourself and avoid getting into any casual conversations."

James was expecting something swank when they

stepped out, but the temple restaurant was a basic canteen-type deal, although the chunky wooden tables looked like they cost a few bucks and there were arty black-and-white photos of the Ark along the walls.

A titchy man in a white shirt and black trousers stepped out as they tried getting in. "Excuse me," he said stiffly, clearly not impressed by two boys in school kit.

Rat pulled his necklace out of his shirt and jangled the gold bead.

The man stepped back a touch nervously. "Oh, yes. It's Rathbone Regan, isn't it?"

"Oh yes, it is," Rat mocked. "Is my stepmum here?"

"She usually prefers to eat alone. I wouldn't . . ."

Rat ignored this and led James between tables, towards a stunningly beautiful woman eating a bowl of minestrone soup. She had long dark hair and her carefully made-up face suggested that her life didn't run on the frantic schedule of a Survivor.

"Hello, Rat," Susie said. Her accent was American and her voice indicated a mixture of suspicion and pleasure at seeing her stepson. "Why don't you both sit down?"

James reckoned he'd recovered enough to sit down, but Rat shook his head. "I'll stay on my feet, if that's OK."

Susie smirked. "Oh dear, how many did you get today?"

"Thirty-nine."

"Phew," Susie said, shaking her head as she looked at James. "I think he rather enjoys it, James. A bit of a masochistic streak."

James wondered if there was some truth in this. Rat

had practically begged James to beat him up in the shower.

"I *don't* enjoy it," Rat said angrily. "I just want people to know that hurting me makes no difference."

The restaurant was self-service, but Susie's elevated status warranted a waiter. The man was dressed the same way as the dude at the door.

"Are these two bothering you, Mrs. Regan?"

"Do I *look* bothered?" Susie yelled back, startling James with the unexpected flash of anger. "Ask the boys what they want to eat and make sure they get it."

Because the restaurant was supposed to be self-service there was no menu. James didn't know what they had, so he let Rat order a burger and fries, with an ice-cream float and Pepsi for both of them.

"And get Rat a rubber ring to sit on," Susie said, making James smile at the thought.

Susie didn't seem anything like a Survivor, but her obvious taste for expensive clothes and jewelry did make her look like the type of woman who'd give up a modeling career to marry a seventy-five-year-old billionaire a few weeks after her twenty-third birthday.

"How'd you know my name?" James asked.

"Your arrival was big news in our little community, James."

Rat noticed that Susie was through with her soup and sensed he was running out of time. "I'm here to call in a favor," he said.

"You surprise me." Susie smirked.

"Ahem," the waiter said.

James looked around and was surprised to see the man

holding an inflatable rubber ring. He'd assumed Susie was joking, but apparently the restaurant kept a few around for the benefit of the recently paddled.

Rat grinned as he settled cautiously onto the ring, making sure that he didn't put any weight onto the tenderest areas of his bum. Moments later, burgers, fries, and a giant pitcher of Pepsi were slid onto the table. It looked better than anything James had eaten since moving into the Brisbane commune more than a month earlier.

"So what's this favor?" Susie said as she stood up to leave. "Spit it out, I haven't got all day."

"James needs a work assignment," Rat explained. "He'd like something that doesn't involve poo or back-breaking physical labor."

"My sister too," James added, then more sheepishly, "if that's OK."

"What's in it for me?" Susie smiled as she hooked a dinky Louis Vuitton backpack over her shoulder.

"You'll want more papers and backup disks nabbed from the office sooner or later," Rat whispered.

Susie looked around anxiously. "Tell the whole world, why don't you."

"But the best thing is"—Rat grinned—"it'll get right up The Spider's nose if you start interfering with the new arrivals."

This comment brought a huge smile to Susie's face. "Yes it would, wouldn't it? OK, I'll make a couple of calls and sort you both out."

Rat pointed at his food. "I'll miss afternoon service if I stick around to eat this."

"You're covered." Susie nodded. "Tell them you were on assignment from me. Enjoy the food and *try* staying out of trouble for once."

James nodded appreciatively at Rat as Susie strode away. "That was slick, Rat. Thanks."

"No worries, mate. You've no idea how good it is to finally have a member of the human race to talk to."

CHAPTER 28

ASSIGNMENTS

James and Rat's brutal paddling was the only surprise of Lauren's first day inside the Ark. The Survivor school taught regular subjects, in classrooms that were air-conditioned and equipped with computers and modern textbooks, although the outside world was cut off: The computers didn't have Internet access and there was no TV, magazines, or newspapers. There was a heavy emphasis on rote-learning of passages from *The Survivors' Manual* and you were out of luck if you wanted to know about anything that had happened since World War One in history class.

Lauren hadn't spoken to James, so she didn't understand why her job in the kitchens got pulled after half an hour. She was told to abandon her rubber gloves, before getting reassigned to a cushier job as an office assistant. She found herself working alongside Rat and her main duties were retrieving files, passing messages, and making coffee for the adults.

The low point of the Ark routine was undoubtedly the food. Lunch had been a gritty pasta salad with black olives, which were one of Lauren's pet hates. Dinner was a dried-out baked potato sitting in a puddle of baked beans, followed by vanilla ice cream and a square of sponge cake that had all the culinary virtues of a seat cushion. As always, there was plenty of sugar-rich orange juice and cola to keep up the youngsters' energy levels.

The school didn't give homework, so after the early evening service Lauren spent time playing skittles and basketball, before getting introduced to a bunch of weird skipping and chanting games. The other girls were polite and ready with hugs and compliments for the new girl, but their words and smiles seemed flat. Lauren began to imagine that she might be able to peel off their faces and uncover a robot army with flashing diodes and microchips inside their skulls.

Lauren's second morning at the Ark began with a shout, shortly after sunrise. She felt a sense of dread as she forced open gooey eyes. The Survivors' schedule was relentless, and Lauren knew she wouldn't get a rest until she returned to bed in sixteen hours' time. On top of that, she couldn't see a clear path forward for their mission and was worried about what would happen over the coming days, especially when every chance they took meant running the risk of a paddling.

The girls around her were already out of their beds, pulling on the grubby kit they'd worn for sports the night before.

"Come on, drowsy," a girl called Verity said brightly. "It's a new day. The Lord has set challenges for us."

The words reminded Lauren of the sickly phrases you get inside cheap birthday cards. She would happily have told God to stuff his challenges, in return for a couple of hours lying in bed watching bad TV, followed by a lazy session pottering around a kitchen whipping up her favorite pancakes, stuffed with Nutella and icing sugar.

Still, Lauren had a job to do. She pulled on her stinking yellow socks and rugby shirt before peeing and chasing the other girls outside onto the exercise yard behind the accommodation blocks. James was already there with the Blues, lined up beside Rat.

Lauren was desperate to speak to her brother, but girls and boys slept, ate, learned, worshiped, and played separately, so it wasn't going to be easy. There was no opportunity during the exercises, nor in the formation lap that followed, but she finally got a chance as they broke free to run the high-speed laps of the compound.

"How's your butt?" Lauren asked, deliberately keeping her speed down so that they dropped behind the charging hordes.

James was out of breath. "My arse is black and blue, but it looks worse than it feels."

"Were you really perving at girls in the shower?"

"It's a long story," James said, not wanting to repeat it

because it made him look dumb. "More importantly, the guy I got paddled with is Joel Regan's son. You and me need to meet up so I can explain properly."

"The earliest will be tonight," Lauren said. "We can sneak off during sports time, between the buildings or something."

They turned a corner and heard a sharp popping sound. Lauren immediately stopped running and hopped on one leg, as though she'd twisted her ankle.

James thought she was really injured. He stopped and turned back anxiously. "Are you OK?"

Lauren spoke through gritted teeth. "Look around, idiot head. It's the signal from John."

With all that was going on, James had forgotten that John was going to try and get the miniature radios to them. It made perfect sense for it to happen at a corner, because the runners ahead of them had no reason to look backwards and the runners behind would be blindsided by the corner.

As Lauren sat down on the pavement, ripping off her trainer and clutching her foot in mock agony, James scoured the floor. He noticed a golden cigarette packet at the edge of the tarmac path that clearly had no business in the middle of the outback.

James realized the pop must have been caused by something firing the carton from between a couple of boulders a few meters away. As he snatched the packet, he had to unhook a nylon cord that must have been there to wind the carton back if things had gone wrong.

He tucked the cardboard pack inside his shorts and wondered how it had managed to get where it was and pop out at exactly the right moment. But there wasn't time to stand around trying to figure it out, because a couple of stragglers and a teacher who always ran at the back had just turned the corner.

Lauren stood on one leg, leaning against the Ark's perimeter as the mustached teacher stopped running and smiled at her.

"What's the matter?"

"I put my foot down funny and went over on my ankle . . . I don't think it's bad, though."

Dana staggered in from her run around the Brisbane mall. She always finished half a lap ahead of the other girls and was surprised to see Abigail standing outside the shower room waiting for her.

"I'm out working all day," Abigail explained hurriedly. "They're really busy over at the warehouse. I got these off Michael last night."

"Who's Michael?"

"He's our liaison with ASIS now that John and Chloe have headed off to the Ark."

Abigail passed Dana a rectangular white strip, which looked like a small bookmark.

"Fat lot of use that'll be to me," Dana said sullenly. "I just hope James and Lauren got theirs OK."

"Apparently they've rigged up a gadget, using a radio-controlled buggy with a video camera and a hydraulic gun mounted on it."

Dana half smiled and shook her head. "James Bond eat your heart out."

A couple more runners had finished and were heading

into the changing room. As Abigail turned and hurried away, Dana gave them her sweetest Survivor smile.

"Great work, girls."

"Thank you, Dana," Eve said as she swept long red hair off her face.

Instead of going into the shower, Dana locked herself into a toilet cubicle. She sat down and slid the radio out of its bag. It was flexible, less than a millimeter thick and five centimeters long. The back had a small solar panel, like on a calculator, and two flat buttons: an on/off switch and one you had to press down to transmit.

She folded open a narrow sheet of instructions:

Ultra low power, multispectrum transceiver.
Range: under 2 km.
Battery Life: 2 hours.
Solar panel recharge: 12 hours.
Quick charge: 15 minutes' bright sunlight will provide
    10 minutes' emergency talk/receive.
Conserve power by leaving the unit off when not in use.
Keep transmission time to a minimum.

Dana scrunched the instructions up and popped them in her mouth. Once they'd turned into a soggy pulp, she spat it into the toilet and flushed.

She felt miserable as she slipped off her trainer, peeled out the insole, and hid the radio beneath it. Dana had finished with top marks in every piece of CHERUB training she'd done, yet she'd never gotten the breaks on any of her missions.

Dana didn't want to hate James and Lauren; they were

good agents and nice people, even if James was full of himself at times. But she was going to be stuck at the mall while they were getting all the glory inside the Ark, and she couldn't help resenting it. Especially Lauren: She already had her navy T-shirt and she was *eleven,* for God's sake.

There was a bang on the door, followed by Eve's voice. "Are you OK in there?"

Dana gritted her teeth. The Survivors didn't even like you getting five minutes to yourself on the toilet without making sure you weren't having any negative thoughts.

"I'm wiping my arse," Dana said irritably, struggling to contain her anger as she pulled her trainer back on.

"Oh," Eve said, disturbed by the graphic description. "It's just that Ween wants to see us after school, so don't go to your work assignment today."

Dana remembered Lauren's comment about Ween having a plan for her, but she was way too cynical to get her hopes up. She poked out her tongue and gave Eve the finger behind the toilet door as she replied cheerily:

"Thank you for telling me, Eve. I'll look forward to that."

James asked around and found out that a paddling was a rare event for any kid who didn't go looking for trouble. Most of his roommates had been at the school for years and had only received a standard dose of a dozen licks on a couple of occasions. Still, while the paddling had made James's introduction to life inside the Ark painful and shocking, it had formed the basis of a valuable friendship with Rat.

After a morning of lessons, a poor excuse for lunch, and the afternoon service, James was hitting his stride and felt a lot more confident as he walked down a sunlit path for his second day of work and met his boss, Ernie, along the way.

"Howdy, partner," Ernie said, clapping his hands happily.

"Yo," James answered enthusiastically.

Ernie was a lively man in his sixties, who'd sold his home, abandoned a bunch of rowdy teenage kids, and switched to the Survivor lifestyle. You could have put him on a Survivors poster: handsome and bronze-skinned with a bushy mustache. The sort of man you'd expect to see playing a friendly grandfather in a TV commercial.

Ernie drove a delivery truck that took letters and parcels to a post office in a one-shop town a hundred kilometers to the east. He'd never had an assistant before and had no idea why he'd suddenly been given one, but Ernie wasn't the sort to ask questions and seemed perfectly happy having James for company.

The delivery van lived beneath the canopy of a vehicle compound, alongside two dozen other cars and commercial vehicles, including Joel Regan's Bentley and the bulletproof limo he'd used for public events when he was in better health.

The sacks of mail ran down a metal chute from the adjacent offices. James and Ernie grabbed the sacks two at a time and hurtled them into the back of the truck. Ernie took the driver's seat and floored the gas pedal as soon as they'd passed through the vehicle gate in the turret.

Ernie claimed that there wasn't a speed trap within five hundred kilometers and cruised at 150 kph, which was about as fast as the truck would go without things getting seriously hairy.

As they jiggled and clattered over badly cracked tarmac, James sat in the passenger seat, watching the plume of dust they were throwing up in the door mirror. It was good to have a couple of hours in his schedule to chill out; just a pity they weren't allowed a radio, because a few tunes would have made it perfect.

CHAPTER 29

HOLIDAY

"Take a seat," Ween said, waving a hand towards the sofa at the back of her office.

Eve and Dana were still in school uniform as they sunk onto the foam cushions.

"Joel Regan believes that women are the key to our survival after the apocalypse," Ween began as she propped herself against the edge of her desk, facing the two fifteen-year-olds. "Most of the senior positions inside the Ark and our communes are taken up by women. Our ceremonies are always conducted by women. After the dark time, girls such as yourselves will become the bedrock of our new civilization: mothers, wives, and leaders."

Dana had been with the Survivors long enough to know that this kind of flattery always led up to somebody wanting something.

"I'm sorry you couldn't go to the Ark boarding school with your siblings, Dana. Eve, you're easily bright enough to attend yourself, but your work with our most difficult teenage recruits has been magnificent. We simply couldn't spare you. But we have found a special project that suits both of your talents. It will only take a few days, but it will get you both noticed at the highest level inside the Ark."

Dana glanced at Eve's excited face. She found it extraordinary that someone as bright as Eve could have mastered all the manipulative skills of the cult, without being able to see that she was being manipulated herself. Nevertheless, Dana was intrigued and felt slightly excited herself. Maybe it wasn't just James and Lauren who'd have a role in this mission.

"The Survivors is a vast organization," Ween continued. "Our financial obligations are equally vast. The Ark under construction in Nevada will cost seven billion dollars and the planned Arks in Europe and Japan will require the purchase of huge tracts of land in countries where space is precious.

"Our church desperately needs money to complete these projects and you girls have been selected to help. Before I can continue, you must swear to absolute secrecy. You'll have to hide the real purpose of your mission, even from your friends and family."

Ween reached across her desk and grabbed a Bible and a copy of *The Survivors' Manual*. "You must take these books and swear our highest oath."

Eve clutched the two books to her heart and looked at Dana, as if to say, *Oh my God, isn't this the most amazing thing ever?*

"I swear on these sacred books as an angel, on pain of eternity in a fiery hell."

Dana took the books and tried to add gravitas to her voice as she repeated Eve's oath.

"You mustn't tell a soul," Ween repeated. "Tell your parents and siblings that you are being taken for a short course at the Sydney commune."

"But what exactly *is* the mission?" Dana asked.

Ween shook her head. "I am not allowed to know. But the request came directly from Susie Regan: two girls, strong athletes, and strong swimmers. If you both accept this honor, I'll arrange for immediate flights to Darwin."

Lauren had no time for boys: she found them loud, obnoxious, and didn't care for either their obsession with sports or their apparent reluctance to wash after playing them. Even when her best friend Bethany briefly took leave of her senses and got off with a boy called Aaron—whose breath always smelled of cheese and onion crisps—she wasn't tempted by any of the invitations for a double date.

So it surprised Lauren that she found herself liking Rat. He was big for eleven and stood with the tip of his nose just level with Lauren's eyes, which somehow seemed exactly how it should be. Rat was good-looking apart from the squashed nose, obviously clever, and the way he stood up for himself against the odds made him seem heroic and vulnerable at the same time. Above everything else though, Rat was a good laugh.

As Lauren worked efficiently, delivering messages, mastering the photocopier, and generally being an obedient little Survivor, Rat constantly mucked around. Two staplers became yapping dogs that skidded around a desktop farting and humping each other. Rat demonstrated his toughness by betting Lauren that he could put the tip of his tongue on the hot bulb inside a desk lamp and hold it there for ten seconds. He lasted less than three before sprinting off to the water cooler in agony. He also proudly gobbed into the steaming coffee mug of a barrel-shaped accountant who'd scolded Lauren for fetching the wrong file.

Of course, boys always showed off and tried to get attention, but Rat was easier to swallow because his outcast status meant that he didn't have a line of idiotic mates pushing him to take things too far.

As six o'clock and the end of their work assignment drew near, Rat approached Lauren holding out a slim leather binder.

"How'd you like to meet *Le Grand Fromage*?"

Lauren smirked: She knew it meant *the big cheese* in French. "Joel Regan?"

Rat nodded as he opened the binder, revealing freshly printed letters and checks stacked inside rows of cream-colored slots.

"My dad has to sign this stuff. You just take it out to the residence, knock on the door of his room, and wait by his bed while he deals with it."

Lauren nodded enthusiastically. She realized that

the walk to the residence and back would probably make her late for dinner, but she'd heard tons of stories about Joel Regan's mega-opulent residence and there was no way she was going to turn down a chance to meet him.

Rat, who appeared to have intimate knowledge of every underground tunnel and room inside the Ark, drew the quickest path from the office to the residence on the back of a compliments slip. The journey involved taking a spiral staircase two floors below ground level and then heading several hundred meters along a cramped passageway that had condensation on the ceiling and patches of mildew on the walls.

This ended at a heavy doorway, which budged after a few worrying seconds during which Lauren thought she wasn't strong enough and might have to walk all the way back. The door took her into the luxurious ambience of the residence.

There was none of the woodchip wallpaper, growling air vents, and acres of magnolia paint that dominated the rest of the Ark. The broad corridor was lined with white marble and the air was scented with vanilla. At one edge, there was a twenty centimeter gutter into which water trickled and fresh white flowers bobbed around in floating glass pots.

Lauren saw that Rat had drawn a left-facing arrow, followed by a long curve, on his set of directions. The curve was an upwards ramp. One side was fronted with floor-to-ceiling glass and overlooked an outdoor spa. The other was hung with large paintings. Lauren was no art buff, but even she realized that anything three meters wide with Picasso's distinctive signature in the bottom corner must have cost millions.

"Can I help you, young lady?"

Lauren looked up to see an Asian man dressed in a three-piece suit, leaning over a chrome railing.

"I'm from the office," Lauren explained, feeling underdressed in her scruffy rugby shirt and oversized shorts.

"Ahh," the man said. "Where is Rathbone?"

Lauren answered as she turned on to a flight of stairs and began stepping up on some extraordinarily deep carpet. "He got held up doing some filing, so they sent me."

The butler walked in front of Lauren. His white-gloved hands were joined behind his back, except when he leaned forward theatrically to allow her through one of the solid maple doors.

Several turns and five doors took the pair into a darkened room. The curtains at two giant windows were closed. There was a bed in a gloomy corner, containing a breathless man, who sat up dressed in silk pajamas.

"Your correspondence, sir," the butler said grandly. Then he looked at Lauren. "I'll wait outside and lead you back."

As Lauren stepped up to Joel Regan, she caught a whiff of disinfectant and noticed that the old man had an oxygen tube running out of his nose.

"You must be Lauren," Regan wheezed.

Lauren was surprised that Regan knew who she was, and must have looked it.

"I may be frail, but I still keep up with the gossip— Come closer."

As Lauren stepped forwards, Joel wrapped his silk-covered arm around her back and pulled her into a hug.

She hated this, because his face was covered in bristles and his pajamas smelled vaguely of sick.

"You're a beautiful angel," Joel said as he let Lauren go. "I sense great power in you and a dazzling future."

"It's so *amazing* to meet you," Lauren said, gushing like she knew a Survivor should.

But all she could think about was the smell and the miserable, wasted lives of thousands of Survivors around the world.

"Specs and pen," Regan said, pointing his finger towards a bedside chest.

Once Lauren had fetched them, Regan pushed the glasses up his nose and began slowly pulling the letters and checks out of their slots. He signed his name with a trembling hand and shooed Lauren away when she leaned in to steady the signature book.

A side door opened without a knock and Susie Regan stormed to the bedside. She snatched the signed letters and began inspecting them. Lauren hadn't met Susie before, but recognized her from photographs.

"Are you reading these, Joel, or just signing whatever she puts in front of you?" Susie asked aggressively. "Have you seen this one?"

Joel downed his pen and looked wearily at his young wife. "Sweetheart, Eleanor knows what she's doing."

"Does she," Susie said. "This one is a power of attorney for our shares in Nippon Vending Industries. Shouldn't I at least fax it to Brisbane and get our people to check it out?"

Joel shook his head. "Our people? Don't you mean *your* people?"

"The Spider is trying to cut me out," Susie said, clacking

the heel of her leather boot against the wooden floor. "You might be dying, husband, but I've still got a lot of living to do and that bitch daughter of yours wants me on the first flight out when you croak. Is that what I deserve? Do you want to see me spending the rest of my life in squalor? I want joint control over the companies. How many times do I have to say it?"

Joel swiped his hand in front of his face. "You'll be provided for, petal. Eleanor *is* my daughter."

"Pity she's not the one over here at four in the morning, calling out your doctor and swabbing chunder off your face."

Joel pointed at Lauren. "Can we not do this when the girl is here? You're embarrassing her."

"*Don't* try weaseling out of it that way."

"I'm sick of this!" Joel shouted, his voice carrying surprising power for such a frail-looking man. "I need rest to get my strength back, not this constant earache from you."

With this, Joel picked up the leather binder and flung it at his bedside cabinet. The letters fluttered out in all directions and the binder hit a vase of flowers. Lauren jumped back as it hit the ground near her feet. She expected the vase to shatter, but it bounced off the floor and the water inside began pouring out.

After standing the vase up, Lauren instinctively grabbed a handful of disposable towels off the cabinet and crouched down to mop up the water before it spread.

"What are you doing?" Susie shouted, turning her spite on Lauren. "Did I ask you to do that? *Get* out of here, you foul brat."

Lauren straightened up abruptly, shocked by the tongue-lashing.

"What about the letters?" she asked edgily.

"Tell the office that Susie Regan will show them to her husband when he's well enough to deal with them."

Lauren nodded, before turning and hurrying for the exit. As she reached for the doorknob, Susie came charging across the floor and grabbed Lauren by the neck, clawing her with painted nails.

"You speak to Rat," she spat. "You tell him that if he wants favors from me, then it better be him that comes with the letters from now on. And when he does, he brings them to *me*."

"OK." Lauren nodded as she felt her pulse hammer inside the tightly wrung skin around her neck.

"And," Susie added, sinking her nails in deeper, "you keep your mouth shut, madam. If you spread around what you just saw here, I *will* find out about it. I'll call up the school and have them paddle you so hard that you don't walk for a month. Understood?"

Lauren nodded as Susie let go and shoved her towards the door.

CHAPTER 30

FLOWERS

Dana used the radio in her trainer to brief Michael on her flight details before getting into the cab to Brisbane airport. He said he'd arrange for an ASIS team to cover them when they arrived in Darwin. The agents would then tail her to wherever she ended up and keep watch from a position close by.

Eve always acted confident around the mall: efficient nods, tight-lipped smiles, and a purposeful walk. But the sudden absence of routine turned her into a wreck. She'd lived in the commune since she was eight years old and her head was so full of devils, angels, and other Survivor gibberish that the real world spooked her.

Eve fretted over safe keeping of the hundred-dollar

note she'd been given as spending money for their journey. She kept asking Dana questions: what kind of food would they find in the airport, whether airplanes had toilets on them, if the takeoff would make her sick. In the crowded check-in area at the terminal, she gawped in all directions and insisted on linking her arm around Dana's so that they didn't get separated.

The way the Survivors messed people up made Dana mad. If you got caught giving a little kid a bag of drugs you'd go to prison, but cults messed kids up as badly, and nobody seemed to care.

Still, getting bugged by Eve wasn't enough to quell Dana's excitement at finally getting her big breakthrough. She had no idea what this trip north was about, but the high level of secrecy meant it had to be dodgy.

The 737 took four hours from Brisbane on the east coast to Darwin, capital of Australia's sparsely populated Northern Territory. It was close to midnight when they landed.

As the girls headed into the Darwin International arrivals lounge, carrying small backpacks containing a few personal items and a change of clothes, a man held up a sheet of cardboard with their surnames on. He was powerfully built, very tall, with blond hair tied back in a bunch.

Dana knew the face from somewhere, but it took a few seconds to place him in a surveillance photograph: It was the dude Bruce Norris had beaten up in a Hong Kong hotel room three months earlier.

"Welcome to Darwin," the man said as he reached out to shake Eve's hand. "The name's Barry, Barry Cox."

• • •

Next morning, Dana woke in a comfortable double bed. The shower was running in the bathroom next door and someone was moving in the hallway. She stepped onto a wooden floor that creaked under her bare feet and headed up to the window to check out the neighborhood. They were half an hour's drive from the city, and it had been pitch-black when they'd arrived the night before.

She ripped back a curtain and peered through a dusty sheet of mosquito netting towards the next house along. The shabby home was thirty meters away, after a stretch of baked earth scattered with rusted-up junk. The bright yellow van on the neighbors' drive had a picture of a satellite dish on the side with RAY'S ANTENNAS painted underneath.

Dana reckoned she'd like to live somewhere like this: a slightly run-down house miles from anywhere, where you could do whatever you liked without anyone hassling you. Go into town once a week for groceries, a good-looking boyfriend who pumped weights in the garage, kept himself to himself, and read a lot of books. Two or three dogs, *definitely* no kids . . .

The door clicked. It was Eve, dressed already and looking at her watch. "It's service time back at the mall, Dana. I think we'd gain strength against the devils if we prayed together."

Dana was cheesed off at Eve for shattering her little fantasy. The girls sat on the edge of the bed and hugged. Eve read a couple of paragraphs from *The Survivors' Manual*, then they both closed their eyes and repeated the ten-sentence chant.

"Good morning, Lord. We are your angels. Here to serve you. Make us strong. Please protect us. Our souls are honest. Our thoughts are pure. We are leaders. We will take humanity. Through the darkness."

A woman called Nina stood in the open doorway when the girls opened their eyes. They'd met this middle-aged woman briefly before going to bed the night before. She had a long red face and you could tell she was a hardcore Survivor from the mass of beads on her leather necklace.

"Angels." The woman sighed dramatically. "Coming in here and seeing two beautiful young girls praying like that . . . I think that was one of the most amazing things I've ever seen."

Dana was tempted to throw up at the syrup, but she copied Eve and broke into an enthusiastic smile. Nina rushed into the room and gave the girls a big hug accompanied by an *ahhh* sound.

"God protect us," Nina said, and the girls repeated the words before saying a round of *Amens*.

"Now, Dana, get yourself dressed and both of you come through to the kitchen. Barry and I will explain our task over breakfast."

James sat facing Rat, with bowls of frosted cereal and beakers of orange juice on the table between them. The two boys had wet hair from the shower and were still puffed from morning exercises.

Rat's expression suddenly wilted. "Oh, crap."

"What?" James asked, but a glance over his shoulder answered the question before Rat got the chance. Georgie was steaming their way.

"Why do you do it, James?" Georgie asked.

"Do what?" James asked defensively.

"I'm talking about your friendship with Rathbone. It does you no credit. It will lead to trouble and when it does, I'll be on you like a Rottweiler."

There was nothing James could say without upsetting either Georgie or Rat, so he diplomatically crammed a spoonful of cereal into his mouth and crunched.

"I got a message from the office," Georgie said. "Ernie's taking the truck out for a special delivery run this morning. He reckons there's going to be some heavy lifting, so he wants you along for the ride."

"Bless you for passing on the message," James said politely, doing his best impression of a good little Survivor.

But Georgie didn't appreciate the sentiment. "Finish your breakfast and get over to the vehicle compound. Chop, chop."

James smiled at Rat once Georgie had walked off to intimidate someone else. "Sweet, dude. No lessons for the big J."

Rat shook his head and gave James the finger. "Swivel on it, smart-ass."

Two thousand kilometers north, Dana, Eve, and Nina sat around a molded plastic table with cutlery laid out in front of them. Barry Cox wore a white vest and a pair of swimming shorts as he cooked up a breakfast of bacon, hash brown, scrambled eggs, and mushrooms, but the sizzling food was overpowered by the unappetizing tang of strong bleach.

"Get your stomachs filled," he said cheerfully. "Today's really gonna be something. If it goes to plan, our masters will be very happy."

A CHERUB agent always has to be careful about how much they pry, but Barry's comment seemed like an invitation to enquire.

"You're not wearing a leather necklace," Dana said. "So who is your master?"

"I'm an environmentalist," Barry said. "The planet is my master. I assume you've all heard of Help Earth?"

Eve shook her head, so Dana explained to her. "They're a terrorist group that targets the oil industry. If you'd seen a newspaper or the TV news over the last three or four years, you'd have heard of them."

"I most certainly *haven't*," Eve said indignantly. "The lives of devils are not my business."

"Haven't you even heard it mentioned at school?" Barry asked.

"If they talk about things like that, I do a chant in my head to block it out," Eve said. "We mostly hang out with the other Survivors anyway."

Barry smiled as he turned around from the hob and began dividing a saucepan of scrambled eggs between four plates. "We prefer not to think of ourselves as terrorists. But the traditional environmental groups are constantly outmaneuvered by corporations and governments with billions of dollars in their pockets. We can't fight back effectively unless we're prepared to use extreme methods."

"But you're not angels," Eve said suspiciously.

Nina broke into a big smile. "Eve, darling, you know

Joel Regan and his wife are extraordinarily passionate about environmental issues. The request to send you girls up here came from Susie Regan herself. What we're going to do today will be historic. This is an opportunity for us to strike a blow for the environment as well as raising a significant amount of money towards building more Arks."

"Does Joel Regan know we're doing this?" asked Eve with excitement. "I mean, will he have heard my name and everything?"

Nina smiled. "Of course he has, sweetheart. I wouldn't be surprised if there was some sort of reward in this. A personal presentation, maybe even a platinum bead for your necklace."

The prospect of a platinum bead—the highest award a Survivor can receive—had Eve bouncing in her chair.

"I can't believe this is happening to me," she squealed.

Dana faked a grin and patted Eve on the back. "You haven't earned the bead yet, mate," she said, before looking across at Barry, who'd finished dishing up and was taking his seat to start breakfast. "So what have we got to do?"

Barry smiled. "Nothing too tricky: just blowing up a couple of supertankers."

CHAPTER 31

TRAINING

Ernie never slowed down. James felt his seat belt straining to one side as the truck took a hard turn off the tarmac onto a dirt track marked out by nothing except the marks laid by vehicles that had gone before it. There was a house and a large outbuilding on the horizon.

"You been here before?" James asked.

Ernie nodded. "I drop their mail by once a week. Couple of American fellows, but it sounds like they're shipping out pretty soon."

"What do they do out here?" James asked.

"They make paint."

James looked surprised. "Why make paint in the middle of the outback?"

Ernie shrugged. "It's pretty easy to get Australian citizenship if you agree to start a business in the outback. Brian showed me around once; it's a good little business. They're not churning out five-liter tubs of emulsion. It's all very specialized: natural pigments and stuff for restoring paintings and antiques."

"How come you collect their mail for them?"

"You're a curious little Dickens this morning, ain't you?" said Ernie. "I think they're friends with Susie, or something."

"Just making conversation," James said, giving a couldn't-care-less shrug.

James realized he couldn't push any further without seeming suspicious. It took five more minutes of Ernie's psycho driving to reach the buildings. The house looked as if it had stood for decades, but the windowless rectangle next door was a recent addition. It was built from prefabricated sections with a corrugated metal roof.

Ernie blasted the horn as James flung open his door and jumped out of the cab. It was getting close to the hottest part of the day, and he had flies swarming around within a second of his feet touching the red dust.

"They must be around here somewhere," Ernie said, craning his neck to look behind the building. "I'll try the workshop, you see if they're in the house." As Ernie jogged off towards the concrete shed, James stepped onto a wooden porch and rapped on a screen door.

"Anybody home?"

He pushed the door open and found himself in a kitchen. There were a couple of suitcases on the floor and boxes packed with cutlery and utensils stacked up on the countertops.

"Hello!" James yelled.

As he stepped farther into the house, James noticed a few photographs tacked on the fridge door. Most of them were regular scenes: two little dudes wearing armbands beside a swimming pool, a school photograph, an elderly couple sitting in a restaurant at some sort of family event. But one of the pictures made him gasp.

"Oh, *shit*."

James instantly recognized the little lad who stood on a pebble beach on a drizzly English day. James had met him two years earlier, on his first CHERUB mission. His name was Gregory Evans and his father was Brian "Bungle" Evans, a Texan biologist and a member of Help Earth who'd tried to kill two hundred oil executives and politicians with deadly anthrax bacteria. Brian was one of the world's most wanted men, but he'd never been found. Nor had the laboratory or any of the equipment used to manufacture the anthrax.

James's brain raced. Everything made sense: Eddie said that one of the men who lived here was called Brian and paint production involves mixing up chemicals, making it a perfect cover for a facility that produced biological weapons or explosives.

This was a big result. Uncovering the Help Earth laboratory would be front-page news all around the world, but James faced a massive problem: He'd met Brian Evans on several occasions when he'd been working in Wales under the name of Ross Leigh. As soon as Brian saw James's face his cover would be blown apart.

241

James felt his stomach shrink into a tight ball, knowing things could turn nasty any second. He realized that the best strategy was to grab hold of the biggest weapon he could find and he figured there would be knives in one of the cardboard boxes on the table. But before he had a chance to grab anything, he heard footsteps and a voice with a familiar Texas twang.

"Hi there, son."

After breakfast, Dana, Barry, Eve, and Nina headed off to train for their attack. Barry took them to a deserted stretch of beach in a Subaru wagon, towing a three-meter dinghy behind the car.

They pulled up on a stretch of squishy sand. There was a strong breeze and the sea looked choppy. Once the four of them had hauled the dinghy off the trailer, Barry and the girls sat on the edge of their car seats and changed into wet suits. Nina stayed behind with the car as the others set out to sea.

As the shore receded and the outboard motors threw up a giant wash, Barry began speaking in a monotonous voice. "What you're going to learn this morning is not complicated, but you must listen or we'll fail in our operation tonight."

He started off explaining how to use the twin outboard motors and gave each girl a few minutes' practice steering the boat and controlling the throttle. Next, he pulled out a couple of GPS receivers and showed the girls how to use them for navigation. He gave Eve a set of coordinates from a waterproof chart and told her to find it.

A five-year-old can navigate with a GPS, so it took less

than ten minutes to reach their target, a natural harbor shielded from the waves by two lines of jutting rocks. The water was clear and the upturned hull of a recently stricken motor launch shimmered a couple of meters beneath the surface.

"OK, cut the power," Barry said. "Put the GPS back in its pouch and pay attention."

Barry unzipped a backpack and pulled out three chunky metal discs.

"It's not easy to sink a large boat," Barry began. "When you're talking about something that weighs over a hundred thousand tons, with watertight compartments and a double hull, you're either gonna need a whole boat packed with explosives crashing into it at speed, or you've got to position your explosives very carefully."

"What about oil spills?" Dana asked.

"Help Earth only attacks empty tankers, but they've really upped the security. Every navy in the world is keeping tabs on them. This time we're trying a different tack and going for LNG."

"LN what?" Eve asked.

"Liquid Natural Gas. This region has some of the world's largest natural gas deposits. Japan, on the other hand, has no natural gas of its own but is the world's second largest consumer of the stuff.

"Natural gas explodes under high pressure, so the only way to move it over long distances is by chilling it to about seventy below zero, when it turns into a liquid. It has to stay at that temperature until it reaches its destination. The liquefaction process has to be done in a special facility that costs billions of dollars to construct. Then it's shipped off in refrigerated tankers that cost another hundred million a pop to build."

"Big bucks." Dana grinned. "I've never even heard of the stuff."

Barry nodded. "You won't meet a lot of people who have, but LNG is a massive industry. Not only does an attack on an LNG facility hit the oil companies in the wallet, the exploding gas burns cleanly and does little lasting damage to the environment."

Dana smiled. "No oil slicks or gooey black birds, then."

"That's right."

"You said *facility*," Dana said. "I thought we were going for a tanker."

Barry nodded. "If you take out the boat when it's refueling, the explosion will take a nice chunk of the terminal with it."

Dana looked solemn. "But if we get caught, they'll lock us up and throw away the key."

Eve hit Dana on the back and spoke furiously. "Don't say that. Don't even *think* that. It's *so* negative. We're Survivors. We have honest souls and God will protect us."

James turned anxiously to face Brian Evans, but it wasn't him. Same accent, similar face, but a younger-looking dude with curly hair.

"Name's Mike," the man said. "You here with my man Ernie?"

James nodded.

"I see you're admiring the picture of my little nephew."

"Yeah, he's cute," James said. "That's Brighton, isn't it? I recognize the pier in the background."

"I wouldn't know, it's my brother that married the limey girl. Are you from England?"

"Nah, but I've lived there for most of the last three years."

"Certainly picked up the accent. You sound like a genuine Cockney boy."

Ernie came in through the screen door wearing his usual smile. "So you've found each other. Didn't you hear the truck arrive, Mike?"

Mike nodded. "The screeching brakes and the blasting horn were a giveaway, but I was up in the roof fetching down some boxes of documents."

"Brian not here?" Ernie asked.

"He'll be landing back at the Ark this evening and running a few final errands here before shipping out himself," Mike said, to James's massive relief.

"Well, I sure hope your business takes off down south," Ernie said. "I'll miss chatting with you guys."

"Thank you kindly." Mike nodded. "We've got customers all over the world; I reckon we'll do all right." He turned and looked at James. "I hope you've got some good muscles on you, young fellow. Gonna work up a sweat clearing out that workshop."

Ernie smiled at James. "You don't need to worry about the boy. You should see him throwing my mail sacks around. Tough as a bull, ain't you, son?"

James hated it when adults patronized him, but he couldn't help smiling at being compared to a bull.

Dana sat on the side of the dinghy and flopped backwards into the water, clasping the metal can to her chest.

This was her fifth practice, but her first wearing a near-black visor designed to simulate diving at night. Even in the bright sunlight, all she could see were a mass of gloomy outlines.

She swam four strokes with one arm, before pulling up and going into a doggy paddle. She felt around with her toes and was reassured to feel the sunken white bow beneath her feet. It hadn't even been underwater long enough to rust.

After a couple of deep breaths to oxygenate her blood, Dana tipped forwards and plunged blindly underwater. As her fingers felt along the metal hull, she pulled the heavy can away from her chest. Its powerful magnetic base took on its own momentum and clamped itself to the hull with a hollow thunk. She sensed a rush of water from some unseen sea creature disturbed by the noise.

Once the dummy bomb was in position, she fumbled until she found a switch, which was locked in place with a steel pin to prevent accidental activation. Dana was getting desperate for breath, but she knew it would be a nightmare relocating the device after surfacing, so she stayed under.

It was always fiddly getting the pin out and not being able to see made it harder. When it finally twisted away, Dana flipped the switch and kicked her feet against the hull, filling her lungs with air as her face broke the surface.

The boat had drifted a few meters, meaning she faced a longer swim back. She grasped the rope on the side of the dinghy, expecting to clamber back aboard, but found Barry holding another dummy bomb in her face.

"Not too bad," Barry said firmly. "But you've got to

release the charge slowly. I heard that magnet thunk against the hull from up here. Remember, there might be people standing on deck twenty or thirty meters above your head. They would have heard a noise like that."

People you're happy to kill, Dana thought to herself as she sighed and swept a strand of hair away from her face.

"Let me catch my breath for a second."

Barry shook his head. "Get back out there. You've got to make three dives in rapid succession tonight, so you'd better get used to it."

CHAPTER 32

CONTACTS

James, Ernie, and Mike took half an hour loading the truck with household stuff and metal trunks containing heavy equipment from the outbuilding.

James was desperate to contact John and tell him what was going on, but even if there'd been a chance to get away from the two men, his tiny radio didn't have enough transmission power to get picked up this far from the Ark.

It was noon when they arrived back. Ernie charged the truck through a broken section of fencing around Joel Regan Airport. The only aircraft in town was a small cargo jet. Ernie pulled up to a screeching halt beside it.

While the turbofans whined above their heads, the

co-pilot opened up the hold and lowered a power-assisted ramp. Loading up was a laborious process, hindered by the jet exhaust making the air even more unbelievably hot that it was already.

Every piece of cargo had to be weighed before they pushed it up the ramp. It then had to be manhandled across the shiny plastic floor inside the hold and strapped down. The co-pilot refused to muck in and stood with a clipboard and smug look, calculating the weight of the payload.

James had sweat pouring out of his hair by the time everything was packed securely inside. Ernie looked at his watch as the jet taxied towards the runway, with Mike Evans and the two pilots on board.

"You might as well head through the terminal, catch a service and some lunch," Ernie said. "I'll take the truck round the back to the compound and see you over there at one for the delivery route."

"Gotcha, boss," James said, faking enthusiasm.

As Ernie pulled away in the truck, a deafening roar erupted. The pilot had opened up the throttles for takeoff and the jet powered past less than twenty meters away. James squeezed his palms against his ears as the gray haze choked him. Once the worst was past, he rubbed his stinging eyes and spat on the tarmac to get the acrid taste of jet exhaust out of his mouth. Then he jogged off towards the terminal.

By the time he'd made it inside, Ernie's truck was out of sight and the jet was a gray dot on the narrow end of a plume in the sky. James had got over the initial shock of stumbling into Help Earth's laboratory, but he couldn't relax. There was still a chance that an encounter with Brian Evans would blow his cover and the contents of the weapons lab were currently heading away at several hundred kilometers an hour. He desperately needed to make contact with his mission controllers and tell them what was going on.

Although there was no one around, James couldn't rule out the possibility of surveillance cameras inside the terminal building, so he cut into the first toilet he found. He figured he could spare a few seconds to splash cool water on his face, but he turned on a tap and found it was dead. So were the next two along.

Abandoning this idea, James locked himself into a toilet cubicle. There was no water in the bowl and a nasty funk rising out of the hole, but time was tight so he had to live with it. He flipped the toilet lid down to sit on, pulled off his trainer, and reached under the soggy inner sole to retrieve the radio.

He pressed the on button and held the thin plastic strip up to his ear. It was warm and smelled like his feet.

"John, are you out there?"

Chloe's voice came back through the tiny loudspeaker. "Loud and clear, James."

"Where's John?"

"He had to fly up to monitor Dana in Darwin."

"What's she doing up there?"

"No idea yet." Chloe shrugged. "Ween sent her up there on some special mission."

"OK," James gasped, as he tried to digest this surprising piece of information. "Listen, I don't have much time. The Help Earth laboratory was located in an outbuilding off a dirt track seven kilometers away from the Ark."

"*Was* located?"

"I just helped pack it up. It's on a jet, tail number A0113D. I've got no idea where it's heading."

"OK," Chloe said. "I'll get that information to ASIS. They should be able to track the aircraft transponder."

"Provided they haven't switched it off."

"Which is entirely possible, maybe even probable," Chloe acknowledged. "I'm glad you called in again. I've been in contact with ASIS this morning. They've been monitoring the Survivors' financial dealings through Lomborg financial. They're trading heavily in the Japanese stock market, buying into companies whose shares will go up if there's a sudden rise in energy prices, like you get whenever there's a Help Earth attack."

"Any idea why it's focused on Japan?"

"Not yet, James."

James thought for a second. "Help Earth's target must be big if they're investing this much money."

"Exactly," Chloe said. "The Survivors seem pretty confident: They've borrowed millions from merchant banks, and they're buying derivatives instead of shares to maximize their profits. A lot of these investments are short-term futures contracts, which means this thing has to happen in the next day or two for the Survivors to make the big bucks."

"Right," James said. "I'll find out what I can and try getting in touch again later. I can't promise though, you know how awkward it can be getting time to yourself around here."

Barry Cox ordered the girls to get some sleep when they arrived back from the beach. Dana took the radio out of her trainer and lay under her duvet with the microphone up to her mouth.

"Anybody out there?" she whispered.

She was reassured to hear John's voice come back in her ear, "Loud and clear, Dana."

"Thank God," Dana gasped. "Listen, John, this is *red* hot. I'm right in the middle of a Help Earth operation. It looks like we're gonna be attacking a supertanker terminal, either late tonight or in the early hours of tomorrow morning."

"Have you got any idea where it is?"

"No, but apparently the tanker will be docked at a terminal that produces a kind of refrigerated gas called LNG. Have you ever heard of that?"

"Can't say I have, but that probably makes it easier for us to identify your target. Give me two seconds, I've got an ASIS agent sitting alongside me, she's a local girl."

Dana anxiously waited for John's voice to come back.

"OK," John said. "She says there are only a handful of LNG terminals in Australia. Apparently they export the gas to China and Japan. The nearest is only about thirty clicks from here. It's one of the biggest employers in town."

"Sounds like our target," Dana said.

"She says it's the only one in northern Australia, so it must be. By the way, I was watching you down at the beach through binoculars. Can you confirm that it's Barry Cox you're with?"

"Sure, I recognized him as soon as I arrived. You know, his jaw still makes a funny clicking noise from where Bruce busted it."

"That's a pain," John said. "If I'd known he was here, I would have sent Chloe up from the Ark."

"How come?"

"Cox eyeballed me in Hong Kong. I'll have to keep my distance in case he remembers my face. The woman who waited with the car on the beach is called Nina Richards. She's a veteran environmental campaigner. ASIS have suspected her involvement with Help Earth for a while, but there's been nothing concrete until now."

This revelation surprised Dana. "Are you sure? She acts exactly like a Survivor."

John laughed. "So do you. My guess is that Help Earth wanted a couple of bodies along for the most dangerous part of the operation and Susie Regan was willing to supply them. Nina must have realized that acting like a Survivor would make it easier to keep you girls in line."

"So what's gonna happen?" Dana asked. "We know the target, and we know it's tonight. How far are we going to let this attack run before we put a stop to it?"

"It'll be easier to nail Barry and Nina if we catch them in the act, but I don't want you exposed to an unacceptable level of danger. I'll have to speak with the ASIS people and work out a strategy. Make sure you call me on the radio again before you leave the house."

"OK, I'll check in later," Dana said. "I've got my own room, so it's a lot easier here than it was inside the commune."

CHAPTER 33

WORK

Most of what Lauren saw around the office was mundane: queries from the communes, transfers of Survivors from one location to another, paying bills, and bulk purchasing the produce that fed and clothed cult members around the world.

She knew some of this information might provide evidence of links between the Survivors and Help Earth, but there were thousands of computer files, rooms lined with filing cabinets, and no easy way to distinguish between routine paperwork and valuable intelligence. Her only option was to stick her nose in whenever she could and hope for the best, but she wasn't optimistic. It might take weeks or even months to get lucky.

Rat hated working in the office. He'd sorted out a regular skive, spending hours of every shift hiding out in a room used to store old bits of furniture. The office was large enough for people to lose track of one another, so it was easy to sneak off.

Rat's favorite scam was to grab a glass of milk and some biscuits from the kitchen and sit under a broken desk reading a paperback. Sadly, reading matter inside the Ark was restricted to the wisdom of Joel Regan and a few classic novels studied by older kids in English Literature classes. Rat's favorite was a paperback copy of *Oliver Twist*, which he'd stolen from a classroom and read more than a dozen times. It was now in tatters and Rat kept an elastic band around it to stop the pages from dropping out.

Lauren enjoyed hanging out with Rat more than doing office work, but she kept herself busy because she knew the mission wouldn't get anywhere while she sat around chatting. Still, Rat could be persistent and he managed to talk Lauren into spending half an hour sitting under the desk talking about different kinds of video games. Rat had played them on airplanes when he was a toddler, but they weren't allowed inside the Ark and he was fascinated by them. He wanted to know every detail, like how many buttons the controllers on different consoles had, what type of things you saved on a memory card and what the most popular games were.

When Lauren finally headed off to do some work, she heard voices on the other side of the door and held back, not wanting to give away Rat's hiding place. She waited for the talking to stop, but instead it started turning into a row.

"Who is it?" Rat whispered.

Lauren got excited when she realized the voices belonged to Joel Regan's wife and eldest daughter.

"It's Susie and The Spider."

Rat enjoyed a good bit of gossip and crawled out from under the desk. The two kids had their ears almost touching the door and sprung away as Susie backed into it.

"Get your freak hands off me, Spider!" Susie shouted.

"I've found a hole!" Eleanor shouted. "Seventy million dollars have vanished over the last five days."

"So what's that got to do with me?" Susie yelled.

"My father and I were the only ones who had access to those funds. Now, Lomborg Financial is draining it."

"Why don't you ask your father before accusing me?"

"Don't bullshit me, Susie, I wasn't born yesterday. I know you gave my father grief until he let you have control over that account. He's a sick man and you're abusing his trust."

"Arnos Lomborg has made us a *lot* of money!" Susie shouted back. "You don't mind when it comes rolling in, do you? Your precious Ark in Nevada would still be a blueprint if it wasn't for me. Japan and Europe would be pipe dreams."

"But where does this miraculous ability to make money come from?"

"Investments."

"Pull the other one; it's got bells on. I'm no financial whiz, but it doesn't take one to know that two hundred percent returns on a three-week investment aren't legitimate."

"Just count your money and shut your mouth," Susie

256

snapped. "The only reason you don't like this is because *my* people set up the contacts with Lomborg. What did the Survivors have before I started taking an interest? Vending machines, collection tins, and red bills from the electricity company. Joel nearly bankrupted us trying to turn this godforsaken stretch of desert into some pathetic copy of Disneyland."

Rat grinned at Lauren and shrugged, as if to say *I don't understand any more of this than you do.* He had no reason to suspect that Lauren understood the implications of every word: Susie Regan was behind the links between Help Earth and the Survivors. Joel was too ill to make decisions, and The Spider was out of the loop.

"Besides," Susie said, "all this talk about your precious father, when did *you* last spend a night looking after him? When did you last even visit him?"

"I can't get near him without you standing two meters away trying to score points off me."

"Get out of my face, Spider," Susie said, sounding exasperated. "Haven't you got a service to conduct, or some stupid little beads to hand out?"

"Devil!" Eleanor screamed. "It sickens me that my father takes to his bed each night with an unbeliever."

Susie chuckled. "Oh no, *here* we go. Your daddy didn't meet God, Eleanor. He invented the Survivors as a way to make a bit of cash."

Rat broke into a huge grin when he heard this blasphemy. Lauren pretended to be shocked.

Eleanor sounded genuinely upset and made a big sob. "My father is a great man. A prophet. God *will* punish you for what you've done to us."

257

Lauren knew all about the power struggle between Susie and Eleanor, but only now was she realizing how different the two womens' opinions about Joel Regan and being a Survivor were.

"I'm not even interested in arguing with you," Susie said finally. "Piss off out of my way."

The Spider pounded angrily on the door. Lauren and Rat scurried back towards the desk, half expecting her to come into the room, but after a few seconds silence they realized Eleanor and Susie had moved on.

Lauren gave Rat a relieved smile, followed by an excuse about having some photocopying to do. She dived off to lock herself in a toilet cubicle, grabbed the radio out of her trainer, and called Chloe to tell her about Susie and Eleanor's conversation.

"What you say about Susie confirms the picture ASIS have been getting from other sources, including your brother," Chloe said. "But we didn't realize that Eleanor and the other devout Survivors knew nothing about the links."

"Did Susie have anything to do with environmental groups before she came to the Ark?"

"Not really," Chloe said. "The only thing the Americans turned up was that Susie refused to wear fur when she worked as a model, but a lot of models insist on that. We've got no idea if Susie cares about the environment, or if she's skimming the proceeds to line her own pockets. Whatever the case, she's definitely been using Survivor money to fund Help Earth."

Lauren hadn't been in touch with James since the morning run, so Chloe brought her up to speed on everything that was going on, including James finding the laboratory and the latest news from Dana.

"Do you know where your brother is?" Chloe asked.

"I expect he'll go for dinner and evening service as soon as he gets back from his delivery run," Lauren replied, keeping her voice really low because one of the admin staff was washing their hands on the other side of the cubicle door.

"Right, do you think you'll be able to ditch your schedule and meet up with James as soon as he arrives back?"

"I guess," Lauren said warily. "This office is right next to the vehicle compound, but the teachers at the boarding school keep close tabs on us. We'll get asked questions if we disappear for long and skipping a service is a paddling offense."

"OK," Chloe said. "Try not to worry about that. ASIS would prefer to wait while you guys and some of their other operations gather more evidence, but the Australian government now know that a Help Earth attack is imminent. If the public found out that the government knew in advance and didn't warn them, the political implications would be enormous."

"Right," Lauren said. "So what docs that mean for us?"

"The Intelligence Minister will make a televised statement at eight thirty this evening, putting the country on its highest state of alert. Every oil facility is going to be evacuated of all but a few essential staff. Dana and her terrorist buddies are going to be picked up when they try to set off in their boat. The Ark is going to be stormed and all the senior personnel will be detained for questioning."

"Stormed by who?"

"The Australian military have had their Tactical Assault Group training for a surprise raid on the Ark ever since the link with the Survivors was first uncovered. They're afraid that information will be destroyed, or that there'll be a siege situation if they move in on the Ark by road. So they're using a small airborne force: four helicopters, sixty TAG commandos, and a dozen backup personnel from ASIS. The aim is to land troops inside the Ark's perimeter and take control before the Survivors can do anything to stop them."

"Sounds dodgy to me," Lauren said, grinding her palm against her forehead. "They've got armed guards in all six watchtowers, Rat says there are heaps of illegal weapons hidden inside the compound and there's *nothing* going on around here. You'll hear the choppers coming in from miles off."

"They're experts, Lauren, we have to trust in their abilities. I'm sure they've put a lot of thought and training into it, but I'd still rather you and James weren't around when it kicks off. The assault team's ETA is around eight this evening, just after it gets dark. That gives you and James a little over two hours to get out.

"I want you to meet up with him as soon as he gets back with the post. If you think it's safe, I'd like you to try getting into Susie Regan's office and making copies of any interesting-looking data first. She's bound to start destroying evidence when the helicopters approach."

Lauren thought for a second. "I've only been up to the residence one time . . ."

"Talk it through with James. If you think it's too risky, don't do it. My number one priority is to get you two out of harm's way. Steal a car, bluff your way out through one of the turrets, or whatever, but *get out*. Radio me before you leave, and I'll pick you up somewhere nearby."

"Right," Lauren said as the magnitude of what was going to happen over the next few hours began sinking in. The commando raid on the Ark and the links between Help Earth and the Survivors would be the top story on every TV news in the world.

"I've never tried to get out before," Lauren said. "But I don't think it'll be hard. There's only a couple of guards on each turret. They'll be easy enough to take out if we sneak up on them."

"Great; and remember, safety first."

"Gotcha," Lauren said, taking a quick glance at her watch. "I expect I'll be seeing you in a couple of hours."

A cherub usually carries a few basic computer hacking tools, but the strict rules on personal possessions inside the Ark made it impossible to bring anything with them. As the end of her shift approached, Lauren sneaked into the stationery cupboard. She grabbed a spindle of blank CDs and headed into the post room with them.

"You wanna head back to the school with me?" Rat asked, giving Lauren a start as she turned to leave.

"Haven't you got to take the signature book across to Joel Regan?"

Rat shook his head as he picked up and inspected the

spindle of CDs. "Apparently the old man's taken a turn for the worse. Susie reckons he's in no fit state to look at any letters."

"Right," Lauren said edgily.

"What are these disks for?" Rat asked.

"Oh," Lauren said, stumbling for an excuse that she realized she ought to have thought up in advance. "I was supposed to take them to one of the accountants."

"Which one? I can run them over for you if you're doing something in here."

"No, no," Lauren said, as she reached out to grab them back. "He's gone off for the day now, anyway."

Rat broke into a big smile. "You're up to something, aren't you?"

Lauren tutted. "Give over, I'm not up to anything."

"You can't pull the wool over my eyes," Rat said. "Did I ever tell you that I have an IQ of one-ninety-seven?"

"Hmm, let me think." Lauren grinned, putting a finger over her lips and scowling as though she had to think hard. "I think you might have mentioned it thirty-six or thirty-seven times over the last couple of days."

Rat looked offended as he put the tub of CDs back on the table. "Well, I'm off for some grub. I suppose I'll see you tomorrow afternoon."

"Not if I see you first." Lauren grinned.

She felt sad as she followed Rat out of the post room and walked off, pretending to have one last task to perform. Rat was fun to be with and she'd probably never see him again. She took a left behind a wooden partition and gave Rat a few seconds to clear off before doubling back to the post room.

There was a window set high in the wall behind a

franking machine and she had to go up on tiptoes to look down into the vehicle compound below. The truck must have pulled up while Lauren was gone, because James and Ernie were already heading away. Lauren panicked as she realized that her brother would be out of sight by the time she walked down the corridor, through the fire door, and down the metal staircase. There was no way she'd be able to contact him once he got into the school area, which was strictly segregated by sex.

Lauren grabbed the CDs and crammed them into the pocket on the front of her shorts. As she turned to run out, she remembered the chute used to drop bags of post down to the truck. The flap made a racket as she pulled it open and she clambered onto a polished metal ramp that looked like an oversized playground slide.

The chute was dark, except for a few streaks of light breaking through the fat rubber strips dangling at the bottom. Nobody had bothered smoothing out the joins in the metal for the benefit of mail bags and Lauren's bum juddered over each one as she clattered down. After pushing through the warmed rubber strips, she sprinted into the subdued light under the canopy and yelled out.

"James!"

He was a couple of hundred meters away, walking across a stretch of dirt alongside Ernie.

Lauren waved her arms and sprinted off towards her brother as he looked back curiously.

James realized Lauren probably had some information that wasn't for Ernie's ears, so he said a quick good-bye before jogging back towards his sister.

"Hey." James grinned. "Are you OK? What's going on?"

CHAPTER 34

SILENCED

Dana helped Nina make vegetarian Bolognese for dinner, but everyone was on edge and Barry was the only one who managed to eat more than half the food on his plate. Eve enthusiastically volunteered to do the washing up, but Barry just smiled.

"Heroes don't wash up." He grinned. "And we won't be back here, so why bother?"

Nina reached out for the hands of the two girls sitting on either side of her. "I think we should all say a final prayer."

Eve held out her hand to Barry and grinned at him. "Come on, and your other hand with Dana's. Let's make a circle to ward off devils."

Barry looked unenthusiastic, but they all squeezed hands tightly and closed their eyes.

"We thank you, Lord . . ."

Dana felt like she was floating as soon as she closed her eyes. She shut out Nina's prayer and tried to calm herself down.

She'd radioed John from her bedroom before sitting down to eat. He'd said that ASIS would be tailing every move they made. They'd managed to sneak a tracking device underneath the Subaru and there were police officers stationed at every major harbor along a thirty-kilometer stretch of coast.

Ideally, Barry's team would be intercepted as they boarded the boat and caught red-handed with the explosives and equipment required to complete the bombing. In the unlikely event that they managed to get the boat out, there were three Australian coast guard vessels and an Australian navy patrol boat ready to intercept them before they arrived at the LNG terminal.

All of that ought to have been reassuring, but the spaghetti still refused to settle in Dana's stomach.

"Amen," Eve and Nina said happily.

Dana's hands were released and she joined in, "Amen."

"OK," Barry said, belching loudly as he stood up from the table. "Nice meal that, thanks, Nina. It's time we shipped out, so if you girls want to use the toilet or anything."

"I'm OK." Dana smiled. "Do you need any help loading our equipment into the car?"

Barry shook his head. "Everything on the boat is being set up by our support team. All we'll have to do is climb aboard and set off."

This was a disappointment to Dana, because loading up the boat would have given the police more time to move in and arrest them.

Barry looked at the two girls. "I need one of you to come with me and sort out a little problem. The other one can stay here and help Nina set up the incendiaries to burn out the house."

"Do you really think they'll track us back here?" Eve asked.

"Can't be too careful about leaving fingerprints and DNA behind," Barry said. "We'll set the timer for twenty minutes after we leave. This house is ancient and it's got a wooden frame. It should burn up nicely."

Eve smiled at Dana. "I'll help Nina, if that's OK."

Dana shrugged and looked at Barry. "Seems like I'm with you."

While Nina and Eve grabbed petrol cans, detonators, and a bundle of industrial explosive sticks from the garage, Dana followed Barry into the hallway. He was tall enough to touch the ceiling without a ladder and easily grabbed a handle to pull down the wooden flap over the loft hatch. He went up on tiptoes, reached inside the dark hole and pulled out an automatic pistol with a silencer screwed on the front.

Dana looked shocked as Barry took the clip off and reloaded to make sure it wasn't jammed.

"What's that for?"

Barry broke into a big smile. "Got a little problem with some devils."

"I thought this was the one," Lauren groaned.

She stared into a small cupboard at the end of an

underground corridor. There was condensation dripping off the ceiling and the tiles at their feet were curled up from the damp.

"I remember the map Rat drew. I was sure this was the right one."

James was starting to lose patience. "Admit it, we're lost."

"We're *not* lost. I know roughly where we are, I just think we took a wrong turn when we passed that room with all the stacking chairs in it."

James looked at his watch. "Well it's nearly half six. We've been going for fifteen minutes already and we can't afford to wander around here all night."

"I know; I'm not stupid," Lauren said crossly. "If you'd shut your gob for a minute and let me think . . . I came down the corridor from the office. Took two left turns, down the spiral staircase and then . . ."

James started walking.

"Where are you going?"

"I'm finding the first exit sign, heading upstairs, and clearing out of here."

"I'm sure I can find it, James," Lauren said as she started to follow him. "I recognize all these corridors."

"That's because they all look *exactly* the same."

A door clanked open fifty meters in front of them and a man in a chef's uniform emerged, pushing a metal trolley stacked with tins of mixed fruit. They backed up to the wall as he headed for the exit.

"At least we're not missing a good dinner." James grinned. "I can't stand fruit cocktail."

They gave the chef half a minute to clear out before

moving off again, turning left when they reached the T-junction at the end of the tunnel.

Lauren glanced at her watch as they walked. "James, we've got time. Can't you let us have one last go at finding it?"

James tutted. "Fine, but then we're out of here."

Rat's voice sounded a few centimeters behind their ears, "I'm sure I can help if you tell me where you want to get to."

"*Jeeeeeesus,*" James gasped, as he and Lauren spun around in a state of shock. "Where did you pop out from?"

They realized he'd emerged through a door they'd passed a few steps back.

"I *knew* you were up to something," Rat said, looking at Lauren. "You left the chute open behind yourself in the post room."

James rapidly considered his options. He could easily knock Rat unconscious and bundle him back into the room, but he didn't want to hurt his friend and Rat's usefulness was obvious.

"If I tell you the truth, will you take us to Susie Regan's office?"

Lauren looked anxiously at James. "You can't."

Telling someone about the existence of CHERUB was up with taking drugs and underage sex on the list of things that could get you expelled from CHERUB.

"Can you take us?" James repeated, deliberately ignoring his sister.

"I know every corridor and secret passageway inside this joint," Rat said. "But if I get caught messing around in Susie Regan's office, she'll have me paddled and locked in a sweatbox for a month. So you'd better have a *pretty* good reason."

"We're not going back to the school," James said. "We're escaping; there's a car picking us up. You can come along if you help us."

"Are you serious?" Rat gasped, breaking into a massive smile. But his tone quickly turned circumspect. "But . . . I mean, why do we need to go into Susie's office first?"

"We don't exactly have a lot of time on our hands," James said as he desperately tried thinking up a plausible lie to explain their actions to Rat. "If you start walking, I'll start talking."

Barry cut out the back door, across the dried-out lawn, and began taking huge strides through the overgrown scrubland behind the neighbors' gardens. Dana had to take a little leap every four or five steps to keep up.

"Keep your eyes open," Barry said. "I've seen a few snakes back here since we moved in."

Dana could have done without that particular piece of information. A big man with a loaded pistol was enough to worry about, without poisonous reptiles getting thrown in.

"Are you squeamish?" Barry asked.

"Not really." Dana shrugged. "Where are we going?"

"I got mugged in Hong Kong a couple of months back. Freakish thing: little scrap of a kid surprised me with a knuckleduster. But when I came around I'd been laid out in the recovery position and I was trussed up all neatly, like no kid ever would have done. I think the security services were on my tail and they used the mugging as an opportunity to search my room."

Dana allowed herself a tiny smile. Barry—like hundreds of criminals before him—hadn't even considered that it was the child mugger who'd been the intelligence agent.

"I realized they'd put a tail on me when I arrived back in Brisbane a few days later. I thought I'd shaken them off, but it looks like I was wrong."

"What makes you think that?" Dana asked, struggling to keep cool.

"I grew up around here; an old school mucker works the radio at the local cop shop. I drop him a few bucks if he gets wind of anything suspicious around here. Late last night a routine patrol spotted a couple of guys sitting in a blue pickup truck. Cops stopped and asked the dudes what they were up to. They pulled out ASIS IDs and told the cops to mind their own."

Dana acted innocent. "What's ASIS?"

"Australian Secret Intelligence Service. It's damned lucky she told me, 'cos this whole operation could have been blown out."

Barry stopped walking and crouched down, craning his neck into the gap between two abandoned houses.

"You see that red Holden?"

Dana peeked out at a bulky red saloon car parked on a driveway. The windows were blacked out, but the one on the passenger side was two-thirds open and she could see a man and a woman sitting inside. It was a clumsy position for a stakeout, but the Northern Territory wasn't exactly a hotbed of criminal activity and Dana suspected that an operation on this scale would be using every available officer, experienced or otherwise.

Dana realized the two officers' lives were in her hands. But what could she do? Barry was a powerfully built man who'd demonstrated advanced combat skills during his hotel room encounter with Bruce. He was in a high state of readiness, with the gun cocked and loaded in his hand.

Barry grabbed a Motorola out of his shorts and dialed the house. "Nina, I'm in position. Are you ready to move?"

"All set to burn in fifteen," Nina confirmed. "We're on our way out the door."

Barry switched off the phone and handed it to Dana.

"Take this, walk around to the driver's side of the Holden and tap on the window. Try sounding upset. Your boyfriend just kicked you out of the house, your phone is dead, and you want to borrow theirs to call a cab. That should be enough to distract them for the few seconds I need to get in close to their car. OK?"

"Right," Dana said, unable to control her quaking voice. "Are you going to kill them?"

"What else can I do?"

Dana tried thinking, but her brain felt like a cotton wool ball, clogged up by the sense of dread.

"I can't do this, Barry," she said, not having to put much effort into faking a sob.

"There's no time for games here," Barry said, his voice turning nasty as he pointed the gun at Dana's chest. "You will do *exactly* what I tell you. If you mess this up, the first bullet I shoot will be going in your back. Now stand up and *move*."

Barry shoved Dana forwards, almost sprawling her in the dirt. If it had been Nina, or even a less imposing man, she would have made a grab for the gun. But all she could do was walk dumbly between the houses towards the car. Everything seemed to go slowly. Each time her trainer crunched in the gravel and each swing of her arm took forever. Her skin felt boiling hot, as if she could already feel the bullet that would tear through her if she made a wrong move.

Please God, someone, anyone. Please get me out of this.

Dana glanced into the derelict houses on either side, considering a dive inside. But the windows were boarded and the doors padlocked.

She broke out of shadows into the hot sun on the driveway and walked around the back of the car. Her brain raced as she crouched down and tapped on the passenger window. She could try giving them a warning, but Barry would kill her if he overheard.

As the passenger window whirred down, Dana briefly sighted the two agents, both looking her way. The woman was thin, wearing a lot of makeup. The man—more like a boy, really—was in his early twenties, geeky with a spindly little neck.

You're about to die.

"Listen . . . ," Dana said, then she paused for a fraction of a second, unable to decide whether to go into the spiel about her boyfriend or try saving their lives at the probable cost of her own.

But there was no time for a second word. Barry had timed his run well and already had the silenced pistol nosing through the gap in the driver's side window. He fired into the woman's chest at point-blank range. The young man was startled and got a fraction of a seconds glance at Barry before his heart exploded.

There was less blood than you'd expect and the muffled sound reminded Dana of two cushions banging into one another during a pillow fight. Barry moved the muzzle upwards and Dana scrambled back from the car, shying away from the head shots she knew Barry would administer to finish the job.

As the bullets pulsed inside the car, Dana felt the most powerful emotional explosion of her life.

I just watched two people die.

She thought she was going to throw up. Then everything started spinning. Raw panic: light-headed, barely knowing where she was, with purple and green flashes exploding in front of her eyes.

"Shift it," Barry said as he tugged her arm. The voice sounded like it was coming down a telephone line.

He yanked Dana forward and grabbed the handle of a silver car door. She hadn't even noticed Nina pulling up a few second's before.

"Come on, hurry up."

Dana trembled as the car door slammed and Nina hit the gas. She looked back at the red Holden, hoping— praying—that it hadn't happened.

When she looked forwards, Barry was grinning at her between the front seats.

"Sorry I got rough with you there, sweetheart, but we had to lose those dudes. You held up well."

Dana gawped as she tried to recover. "Is this a different car to the one we were in earlier?"

"Sure is." Barry grinned. "Had it parked in a garage a few houses up these past couple of weeks. Nobody should come looking for us in this one."

Dana had clamped her hands under her arms to stop them shaking. It was *too* awful: The team watching the house was dead and the car with the tracking device was still parked inside the garage, waiting to get burned up in the fire. But Dana knew she had to put this behind her and get hold of herself. Two innocent people had died. She had to make sure they were the only ones.

CHAPTER 35

LIES

Lauren had been right: They were only slightly lost. It took Rat less than three minutes to reach the vanilla scented corridors leading towards Joel Regan's home.

"So your dad's a spy?" Rat said as they walked, clearly far from convinced.

"Not a spy *exactly*," James stuttered, struggling to make his explanation plausible without revealing the existence of CHERUB. "Our dad knows a couple of dudes who work for Australian intelligence. When our mum went nuts and joined the Survivors, he asked them to help us escape. They agreed to help him, on condition that we nosed around Susie's office before we left."

"Right," Rat said suspiciously. "How have they been communicating with you?"

"We've got hidden radios," Lauren said.

"And why exactly is the Australian secret service interested in Susie Regan?"

James shrugged, deliberately sounding irritated by all the questions in the hope that it would discourage Rat from asking more. "I don't know and I don't really care; as long as we can get out of here and go back to living with our dad."

Mercifully, Rat had to shut up because they'd reached the curved ramp leading up to the residence.

"The butler will stop us if we go up there," Rat whispered. "But I know a back way. You two wouldn't have got jack without my help."

"OK," James said. "Stop rubbing it in; I'm sorry I didn't ask you to come with us."

Rat led them through a door that was only distinguishable from the surrounding marble by a recessed catch. The three kids found themselves in a musty cloakroom, the long rails on either side of them lined with empty wooden hangers.

"Keep your eyes peeled and your mouths shut," Rat said, when he reached the door at the back of the room. "As well as the butler, there's usually a couple of cleaning staff and my dad's nurse on duty."

"Who actually lives upstairs?" James asked.

"Only Susie and my dad."

"Right," James said. "Where are we headed?"

"You want Susie's office, so I'm gonna take you right through the basement. We'll come up the back stairs.

When you step off the landing, Susie's office will be the second door on your left."

"Aren't you coming with us?" Lauren asked.

"I've had my arse beaten enough times, thanks very much. I'll wait on the landing."

They crept anxiously through the basement rooms of the Regan residence: a laundry and dry-cleaning area, a disused kitchen large enough to cater for parties of hundreds of guests. Finally, they cut down a narrow corridor and passed the doors of the nurse and butler's cell-like living quarters.

As they went through the last set of doors, they were shocked to see the butler's black trousers and mirror-finished shoes poking out from under the stairwell. Rat looked aghast as James put his hand in front of the butler's mouth to check on his breathing.

"I can't see any obvious injuries," James said. "But I seriously doubt he collapsed under here. Someone must have dragged him."

Lauren nodded. "Drugged by the looks of it."

"How long do you think he'll be out for?" Rat asked.

"Depends what they've given him." Lauren shrugged. "Might be less than an hour, might be a day or more if they used a heavy-duty tranquilizer like Ketamine or something."

James looked at his sister. "Do you think we should carry on?"

"Well . . . ," Lauren said, before stopping to think for a second. "It could be dangerous, but something's going on up there. I reckon we ought to at least try and find out. It could be critical to the mission."

"What mission?" Rat asked.

Lauren realized she'd slipped up. "I mean our escape," she said weakly.

"How does it affect that?" Rat asked. "Why don't we just clear out and tell these spy dudes that we couldn't get into Susie's office? They're hardly gonna send us back, are they?"

"We promised our dad," James said.

"I shouldn't really complain," Rat said, half grinning. "I've spent my whole life moaning that nothing exciting ever happens around here."

As James put his foot on the bottom step, Rat had an idea. He leaned forwards and grabbed a bunch of keys out of the butler's jacket. They headed up four flights of stairs. The first two were bare concrete, the third and fourth covered in deep carpet. Rat opened a maple door and peeked through into a broad corridor.

"Looks good," he whispered.

"Are you coming with us now?" James asked.

"Gotta admit I'm curious," Rat said.

The three kids walked briskly. James knocked when he reached the second door.

"If somebody answers, leg it," he whispered.

There was no reply and the door wasn't locked. It was a large office, gaudily furnished with a marble-topped desk and chairs finished in purple leather. While Lauren kept lookout in the doorway, James walked around the desk and checked out the computer.

"Crap," he gasped, as he saw the computer had the side panel ripped away and a bunch of loose leads dangling across the carpet.

"What's up?" Rat asked.

"They've taken the hard drive out. It's like they knew we were coming, or something."

"Can't we make it work without that bit?" Rat asked naively.

James shook his head. "All the information inside a computer is stored on the hard drive, it's the only bit that matters."

Lauren took her head out of the corridor. "Do you think Susie has links inside ASIS? Maybe someone's tipped her off about the raid."

"What raid?" Rat asked.

James deliberately ignored him. "Well, I packed up the lab this morning. Maybe Susie's shipping out with Brian Evans."

Rat was starting to look angry. "How the hell do *you* know about Brian Evans?"

"What do you mean?" James asked.

"No way," Rat said bitterly. "You guys are holding out on me. How can you expect me to trust you when you're feeding me lies? Why should I tell you *anything*?"

James gritted his teeth. "Please, Rat; I swear you can trust us, but I haven't got time to explain every little detail."

"Why can't you just tell me the truth?"

"Fine," James said, exasperated. "Me and Lauren are undercover agents. We've been sent in to uncover links between the Survivors and a terrorist group called Help Earth. We wanted to get the data off Susie's computer before we left because in less than ninety minutes a bunch of commandos are gonna drop out of helicopters and storm the Ark."

Rat considered this information for a moment.

"That really *is* the truth, isn't it?" he said, breaking into a wry grin. "That's why neither of you got brainwashed, that's why you're both so smart, that's why you're both good at fighting and you know about computers and stuff. Oh *man*, this is totally amazing."

Lauren was horrified that they'd blown their cover, but fairly confident that they'd get away with it: the mission was almost over, they hadn't gone into any specifics about CHERUB, and nobody would believe Rat if he opened his mouth.

"OK," James said. "I told you, now tell us about the Evans brothers."

"I don't know about brothers," Rat said. "But one afternoon I came up to Susie's office with the letters to sign and she's lying over her desk snogging this Brian dude. She *totally* freaked out. Started screaming her head off and threatened to have me killed if I breathed a word."

"I bet that's it," James said. "She's running away with Brian. When I drove in with Ernie half an hour ago there was another jet on the runway. They've drugged the butler and ripped the hard drives from their computers to cover their tracks."

Rat nodded. "That would explain why she didn't want me coming over with the signature book today as well. But I don't see the need for secrecy unless they're up to something else. I mean, Susie's not under lock and key. She flies down to Sydney for shopping trips all the time."

"What else do you think it could be?" Lauren asked.

Rat shrugged. "I haven't got a clue."

"Has either of you heard the jet taking off?" James asked.

"Nope," Lauren said, as Rat shook his head.

"I'll radio Chloe and warn her that Susie is leaving," James said.

"*Aaagghh!*" Lauren gasped, quickly closing the door. "Susie and Brian—they just came into the corridor. They've got massive suitcases and they're waddling this way."

Nina drove the silver car briskly, but not so fast that they attracted attention. Dana kept replaying the shooting in her mind, trying to think of something she might have done differently to bring the situation under control. Although the shooting had shaken her up, she'd finally straightened out her head enough to string together a few coherent thoughts.

They'd set off from the outskirts of Darwin and within minutes they were on a stretch of open road, touching 120 kph. They pulled through a metal gate and onto a dirt track leading to a disused stable block. Dana realized they weren't anywhere near the coast and got seriously worried when they passed behind the stables, revealing a dirt airstrip and a twin-prop airplane.

Eve asked the obvious question. "What is this? I thought we were getting on a boat."

Dana wasn't sure she'd have the stomach for Barry's answer. He looked between the front seats as Nina pulled on the handbrake and yanked the ignition key.

"We'll be getting on a boat, but it's moored off the Wessel Islands, six hundred kilometers from here."

Dana couldn't understand. John had said the only other LNG facility in Australia was over three thousand kilometers away. A boat would take days to travel that kind of distance. She looked around as she got out of the car, hoping for some sign that another ASIS unit had picked up the trail and tracked them. But all she could hear was birdsong and flies, and her view towards the highway was blocked by the abandoned stables.

Barry headed across to the small aircraft, with Dana, Eve, and Nina following. He pulled a weatherproof canopy from around each engine, while Nina took the blocks out from under the wheels.

"So," Dana enquired, sounding as unruffled as her spinning head would let her, "is the journey going to take very long?"

"We'll be in the air about a hundred minutes," Barry said. "We're meeting up with a high-speed boat. If the weather stays fine we should be able to make it across the Arafura Sea in four to four and a half hours."

"Oh." Dana nodded, wishing that she had the vaguest idea where the Arafura Sea or the Wessel Islands were.

Fortunately Eve had a better grasp of Australian geography. "So the LNG terminal is in Indonesia?"

Dana cursed in her head. John and his ASIS colleagues had only considered Australian oil facilities, but parts of Indonesia were just a few hundred kilometers across the sea.

"It's not that we wanted to keep you girls in the dark," Nina explained, as Barry opened up the door on the side of the aircraft. "But everything Help Earth does is on a need-to-know basis."

"Smart," Dana said, as the reality of this rapidly changing situation began sinking in. Her mission wasn't going to end with a neat arrest at a Darwin dockside. Even worse, she was out of transmission range, so there was no prospect of radioing John with an update before takeoff.

She couldn't help but grudgingly admire the combination of excellent organization and ruthlessness shown by Help Earth. They'd consistently shown that they were the most effective terrorist group in the world, and it looked like they'd fooled the authorities once again.

Barry was already belting himself into the pilot's seat. He waved at the others to hurry inside the plane as one of the engines blasted into life. Dana was the last one to step inside and Barry began taxiing as Nina pulled shut the door.

"Settle down and get your seat belts on!" Barry yelled from the cockpit. "These dirt runways ain't exactly renowned for smooth takeoffs."

CHAPTER 96

GURU

"I doubt Susie and Brian will come in here again," James said, thinking hard. "They've already stripped the computer."

"Don't wet yourselves," Rat said, grinning as he walked up to the back wall and grabbed a bookcase. "This was my mum's study in the old days. This leads through to her dressing room."

The bookcase swung forwards, opening up a low door. James was the tallest and had to duck as they passed through.

"I *love* those." James grinned. "When I'm rich, all my rooms are gonna have hidden door thingies."

The room they'd stepped into was lined with open wardrobes. There was a minibar and a dressing table stacked with designer makeup and perfume. The floor was covered in coat hangers where Susie's clothes had been stripped out in a hurry and smoke lurked in the air.

Lauren peered into a large metal dustbin and saw that it was full of ashes. "Looks like they've burned what they couldn't carry with them."

James shook his head, looking a touch sad. "Let's face it, Susie's covered her tracks. We're not gonna find anything useful up here. We might as well leave."

James sat at the dressing table and pulled off his trainer to get the radio. Rat looked impressed when he saw it.

"I'd better sneak a look into the corridor and see where Susie and Brian have got to," Lauren said.

James nodded. "Good idea. If they're lumbering down the stairs with all that luggage, we'd better hole up here until they've gone."

"They might even be coming back," Rat said. "Susie's a clothes nut. She's not gonna want to leave too much behind."

James looked at his radio. "So, when do you reckon I should ask Chloe to pick us up?"

"Perhaps we shouldn't call her until we're sure they've gone," Lauren suggested.

A look of revelation blossomed on Rat's face. "Wait up, while they're sneaking out the back way, there's nothing to stop us going out the front. The butler's unconscious and I'd bet my last buck that Susie has made sure all the other staff are off duty or got whacked on the head. It'll mean sneaking out through my dad's bedroom, but he's asleep most of the time anyway."

Lauren smiled. "And he's not in any state to chase after us even if he's awake."

"Makes sense." James nodded. "So which turret should we leave by?"

"There's only two open this late," Rat said. "There's a chance we'll bump into Susie if we use the airport turret, which leaves the one over by the vehicle compound."

"It's a long walk, but there's hardly any security up there," James said. "Me and Ernie always drive straight through in the truck and nobody even looks at us." Decision made, he pressed the transmit button on his radio, "Chloe, can you read me?"

"Loud and clear," Chloe answered.

"We've drawn a blank up here," James said. "Brian Evans is on site and he's about to ship out with Susie. Looks like they've been shagging behind Joel's back. They've burned up a ton of paperwork and stripped the hard drive out of the computer."

"Pity," Chloe said. "I did notice a jet on the runway. I'll have ASIS put a track on it. They can arrest Susie and Brian wherever they land."

"We're about to set off for the rearmost turret. I'll be driving out in Ernie's truck. I'll meet you on the road about five kilometers out towards where you're staying, if that's OK?"

"Sounds perfect," Chloe said. "How long do you think it'll take to get out there?"

"Twenty minutes, half hour tops." James shrugged. "Just one spanner in the works. We'll have Rathbone Regan along for company. He realized we were up to something and followed us."

"That's not too clever." Chloe tutted. "Never mind, bring him along. We'll have to untangle the mess afterwards."

James pocketed the radio, wanting it handy in case the situation suddenly changed.

"Chloe'll be waiting for us," he said. "Rat, you know the way."

Rat opened a door into a luxurious marble bathroom. The huge tub had gold taps sculpted like swan heads, there was a separate shower and his and hers toilets behind slatted wooden doors.

Lauren pointed towards Joel's fancy-looking shaving brush and razor. "How much do you reckon I'd get for them on eBay?" she asked.

Rat looked mystified. "What's eBay?"

"Don't worry about it," James said, giving Lauren a stiff look, as if to say *stop messing about*.

Rat was sure there was no one except his father inside the bedroom, but he opened the door cautiously just in case. As James and Lauren followed, Rat drew a gasp.

"Dad!"

"*Sssssh,*" James said irritably. "Leave him be. What are you gawping for?"

"He's always pale, but not that pale," Rat explained anxiously. "And someone's taken the oxygen tube out of his nose."

Lauren stepped up to the bed and rested her hand on Joel's forehead. "Stone cold," she said, shuddering at the thought of touching a dead person. "Must have died at least an hour ago."

"Bloody hell," Rat said weakly, stepping back from the

287

bedside, not knowing how to react as James stepped in to confirm Lauren's diagnosis.

"Are you OK, Rat?" Lauren asked gently.

"He was totally dependent on the oxygen. I bet Susie waited for him to fall asleep and just pulled the tube out. I guess that solves the mystery of why they're in such a big hurry to leave."

"Whatever," James said dismissively. "Susie might come back. Let's get out of here."

Lauren was furious. "For God's sake, James, give Rat a minute. He just found out his father died."

Rat waved a hand in front of his face. "James is right," he said, close to tears. "He never gave a toss about me anyway. Let's roll."

Lauren put her arm around Rat's back and rubbed it gently. "I'm sorry. . . . I wish I could think of something to say."

While Lauren comforted Rat, James radioed the news to Chloe. She pondered for a couple of seconds, trying to understand the murder.

"I can only guess that it's a deliberate distraction: people will concentrate on Susie stealing millions and murdering her husband, instead of making the link between the missing money and Help Earth. We might even have fallen for it if we didn't already know the score."

"We're setting off for the vehicle compound right now," James said, glancing at his watch. "We should be OK: We've got an hour until the choppers arrive."

The three kids piled out of Joel's bedroom and began running along the corridor towards the front of the residence.

"This is *so* bad," Rat said anxiously. "The Spider's a nutter. When she finds out that my dad's dead and Susie's legged it, those turrets are gonna be locked down tight. I wouldn't be surprised if she flips out, says it's the end of the world and starts handing out guns and ammo."

"Sensible," James said wryly as they burst through a pair of maple doors. "A bunch of religious flakes versus special forces commandos. I know who my money's on."

Rat sped towards the glass-walled lounge at the front of the residence. He unlocked one of the French doors and led them around an outdoor swimming pool and up to a set of high metal railings at the edge.

"This is a tricky climb," Rat explained as he clutched a metal rail with each hand and began shimmying up. "But it saves us a few minutes."

Lauren and James followed, one on either side. As they swung their legs over the points at the top, they heard a jet engine going to full throttle on the runway less than a kilometer away.

After leaping down onto the baked earth and wading through a tangle of low shrubs, they headed along the paved path, towards the giant church at the center of the Ark. It was a few degrees cooler than the middle of the day, but the low sun blasted them in the eyes and the insects were at their most annoying.

They didn't run, but Rat led them at the typically brisk pace of Survivors with someplace to go. The paths were busy and their youth and school kit earned them a few odd glances: Everyone knew that boarding-school kids were scheduled to be playing games in the exercise yard at this time in the evening.

"Shouldn't we use the tunnels?" James asked, sure that they were about to be stopped and asked awkward questions.

"Keep cool," Rat said, shaking his head. "If anything happens, we just say we're running an errand for Susie."

James knew he'd have to answer some awkward questions about Rat later, but at that moment he was happy to have him on the team.

After walking around the vast limestone walls of the Holy Church, they set off on the path towards the office and vehicle compound. The changeover between evening service and recreational activity was now complete and this area of the compound was eerily quiet.

The only other people on the path were coming towards them: two men and the unmistakably reedy figure of The Spider in a hurry. James expected a grilling, but instead he had to step off the edge of the path to let them steam by.

"What do you reckon on that?" James asked, looking backwards.

"The Spider's got eyeballs everywhere," Rat said. "She'll have heard that Susie packed up a ton of luggage and took off in that jet."

"Remember in the hallway earlier?" Lauren added. "She was going on about that bank account, and Susie said, 'Why don't you go and ask your father?' I bet that's where she's heading right now."

"And she's gonna find that Joel is dead," Rat concluded.

"*Tits,*" James said. "How fast can she lock this place down once she finds out?"

"In the time it takes to make two phone calls to the guards inside the turrets."

James felt a shot of adrenalin as he realized that their window for escaping the Ark had probably just shrunk from an hour to ten or fifteen minutes.

He exchanged a look with his sister and they spoke in unison. "Run?"

"Definitely," Rat answered.

"We need the keys to the truck!" James yelled as they all broke into a sprint. "I know Ernie hangs them up somewhere inside the office."

Rat nodded. "There's a key cabinet inside Rumble's office."

"Who?" James asked.

"It's my nickname for the evil cow that runs the office."

"Rat hates her." Lauren panted as she ran. "She makes him do filing in the basement whenever she catches him mucking about."

It took two minutes to reach the door of the office building. James crashed into it breathlessly, only to find that it had been locked up for the night.

"Might have known it!" he shouted as he kicked the door.

"Mail chute," Rat said.

The three kids ran around the side of the building, beneath the canopy of the deserted vehicle compound. James was first to clamber through the strips of rubber and into the base of the chute. Ten meters of shiny metal stood between himself and the top.

He grabbed hold of the curved sides and made a run for it. After a couple of steps, his feet lost their grip and he slid back, catching Lauren in the mouth with his trainer as he clattered into her.

"Careful," Lauren said angrily, tasting blood and grit as she wrapped a hand over her front teeth.

"It wasn't deliberate," James snapped.

While the siblings scowled at each other, Rat clambered around them and tried a different technique: He placed one leg over the edge of the metal chute and pulled himself up by grabbing the bolts that joined the metal sections together.

"Wait here," James said to Lauren as he followed Rat up; the rusty bolts tearing into his fingers.

"Try getting me some tissues," Lauren said as she wiped her bloody chin on her shirt.

When Rat reached the top of the chute, he swung his legs out in front and booted the flap open with a double-footed kick that made James's ears ring.

"Make some noise, why don't you?" James muttered as he clambered out into the dark post room and fired a dusty mouthful of spit at the carpet.

Rat opened the door and charged out into the gloomy open-plan office, cutting between desks on a fifty-meter dash to the manager's office. James ran a few steps behind. They found the door open, but the key cabinet hanging behind the desk was locked.

"Stand back!" James grabbed a fire extinguisher and took a run up.

It smashed against the clear plastic. The cabinet tore off the wall, hit the floor, and the keys inside jangled off their little hooks, but the lock was still on and the cover only had a tiny crack in it.

"Dammit," Rat snarled, stamping his heel against the plastic to make the crack bigger.

James joined in, and after about five stamps each, the cabinet's hinges sheared away and Rat stripped off the sheet of plastic.

"I need light," James said.

As fluorescent tubes plinked to life over his head, James crouched down and rummaged through the loose keys, looking for the key ring with the little Toyota oval on it. Like always when you're panicking, it seemed to take ages.

"Got it," he said finally. "Rat, get the tissues for Lauren."

Rat grabbed a tissue box off the manager's desk, as James started back towards the post room. As the two boys ran, a great wave of light began flickering across the ceiling. Someone must have been working late or cleaning downstairs and they'd come up to investigate the noise.

James looked backwards, but there was no one in sight. The office was large enough that it would take a few minutes for someone to work out what had happened and where they'd gone. Rat went down the chute first. James followed, catching his shorts on one of the joints. It squeezed his balls as it snagged and tore up a corner of his back pocket.

"Lauren?" James gasped, straightening out his bits as he scrambled through the rubber strips and stood up.

She sat against the side of the building with blood trickling out the corner of her mouth. Rat handed her a bunch of tissues.

"You OK?" James asked guiltily.

"Shit happens," Lauren said, mopping her face as she stood up.

James cut between a couple of Ford pickups and stepped across the open tarmac to the dusty Toyota truck. As Lauren and Rat climbed into the passenger side, James felt intimidated by the half-meter of steering wheel and broad expanse of dashboard in front of him. With power steering, power brakes, and an automatic gearbox it was no more difficult than driving a car, but it was double the length of any vehicle he'd taken on before and the ground seemed a hell of a long way down.

He turned the ignition key, dropped the handbrake, and dabbed the accelerator to roll out of the parking spot.

"Could you drive any slower, James?" Lauren sniped, slurring because she had tissues packed in her mouth to stop the bleeding.

"Better safe than sorry," James said, picking up speed as he pulled out from under the canopy and turned on to the three-hundred-meter slip road that led up to the turret.

It was starting to turn dark, so it took a second to realize that the drawbridge on the outside of the turret was being winched up by its thick chain.

"No *way*!" Rat yelled, kicking the dashboard with both feet.

James thought about hitting the gas, but the drop-down gate had been built to withstand an apocalypse and the truck wouldn't even make a dent in it.

James looked at his bloody sister in the middle seat. "What do you reckon now?"

"I dunno." Lauren shrugged. "Leg it out of this truck and find a safe place to hide, I guess."

CHAPTER 37

SURPRISE

The sky was black as the small plane headed for a beach landing on the Wessel Islands, a two-hundred-kilometer chain that stretched out from Australia's northern coast. Dana had found herself a single seat at the back, two rows clear of Eve and Nina.

She knew there was a chance ASIS had successfully tracked the flight and had a team waiting to ambush them when they landed, but she doubted it. Most likely, everyone would assume that Barry Cox had canceled the attack and gone to ground after discovering that his team was under surveillance.

So it was all down to Dana. At first, the idea scared her. She didn't know anything about tankers or LNG facilities, but guessed that there had to be at least fifty lives at stake. The longer she sat at the back of the plane in her trademark position—arms folded, legs outstretched—thinking about it, the more confident she got.

CHERUB training teaches you that surprise is everything. Barry had thrown her off stride with the double murder and the sudden revelation that the attack was going to take place in a different country, a thousand kilometers from where everyone was expecting it. But she'd have surprise on *her* side during the four-hour ride to Indonesia.

Once the boat was underway, people would let their guard down; maybe even try getting some sleep if things weren't too tense. Dana didn't have any weapons, but reckoned she'd find plenty on a boat: fishing hooks, ropes, kitchen utensils in the galley.

Dana was fifteen and had lived on CHERUB campus since she was seven. She'd been baked, frozen, half drowned, and shot at during training exercises, she'd read eight-hundred-page computer hacking textbooks, learned to speak Russian, and had her nose rubbed in puke by a sadistic training instructor; but all she had to show for it were a string of missions that had fizzled out or only been partially successful.

Now Dana had a chance to prove it had all been worthwhile. She felt like the last eight years of her life had all been building up to what was going to happen in the next few hours.

Chloe sat in a car at the roadside, with the Ark glowing serenely two kilometers ahead. There was no hint of the brewing trouble. The helicopter attack was due in nine minutes. She had a satellite phone at her ear and could barely hear the man talking to her, because his voice was being patched through from a helicopter that was thirty kilometers off, but closing in rapidly.

"Why won't you listen to me?" Chloe shouted. "There are more than a hundred children inside the Ark. I have two undercover operatives who have positively identified an array of heavy weaponry."

"We're aware of their capability, Miss!" the TAG unit commander shouted back patronizingly. "This raid has been planned carefully. We've been in training for two months."

"You're *not* listening to me!" Chloe yelled, growing increasingly exasperated. "I have reason to believe that Joel Regan is dead. You're attacking at the worst possible time. The Ark has been locked down tight and the Survivors are in an emergency state of readiness."

"Well, I haven't received any such intelligence. . . ."

"Yes you *have*. I just told you."

". . . from credible sources," the commando added sourly. "We've trained for this raid. We're an elite unit. Now I know you're worried about your undercover operatives, but this plan has been authorized at Prime Ministerial level."

Chloe groaned. "Is there anyone from ASIS up there in the chopper with you?"

The TAG commander seemed only too pleased to get Chloe off his back and handed the radio across without another word.

"Who are you exactly?" the ASIS officer asked stiffly.

Chloe wasn't about to reveal the existence of CHERUB to a helicopter full of commandos. "I'm on attachment from British intelligence," she explained. "I have two agents inside the Ark and they're telling me that Eleanor Regan has issued weapons to every able-bodied adult. If you go into that Ark tonight, you're going to face a significantly— I repeat, *significantly*—more hostile reaction than the one you're expecting."

"Miss Blake," the ASIS officer said bluntly. "I'm not even aware of any undercover operation inside the Ark, and there's no way we can pull out at this stage. If you're still in contact with your undercover officers, I suggest you tell them to find refuge. The raid *will* commence in five minutes. If you feel we're behaving inappropriately, you can file an official complaint after the event."

"Arsehole," Chloe gasped, losing her temper. "I just hope you live that long."

Chloe ended the call and threw the satellite phone down on the passenger seat in frustration. After a groan, she grabbed another radio that was resting on the glovebox flap.

"James, do you copy?"

"Loud and clear. What's going on, are they still coming?"

"Looks that way," Chloe said. "Eight on the dot. What's your situation?"

"Same as," James said. "Eleanor put out an announcement over the Tannoy that Joel died and told everyone to protect themselves from a possible attack by devils. Everyone here is tooled up and running around dressed like Action Man. When they hear those choppers they're gonna think it's the bloody apocalypse."

"What kind of weapons are you seeing?"

"Automatic rifles mostly," James said. "AK-47s, M16 carbines. There's heavier stuff being set up inside the turrets: twenty-millimeter cannons and rocket-propelled grenades."

"Where are you now?"

"We're in a classroom on the first floor of the adult education center. Rat took us here because it's deserted: It's been mothballed since they stopped letting guests inside the Ark."

"OK," Chloe said. "Can you find somewhere with better cover, like an underground bunker or something?"

"Yeah," James said. "Rat says there's a bunch of tunnels right under here. But we won't be able to see what's going on once we're down there."

"I wouldn't worry about that," Chloe said. "We've got total communication breakdown. The special forces commander won't listen to me and the ASIS officers up there haven't been briefed on the CHERUB mission. In the end I lost my rag and ended up swearing at them."

"That's not like you," James said.

"Sheer bloody frustration." Chloe groaned. "Just get yourselves undercover. Keep calm, keep safe, and don't try anything stupid."

"Would I?" James said, making a weak stab at humor, even though he felt more like throwing up from nerves. "I'll be in touch as soon as there's something to tell you."

Chloe took the radio away from her ear. For a moment she thought she'd left the volume on and was listening to static, then she realized it was the distant pulsing of helicopter blades. She looked at the digital clock in the dashboard: 19:57.

The beach was illuminated with flood lamps, powered from a diesel generator. Barry made a gentle landing on sand leveled by the outgoing tide. As Dana unbuckled her seat belt, a man dressed in deck shoes and loud shorts came jogging towards the small aircraft. She'd not met Mike Evans before, so she had no idea it was him.

As they clambered from the aircraft onto the dark beach and walked the stiffness out of their legs, Mike shook Barry's hand and spoke with a Texan accent.

"Hey, Barry, y'all set?"

"So far so good." Barry nodded. "What's been going on up here?"

"Your boat's all set to run. Weather's good, the sea couldn't be any calmer, so you can drive her flat out if needs be. But watch the fuel gauges 'cos you're squirting eight liters a minute into the turbines when she goes above fifty knots and you won't make it back to Oz at that rate."

"What about the radar?" Nina added.

"Not a dickey bird," Mike said. "The systems on that boat are state of the art. There's nothing unexpected on the screen, either in the sea or up in the air. I'm ninety-nine percent sure nobody followed you out of Darwin."

Mike turned his head towards the girls before continuing. "And why haven't you introduced me to these two beautiful young ladies?"

Barry smiled. "This is Eve and Dana, and I'm extremely proud to have them on our team tonight."

Mike grinned and shook both their hands.

"Are you coming on the boat with us?" Dana asked, not happy at the prospect of having another crewmate to take out.

"I'm sure your company would be a delight, but I'm gonna see you off in the boat. Then I'm gonna pack up the landing lights and fly the plane out of here."

"That's a pity," Dana lied, creeped out by the way Mike was flirting with her.

Mike led everyone on a trek across the beach. They walked for a couple of minutes, when they reached a wooden jetty with a large powerboat moored off the end.

It was dark, so they were less than twenty meters away from the boat when Dana got a proper look. It was extremely cool in a menacing kind of way: twin black hulls with chromed deck fittings. The whole shape was streamlined for high speed and a dinghy—identical to the one they'd trained in that morning—was lashed to a ramp at the end of the rear deck.

Eve and Dana straddled over the deck rail and climbed aboard. As Barry ran up a flight of steps to the bridge, Mike began unwinding the ropes tethering the boat to the jetty.

"Free to go!" Mike shouted, standing to attention and saluting the three females. "Good luck out there."

The catamaran lurched as the turbine inside each hull gulped down the water it would propel out of the stern in a high-speed jet. As Dana headed into the mess room beneath the bridge, Barry cranked up the power and two blasts of spray erupted five meters into the air behind the boat.

CHAPTER 38

APOCALYPSE

The emergency siren inside the Ark began to whine as soon as the helicopters were heard. A minute later it cut to a crackly Tannoy announcement from Eleanor Regan.

"Angels in the southern turrets have sighted helicopters. My father's death has emboldened the devils and encouraged them to attack. They will soon be upon us. Stand firm, defend your positions, and remember that our strength comes from God."

Rat gave Lauren and James a wry grin. "I bet those brave words came from about four levels below ground."

The three kids had their faces at a window in the adult education block. The sky was black, but you could tell the helicopters were close from the vibrating glass.

"Can we make it down to the tunnels in time?" James asked.

"Depends how long we've got." Rat shrugged. "We'll have to head out of this building and run about thirty meters, then down a flight of steps."

Lauren spoke awkwardly, because she still had a wad of bloody tissue jammed into her mouth to stop her lip bleeding. "I don't fancy it."

"Me neither," James said. "The last thing we want is to get caught out in the open. We're better off staying put."

All three kids ducked instinctively as a helicopter skimmed the roof. Two more came into view, looming over the courtyard at the rear of the Holy Church, their positions exposed by the powerful lights illuminating the spires.

One of the helicopters switched its searchlight on, flooding the paved area beneath it with light. It was a big beast, military green, with a dozen commandos standing in open doorways, ready to spring out when it touched down.

As the chopper moved within ten meters of the ground, an orange streak roared out of the church and hit it from point-blank range. The blast knocked three men out of the open doorway as a blaze erupted inside the cockpit.

"Back up!" James yelled.

He knew the window would shatter if the helicopter exploded, so he wrapped an arm over his face and dived under the nearest desk. Lauren and Rat did the same, but nothing happened. James braved a glance. The flames were out and clouds of fire-extinguishing powder billowed out of the helicopter's doorways.

Apparently the helicopter had been saved by its fire protection system, but the pilot was flying blind and had no option but to pull up. That left three bodies on the ground below. Two were engulfed in flames and didn't seem to be moving, but the third rolled frantically in the dirt trying to extinguish his burning uniform.

The other three helicopters were now in plain sight, trying to land in the courtyard but coming under heavy fire. Another streak—James guessed it was a rocket-propelled grenade—ripped off from inside the church. It deflected off the side of a descending helicopter, before spiraling up in a wild trajectory and exploding close to the perimeter wall.

The next shot was a direct hit on the tail rotor of the helicopter closest to touchdown. It twisted violently, its blades centimeters shy of a fatal collision with the side of the church.

As the pilot battled to control his ship without a tail rotor, the other two helicopters pulled up and backed away from the compound, apparently under orders to withdraw. Unfortunately, this left the chopper with the damaged tail as the only target in the sky. Two more rockets slammed home as it tried to pull up, one from the church and one from inside a turret.

This last was a direct hit on the fuel tank. James buried his face against the classroom floor and felt a wave of heat as the sky lit up in orange. A deafening slam was followed by a shock wave that blew out hundreds of panes of glass across the Ark.

Deadly shards sprayed the room around James, as the sudden change of air pressure made his ears pop. If he hadn't been shielded under the table, he would have been sliced to pieces.

Although his eyes stung from the smoke and fuel vapor, he forced them open and looked around desperately for his sister. "Lauren?"

"We're OK!" Lauren yelled back, though James could hardly hear over the ringing in his ears. "You?"

"Yeah . . . I think."

James stood up carefully, avoiding the broken glass. He dashed over to join Rat and Lauren, who'd huddled together in fright.

"I think they've pulled back, for now," James said.

Lauren rubbed her eye. "That poor man burning on the ground," she said, sniffing and looking completely stunned. "There must have been loads more in the one that blew up."

James grabbed his radio and shouted, "Chloe?"

"Where are you?" she asked, audibly shocked. "Did I see what I think I just saw?"

"We didn't have time to get underground, we're still in the education building, and yes you did see a chopper go down."

"I *told* them!" Chloe screamed. "I bloody told them. Are you guys OK?"

"Lauren's shaken up, but we're all in one piece."

"The other three choppers are touching down in the desert near me," Chloe said. "I've got nursing qualifications. They're bound to have injuries up there, and I'm sure I can help out."

The high-speed catamaran had been built as a rich man's plaything, or at least Dana couldn't imagine any woman

305

splurging millions on such an absurd toy. Yet, in another way, she couldn't help admiring it, from its immaculately chromed toilet basin to the soft leather sofas and the compact kitchen with more gadgets and flashing lights than a space shuttle.

Most impressive was the sense of isolation. They might have been skimming towards Indonesia at a hundred kph, with two jet turbines hurling a wall of water ten meters into the air behind them, but when you closed the triple-glazed door leading onto the rear deck, the only sense of motion was an occasional violent jolt when they punched through a big wave.

It was 8:40 now and Dana was certain that ASIS had no idea where she was. That left her with three and a bit hours to overpower her crewmates and take control of the boat.

She made every step count: glancing in kitchen drawers, opening up cupboards in search of weapons, carefully studying the internal layout of the boat to see which doors led where and working out the best places to isolate people so that she could take her companions out one at a time. She didn't think Eve and Nina would present major problems, as long as she retained the element of surprise. Barry was in a different league: he was huge, strong; he'd clearly been through advanced military training and had proved himself capable of killing with the pistol he kept tucked in his shorts.

"Are you with us down there?" Nina asked.

Dana had been thinking and was startled by the remark. She looked up from her leather seat and faked a yawn. "Sorry. . . . Just a bit tired."

Nina nodded sympathetically. "It's been a long day. You girls can go into one of the cabins and get some rest once we've had our briefing."

"I could use that," Dana said. "Are you doing it now?"

"Might as well get it over with." Nina nodded.

Dana got up and took five paces towards a circular table in the galley. Eve was already sitting there and Dana joined her as Nina unzipped a backpack and pulled out a rolled-up diagram.

"Hold the corners," Nina said as she unfurled it.

The drawing was to scale and showed only basic outlines. There was a jagged coast, with the shapes of giant LNG cylinders and the gas liquefaction terminal behind them. A long jetty led out into the sea and there were the outlines of two identically shaped supertanker hulls at the end.

"This is pretty self-explanatory," Nina said. "The positioning and timing of the explosions is critical to the success of the operation. We'll take the dinghy in to about two hundred meters shy of the tankers. For the sake of quiet, we'll cut the engines and row the last stretch, ending up here, hidden beneath the jetty with a tanker docked on either side of us.

"You'll deal with one tanker each. You'll position two magnetic charges in the bow area of each boat, two meters below water level and spaced eighteen meters apart. The devices are designed to puncture the outer hull and inject explosive gas into the watertight space between the tankers' twin hulls a few seconds before detonation. The explosion should be enough to rip the front end off both ships and fracture the outer casing of the pressurized LNG cylinders on board.

"Once the devices are fitted to the tankers, we'll attach two much larger explosives to the jetty itself. The first will be by the refueling gantry that leads out to each boat. The other will be positioned at the opposite end, close to shore. Our aim is to have the devices put in place within fifteen minutes. All six will be timed to explode simultaneously, approximately fifteen minutes after we've cleared the area.

"The terminal is designed so that LNG can be safely vented in the event of a minor accident. However, if our calculations are correct, simultaneous explosions between the front of the boats and along the length of the jetty should completely overwhelm the capability of the terminal's fail-safe systems. The explosion should destroy not only the jetty and the two tankers, but also gas storage facilities on dry land and a significant section of the liquefaction plant itself.

"In order to make accurate positioning of the explosives, you'll each wear a GPS receiver on your wrist. It will be preprogrammed with the exact coordinates for the four explosions."

"Piece of cake," Dana said, doing her Survivor grin.

"Not if you take that kind of casual attitude it won't be," Nina said sharply. "*Please* listen. We'll be working in complete darkness with oil company workers a few meters away from us. We've got to keep our movements quiet and speech to an absolute minimum.

"Now that I've given you the basic outline of the raid, I'm going to talk you through each step in detail. If you have questions, ask them *now*, not during the operation.

"The equipment needed for the raid has already been

loaded into the dinghy. It will be launched off the back of this vessel with an electronic winch. Obviously, the engines have to be switched off before we can do this safely . . ."

Dana stifled a yawn as her brain struggled to absorb the stream of facts.

CHAPTER 36

BENEATH

James had underestimated the Survivors' ability to fend off the TAG units. He'd expected things to get hairy when he'd seen the Survivors' arsenal, but not in his wildest dreams did he think the commandos would lose a ship and be forced to back off before getting a man on the ground.

With hindsight, he realized that the Survivors would have had little trouble getting hold of grenades, mortars, and other heavy weapons. A smuggler could choose from thousands of kilometers of deserted Australian coastline on which to land a boatload of weapons that could be purchased in dozens of war-torn countries around the world.

Twenty minutes after the crash, smoke still poured out of the helicopter's mangled chassis. The surviving soldier, who'd fallen from the first helicopter and extinguished his flaming clothes, had been peeled off the ground and dragged inside as a hostage.

There was much less smoke around now and the air inside the education block had completely cleared. Lauren and Rat had tipped one of the desks onto its side and pushed it around like a snowplow, sweeping all the broken glass to one side of the room.

James peered through a shattered window. After the explosion there had been people running everywhere, but now the Survivors and their weapons seemed to have retreated into buildings and tunnels.

"What do you reckon?" James asked. "Looks pretty calm out there now, shall we risk a move?"

"Are you sure we're not better off here?" Lauren asked. "We've got no idea what's going on in the tunnels."

James shrugged. "I can only see this ending one of two ways: either the Survivors are going to surrender and we all walk merrily out the front gate—which seems unlikely—or those bad-assed soldiers who just lost twenty of their colleagues are gonna wait until they've got reinforcements and some armored vehicles and then they're gonna storm this place.

"Whether that happens tonight, tomorrow, or at the end of a long siege, I don't want to be sitting in a building made from wood and plasterboard."

Lauren nodded reluctantly. "I guess you're right. But Rat, you know this joint, are you *sure* there's not a secret passage or some other way out of here?"

Rat shook his head, "This whole place is built for a siege. The turrets are the only way in or out."

"So we're agreed," James said. "Lets move."

James led the way down a short corridor between two classrooms. He cautiously opened the door on to an outdoor landing and studied the shadows below before setting off down the metal steps.

An ammunition cartridge inside the burning helicopter chose that moment to pop and the three kids raced down and hit the ground at the bottom. It sounded exactly like they were being shot at.

"False alarm, I think," James said warily.

"I *hate* this," Lauren whispered, holding a clammy hand over her heart.

Rat knew the way, so he took the lead on the thirty-meter dash, crunching across a path strewn with broken glass, before heading down a flight of metal steps cut into the ground. When they reached the thick metal door at the bottom, Rat rested both hands on the rubber handle and pushed down. The mechanism clanked, but he shoved hard and it wouldn't move.

"You want me to try?" James asked. "I'm stronger than you."

Rat shook his head. "You won't do it. The bolts must have been put on inside."

Lauren tutted. "Isn't there another way in?"

"I doubt it," Rat said. "Every second or third building's got a door out back that leads down into the tunnels, but if this one's been locked I'd guess that they all have."

"So now what?" Lauren asked, looking at James.

"We could try a couple more doors," said James. "If

not, we'll have to go back to the classroom. Maybe we can pile up the tables and make some sort of shelter, or something."

Lauren looked at her brother like he was an idiot. "Yeah, desks are notorious for their bullet-stopping ability."

"Well, sis, if you've got any better ideas my ears are *wide* open."

"Shut it," Rat gasped. "Something's up there."

A torch lit up their faces as a shout came from the top of the staircase. "Turn around, put your hands on your heads."

James recognized the voice and smiled with relief. "Ernie, thank God it's you."

He felt confident until he heard the safety catch of an automatic rifle being removed.

"Hands on heads," Ernie repeated stiffly. "I don't know what's going on with you three, but Miss Regan's had a dozen people out searching for you. Now, come up them steps nice and *sloooow*. No sudden moves."

Everyone they passed in the dimly lit tunnels wore body armor and most had a gun slung over their shoulder. *The Survivors' Manual* said there was no such thing as an angel who wasn't prepared to defend the Ark by any means necessary.

The combo of ragged Survivor clothes, middle-aged spread, and automatic weapons had a comic air, like a bunch of accountants dressing up to re-enact some famous battle. But James didn't find it funny: These were Joel Regan's most fanatical followers and they'd already shown what they were capable of.

The Spider's bunker was three levels beneath the church. Her garb was pure theatre: camouflage baseball cap, flak jacket, a small machine gun hung off her spindly shoulders, and two grenades hooked over the waistband of her cutoff jeans.

The three kids lined up stiffly in front of her desk. Some of the Spider's cronies sat behind them on stacking chairs, including Georgie, who now sported a backwards baseball cap and an assault rifle.

"The three of you were seen clambering out of the residence," The Spider said. "What were you doing up there?"

"Susie ordered us up there to help her pack," James explained.

"But you clambered out and didn't return to school," The Spider said severely. "Sneaks clamber, honest souls use the front door."

James didn't know how to answer and Rat took up the slack.

"I ripped one of Susie's skirts pulling it off its hangar," he lied. "She started going *insane.* Screaming and shouting about how much money it cost and threatening to have us paddled. She threw a makeup case at Lauren's head and we just legged it. We didn't want to disobey her, honestly. But we were scared. We'd seen what had happened to the butler, and we really thought she was going to hurt us."

"I see," The Spider said, leaning across the desk and locking her fingers together. "And then you were seen in the truck. I can only assume you were trying to escape."

"We were scared Susie was after us," Rat explained.

"James said he knew how to drive the truck. He said he'd be able to take us as far as the nearest town and phone his dad for help."

James couldn't help admiring Rat's intelligence. The excuses were ten times better than anything he could have come up with.

The Spider hummed as she tried to find the flaw in Rat's story. "But you must have realized that Susie and Brian had left when the jet took off. Why did you stay in hiding?"

"I thought she might have left orders for Georgie to punish us when we got back to the school."

"Well . . . ," the Spider said, breaking into an uneasy smile. "That seems to explain the great mystery. You'll be happy to learn that I don't think we'll be seeing Susie Regan inside the Ark again."

Georgie cleared her throat, making it clear that she wanted to speak.

The Spider nodded. "Yes."

"I don't mean to speak out of turn, Eleanor, but you'd do well not to believe *every* word that comes out of Rathbone's mouth. He's a notorious liar. I've had to paddle him more times than the rest of the Blues combined."

The Spider's face stiffened and she reared up in her seat. "Georgie, I don't much care for your tone. I know Rathbone can be a handful, but you ought to remember that he is of the blood. He *is* and shall *always* be Joel Regan's son and my own half brother."

Georgie's bulbous frame seemed to wilt under the Spider's glare. "Of course," she said weakly. "I understand."

"Take the three of them back to the school," The Spider

ordered. "And make sure you don't lose them again."

As soon as they were a hundred meters clear of The Spider's office and heading down a tunnel towards the school, Rat couldn't resist giving his arch enemy a cheeky grin.

"Eyes forward, Rathbone," Georgie said acidly. "You might have sweet-talked your big sister, but I *always* know when you're lying."

"How do you reckon on that?" Rat asked.

"Because every filthy word out of your devil mouth is a lie."

"Maybe I should talk to my big sister about you." Rat grinned. "I sense a serious lack of respect for my elevated status."

They reached the tunnel beneath the boarding school two minutes later. All the kids were confined to their dorms because of the emergency. Lauren gave James a worried look, thinking she was about to be separated from the boys and sent off to her room with the Yellows. But Georgie had other plans and unlocked the door of an underground room.

It was a nursery, set up with cushions and toys. The dank space, which smelled like waterpaint and milk, was home to five kids whose parents worked inside the Ark but weren't old enough to attend the school upstairs. There were no other adults around and Georgie had simply locked them away, under threat of a good paddling if they misbehaved.

"I don't want you three running off again," Georgie explained. "You can stay here, where I can keep my eye on you."

A cute little girl holding a comfort blanket had strolled up alongside Georgie and tugged at her trousers. "Miss, Martin took my pacifier."

Georgie glowered down at the girl. "I'm not your nursemaid, Annabel," she growled. "Find another one or go without."

The little girl scowled at a plastic tub on a high shelf. "Can't reach that."

Georgie wagged her finger. "I'm not in the mood to put up with your *shit* tonight, Annabel. Do you want a whack on the arse?"

The little girl's face crinkled up like she was about to cry, but she reconsidered when Georgie raised a threatening hand.

Lauren intervened, crouching down and smiling at the toddler. "Why don't you show me where the box is?"

Georgie grabbed Lauren's T-shirt and dragged her back. "If you're gonna start playing with the little ones, don't wind them up. It's late and it does my head in when they start screaming and chasing around."

Lauren nodded politely. "OK, Miss."

"I'm going upstairs for a smoke," Georgie said, scowling at James and Rat. "Behave yourselves, or there's gonna be blood and snot all over the place when I get back here."

Georgie backed out of the nursery, slamming the metal door and turning the key in the lock.

CHAPTER 40

TIME

Eve was in the top bunk with her eyes closed, but Dana doubted she was asleep. Who'd be able to, an hour and a half before you were supposed to climb into a little boat and blow up a couple of supertankers?

Dana threw back her duvet, quietly grabbed her cargo shorts off the floor and was slipping her socked feet inside trainers when the boat hit a huge wave, knocking the back of her head against the frame of the upper bunk.

Eve's eyes flicked open. "*Oooh* I heard that," she said. "Are you OK?"

"Yeah. It sounded worse than it felt," Dana said as she tried rubbing away the pain.

"Why are you getting dressed, it's not time, is it?"

"No, I need the loo again."

Eve sounded confused. "You don't need to get dressed for that."

"I guess," Dana said. "It's just being on a boat I suppose . . . with Barry around and that."

"That's at least the fifth time you've been. Are you OK?"

"My stomach always goes crazy whenever I'm nervous," Dana lied. "Last year, the morning before my exams, I must have gone about twenty times."

"Maybe we should pray," Eve said. "Thinking about God always helps me to relax."

Dana stood up. "We'll pray when I get back. How about you? Are you nervous?"

"I just hope I can live up to God's expectations," Eve said. "Nina said they might name a room inside one of the new Arks after us. Can you *believe* that?"

This kind of Survivor speak made Dana nuts. In Eve's head, a platinum bead and a room named after you inside an Ark meant more than six numbers on the lottery.

As Eve slumped back on to her pillow, Dana took three steps down a narrow corridor and slid a bolt across the bathroom door behind her. She raised the lid and sat down to pee, but that wasn't the reason behind this visit to the bathroom, or any of her previous excursions out of her bunk.

Dana opened the cupboard under the sink and began pulling out the stash she'd gathered on her wanderings around the boat: a key, a saw-toothed hunting knife, a small aerosol canister of oven cleaning spray, and some strong nylon cord. She'd already chopped this into lengths suitable for tying a person up.

Everything fitted into her pockets, except the rope. She stared at herself in the mirror over the sink, breathing deep and trying to think calming thoughts. In ten minutes' time, Dana knew she'd either have taken control of the boat, or she'd be dead.

James, Lauren, and Rat had been locked in the nursery for almost two hours. The space had its own bathroom, with little sinks barely half a meter off the ground and kiddie-size toilets. For some reason the stall nearest the rear wall was the only spot in the whole nursery where James could get a decent signal on his radio. There were no locks on the doors, so Rat had to stand with his back against the bathroom door to stop the little kids from coming in and seeing what he was up to.

"Chloe," James whispered. "Any news?"

"Negative," Chloe said. Her next sentence disintegrated into static.

"Sorry, can you repeat that."

"I said the first reinforcements should be landing within an hour. More will be coming by road and it looks like the media have caught on to the story as well. One of the TAG commanders wanted me to ask if you have any idea what's going on inside the towers?"

"Afraid not," James said. "We're totally isolated here. Georgie's been in and out a few times, but she never tells us anything. Why, what do you think's going on?"

"The commandos are looking into the turrets with heat-sensitive cameras. It looks like the Survivors are moving out a lot of weapons, maybe even abandoning the turrets altogether."

"Is it the same in all of them?"

"We think so, yes."

"So are you getting any idea of what the TAG units are planning?"

"They're—"

"Sorry, Chloe, you dropped out again."

"Everyone here is in shock: The TAG units lost a quarter of their manpower when that chopper went down. The commander, who wouldn't even *listen* to me earlier, knows he's messed up and he's running around like a headless chicken. Nobody's prepared to make any decisions. They're flying in a hostage negotiation team to take over the show, but they're not due here for another three or four hours."

"The Survivors down here are totally hard core," James said. "They'd sooner starve than leave the Ark. It's hard to see a happy ending."

"I know this is a bad situation, James. I wish I could be of some comfort, but I feel the same way you do. Keep in touch and do let me know if you get any information about what's going on inside the turrets."

"OK, Chloe, over and out."

As soon as James pocketed the radio, Rat let in six-year-old Joseph, who'd been thumping on the door. He wore a set of faded pajamas that were way too small for him.

"What are you doing?" Joseph asked angrily, rubbing his tired eyes.

"Just messing around," Rat said as the kid stepped up to a urinal and started peeing.

Joseph looked around at Rat. "What are you staring for?"

"Hmm?" Rat blinked. "Oh, nothing."

James led Rat back out towards Lauren, who sat on the carpet with her back propped against a beanbag. Three-year-old Annabel and her four-year-old brother Martin were cuddled alongside her, fast asleep with their heads resting in her lap.

"Sewage." Rat grinned cryptically as Joseph ran between them and leapt noisily into one of the little beds set against the back wall. "Something just occurred to me. A way out, maybe."

"Really?" James said.

"I wanna see what Lauren thinks, too. I'm not going through it twice."

James stepped up to his sister and tapped her cheek. She wasn't asleep, but her eyes were shut.

"Come over here a minute," James said.

Lauren shuffled out, gently shifting the two warm little bodies onto the beanbag, trying not to wake them up. Annabel took a sudden breath and opened her eyes.

"Where are you going?"

"Not far," Lauren answered gently. "Go to sleep. I'll be back in a minute."

"You're nice, Lauren," Annabel said, smiling as the need for sleep overpowered her and her eyes rolled shut.

Lauren looked back at the two kids as she walked over to James and Rat. "They're *so* cute."

"Sewage," Rat said again, clearly excited by something. "You know when you asked me if there are any other exits apart from the turrets? When I saw Joseph peeing, I remembered something from a few years back.

"All the Ark's drains feed down into one big sewage tank. A few years ago, we kept getting this horrible stench whenever there were a lot of people inside the Ark. They had to dig it up and put in a bigger tank. I saw it arrive; it's huge. I mean, you could walk through it standing up."

"So?" Lauren said. "What good does that do us?"

Rat smiled. "The truck comes in twice a week and pumps our sewage and waste water out of the tank. It backs up to a metal hatch on the *outside* and they attach a pipe to suck it out. You see the hatch when we do our morning run. It's just past the fourth turret."

"I think I know the one you mean," said James. "It's easily big enough to climb through."

"Hang on," Lauren said, raising her hands. "We're talking about a sewer here, right? We're talking about escaping by wading through the stuff that gets flushed down the toilet?"

James shrugged. "Lauren, there's two sets of people with guns and we're stuck between them. If there's really a way out, I'm taking it."

"Well . . . I suppose," Lauren said uneasily.

"What's better?" James asked. "Doing something gross or getting a bullet through your head?"

The three kids turned towards the door as a key clattered in the lock.

"What are you three plotting?" Georgie asked sarcastically as she plunged a fat finger up her nose and slumped in a chair.

Dana got a fright as she stepped out of the bathroom. Nina was right outside the door.

323

"Are you OK?" Nina asked. "I keep hearing you moving around."

Dana put a hand over her stomach. "Nervous tummy."

Nina nodded. "What's with the cord?"

This really put Dana on the spot. She considered laying Nina out, but her plan worked best if she had Barry's gun in her hands before showing her true colors.

"It fell out of the cupboard when we hit that big wave," Dana said, convinced she was giving the crappiest excuse in history. "I thought I'd stick it in one of the cupboards in the mess so that no one trips over it."

"Right," Nina said. She clearly found this explanation odd. Fortunately her desire to pee was greater than her curiosity and she hurried into the bathroom.

Dana rushed out, cutting through the galley and the luxurious mess room. A blast of noise and sea air hit her as she slid open the glass door at the back of the mess and stepped onto the rear deck. There was light coming from inside, but it was still a fiddle getting the key into the lock and turning it. Eve and Nina would be able to climb out through one of the windows if they got suspicious, but the locked door would slow them down.

Dana headed briskly up a flight of stairs, ditching the bundle of cord at the top of the staircase before stepping onto the bridge. The small space was as luxurious as the rest of the boat, with leather seating along three sides and a chrome steering wheel set in the control panel at the front. The main lights were off and Barry stood in silhouette, bathed in the blue light coming off the instruments.

"Hiya," Barry said cheerfully. "Come to pay me a visit?"

Dana smiled. "You don't mind, do you? I'm too wound up to sleep."

"Not much to see up here at night," Barry said. "You set the coordinates on the GPS and this baby finds its own way. You just have to keep an eye on the radar screen to make sure you don't hit anything."

"It's a fantastic boat," Dana said as she stepped up to the steeply raked front screen and stared at the spray ripping up around the two hulls.

Barry shrugged. "It's a good tool for our mission, but to be honest I find this kind of thing repulsive."

"Really?"

"A media big shot owned this boat. Spent millions building it. After a few years he got a better one and sold it on. Now, anyone with ten thousand bucks in their pocket can hire it for a day. Meanwhile, on the other side of the world, there's a little continent called Africa where millions of people die every year because they can't get a few cents' worth of medicine."

"I guess . . . ," Dana said, eyeing the gun tucked into Barry's shorts and trying to think up the best way to get close. "I kept thinking about those two cops in the car earlier. I know they're only devils, but they were just doing their job. . . . You know?"

"That's the trouble with the world we live in, Dana. It's full of people *just doing their job* and ignoring what's really going on. Care about the rain forest until they get a couple of kids and enough money for a gas-guzzling car, or some fancy hardwood dining furniture. Watch all those wildlife programs and coo over the furry animals, but still eat meat and poultry that was raised in conditions of unbelievable cruelty. I'm sorry, but we live in a relatively free society. The facts are available, but people choose to ignore them. As far as I'm concerned, any educated person who works for the government or a big oil company is guilty through their own selective ignorance."

Dana looked solemnly at the floor. "I guess I'm scared about what's gonna happen."

Barry turned towards Dana, one side of his face lit up blue by the control panel. "You're going to do a fantastic thing in a couple of hours. Help Earth is fighting a war to help make the world a better place and you and the Survivors are part of that. You should be proud."

As Barry said this, he stepped forwards and pulled Dana into a hug. It was *perfect*. Dana could feel the gun pressing into her waist as Barry's hairy hand gently massaged her shoulder blade. She reached around to the back pocket of her shorts, slid out the aerosol, and felt for the little dimple on the nozzle to make sure it was going to spray in the right direction.

The instant the hug broke apart, Dana whipped out the can and began squirting it in Barry's face. Oven cleaner contains sodium hydroxide—a highly caustic substance that burns human skin as effectively as it dissolves the grease inside your oven.

As Barry staggered backwards with the bitter tasting foam bubbling around his eyes and mouth, Dana used her free hand to snatch his gun and expertly clicked off the safety.

"On your knees, prick," Dana demanded. "Quickly."

"You're *dead*!" Barry shouted as he desperately tried to scoop the burning foam out of his eyes.

"That's not how it looks from here," Dana said as she turned the gun on its side and used it to punch Barry in the face. His nose burst and blood spattered Dana's T-shirt as he splayed out over the leather cushions. She stood over him, pressed his head against the cockpit window and took two more slugs with the gun to knock him cold.

Barry's face was pulped. Maybe the last punch had been one too many, but with adrenalin flowing and dozens of lives at stake, Dana figured it was better to be safe than sorry.

The hardest part of the job was done, but there was no time for self-congratulation. Dana ran out the door at the back of the bridge and grabbed the bundle of nylon cord she'd dumped at the top of the stairs.

Back inside, she put the gun down on the cushion and dragged the unconscious body off the sofa onto the floor. As she knelt on Barry's back, binding his wrists behind his back, the boat tilted violently and she slipped off.

It had been five years since Dana learned knot-tying in basic training and she struggled to remember. When she was done, Barry's wrists and ankles were bound and she'd trussed the two sets of ropes together, but the result didn't look much like the neatly tied outline in the CHERUB training manual.

As Dana stood up, she realized that the catamaran was skimming the water at a hundred kph with nobody at the helm. She grabbed the throttle to cut the engines. As the turbines slowed down to idle and the boat became eerily quiet, the door at the back of the bridge slid open. It was Nina, brandishing an evil look and a bread knife.

"Traitor," Nina snarled. "I thought you were up to something with that cord."

Dana spun around to grab the gun off the cushion beside her, but the wave had knocked it across the floor. Nina saw Dana eyeing the weapon and both women lunged.

Dana was closer and got a hand on the barrel, but Nina came crashing down on the outstretched arm as she swung at Dana's head with the knife. The blade skimmed Dana's shoulder and plunged into one of the leather cushions. Despite having Nina's entire bodyweight crushing her arm, Dana tightened her grip on the gun and managed to lock her free arm around Nina's neck, making a chokehold.

Nina fought for breath as both women tried getting control over the gun. As fingers tangled around the trigger a wave knocked the boat to one side and the knife dropped out of the cushion, hitting the deck with a clang. The blade was now within easy reach, but Dana let it be, sensing that her opponent was rapidly losing the fight for air.

On the edge of unconsciousness, Nina finally managed to wrest Dana's fingers off the trigger. She was pinned and couldn't raise the gun off the deck, but she managed to turn it around and fire a shot.

The blast echoed in the cramped space and Dana felt a tearing sensation, as if her foot had just been ripped off. But she managed to keep up the stranglehold for a few more seconds, until Nina's body went limp.

As she freed her trapped arm, Dana rolled onto her back and moaned at the searing pain in her ankle.

The main light was still off. Dana felt queasy as she crawled to the control console and flipped a light switch. With no idea what state her leg was going to be in, she was scared to look down. Her heart was flat out, over two hundred beats per minute, and she was close to collapsing in shock.

When she finally braved a glance, it was a relief. Her leg looked OK, but there was blood seeping from a bullet hole at the tip of her trainer. Oddly, her toes didn't hurt as much as the tendons as the bottom of her leg. She recalled a badly twisted ankle that had caused a similar pain a couple of years earlier and after a second's thought it made sense: The joint must have been torn out of position by the huge force of the bullet smashing into her foot.

There wasn't time for Dana to feel sorry for herself because there was still Eve to deal with. She tucked her gun into the waistband of her shorts—realizing that she'd have been in a lot less pain if she'd taken a couple of seconds to do that when she was tying up Barry—then grabbed the bundle of nylon cord and crawled across to Nina. After checking she was still breathing, Dana rolled the woman onto her belly and trussed her up the same way she'd done with Barry.

Dana was reduced to crawling or hopping, but she had the gun and didn't believe that Eve posed much of a threat. She had no way to get down the steps to the rear deck in her present condition so she figured that her priority was to send out an emergency call. She crawled across the floor and pulled herself up using the arm of the captain's chair.

There was a microphone attached to the console, but

the radio looked confusing and Dana knew nothing about maritime communication. Was there an emergency SOS frequency she should use? Maybe it was already set on the channel, or maybe she'd have to spend ages twiddling knobs until she found someone else to talk to. As all these thoughts spun around, she was massively relieved to discover a satellite phone on the opposite side of the console.

Using the control console as a prop, she hobbled across the bridge, grabbed the handset, and dialed the U.K. code, followed by the number for CHERUB campus.

The female voice came back with a reassuringly Geordie accent. "Unicorn Tire Repair."

"Agent eleven-sixty-two!" Dana yelled anxiously. "Can you patch me through to John Jones?"

"Dana Smith?"

"Yeah."

"OK, I'm trying to get John's mobile in Darwin. It's bloody good to hear from you, pet. We've had full-scale missing agent alert on you. Where are you?"

"Have you ever heard of the Arafura Sea?"

"Can't say I have."

"Nor me, until about five hours ago. I seem to be in the middle of it, halfway between Australia and Indonesia."

"OK, I'm patching you through to John right now."

As Dana heard a beep from the campus switchboard, she looked out towards the rear deck of the boat and gasped in shock: The lights over the rear deck had been turned on and the dinghy had disappeared from the back.

John's voice came through the earpiece. "Dana?" he said, sounding hugely relieved. "Thank Christ, can you hear me?"

"Yeah," Dana said, totally stunned. "I'm here—just."

As she spoke to John she stared incredulously towards the empty space at the rear of the boat. The dinghy hadn't fallen off, because the tarp that had been covering it lay across the deck.

Dana had no idea if the dinghy could last in the open sea, or if there was enough fuel onboard to reach the coast of Indonesia, but she did know one thing: Eve was a fanatical Survivor who'd do everything she could to take out the oil terminal on her own.

CHAPTER 41

explosives

The nursery wasn't big enough for James, Lauren, and Rat to talk while Georgie sat in her canvas director's chair by the door. They spread cushions over the floor and tried to rest, but the evening's events had left them way too tense. At five to midnight, The Spider put another announcement over the Tannoy:

"I'm sorry to have to announce that the forces of the Devil are swelling around the Ark's perimeter. Soon, they will have men and weapons enough to overwhelm us. Since the discovery of my father's murder, I have been praying for guidance. I have also been studying his writings. He taught us that when the dark time came, we must gather at the core of the Ark, in the strong rooms beneath our Holy Church. We must go there now to pray and await our instructions from God. When we emerge, be that in days, months, or years, it will be into another world. Our task will either be to rebuild this world, or face judgment in the next."

Georgie shot up as soon as the Tannoy cut out. She flicked on the lights and stepped towards the kids.

"You heard our new leader!" Georgie shouted. "The dark time is upon us. I'm heading up to the school to make sure that the staff up there know what to do. You three wake up the others. Grab the little ones, put them in strollers, and take them up to the church."

Georgie slung her M16 over her shoulder and headed off, leaving the door open behind her. James, Lauren, and Rat rolled off the cushions and onto their feet.

"Don't know about you two, but I don't fancy getting myself barricaded underneath the church," James said as he stuck his head through the door to see what was occurring in the corridor outside.

There was nobody around, but he was shocked to see electrical wire running along the floor, linked up to sticks of explosive spaced out every ten meters.

"That's *not* good," James gasped. "Once that circuit is activated, any TAG units trying to come down here will get blown to bits."

"The rest of the tunnels are probably the same," Lauren said. "The turrets and gates as well, I'd bet."

"So," Rat said, "are we good little kids heading for the church, or do we risk making a dash and try escaping through the sewage tank?"

A little voice came up behind them. "Are we going?"

James looked back at Joseph. "Sure, wake Ed up and get dressed quickly."

"You'd better decide fast," Rat said as Joseph took great delight in waking Ed up by twisting his ear. "Georgie doesn't trust us. She's not gonna leave us down here on our own for long."

James nodded. "OK, we'll vote. I don't fancy getting locked behind a blastproof door until the food runs out or special forces storm in, so I vote sewer."

Lauren waved her hand uncertainly. "I wish there was another choice, but you're right."

Rat had already been outvoted, but his smile made it clear things had gone the way he wanted. "I've spent my whole life trying to get out of here. Let's go."

"Hang on," Lauren said. "What about the little dudes?"

"Eh?" James frowned.

Rat shook his head as Lauren scowled at the two boys. "You're prepared to abandon them down here? If something happened I'd never forgive myself."

"Come off it, Lauren," James said. "They'll slow us right down, it's not practical."

Lauren stepped backwards and waved the boys away. "Fine, you two go. But I'm staying here. I'll do what I can to help them."

James shook his head firmly. "I'm senior, Lauren. I'm *ordering* you to come with me."

"I'm not stopping *you*," Lauren said. "Just go."

James knew his sister was as stubborn as hell and he didn't want to leave without her. "Get the strollers out." He sighed. "We'll take 'em."

The two oldest kids, six-year-old Joseph and seven-year-old Ed, were nearly dressed. Lauren scooped Annabel and Martin from the cushions and popped them into a double stroller unfolded by Rat. The fifth kid was a three-year-old called Joel, who'd been asleep since they arrived. James picked him off a small mattress and gently lowered him into a single stroller.

"Great, you've got them all ready," Georgie said, breaking into a rare smile as she stepped through the doorway.

James thought fast and gave his sister a shove. "Wait for me outside."

Lauren didn't know what her brother was up to, but didn't argue. After everyone was out of the nursery and as Georgie reached to shut the metal door, James spun around in the doorway and dashed back towards the bathroom.

"Just a sec."

"For crying out loud," Georgie said irritably. "Can't you hold it in for five minutes? I want to lock up and get moving."

"I'm really busting," James said as he ran into the bathroom.

James looked around for a weapon. The porcelain lid over the toilet cistern looked ideal. It was up near the ceiling, so that little hands couldn't fiddle with it. James balanced on the toilet seat as he slid it off, making a grating sound that sent a chill down his back.

"Come on!" Georgie shouted after a minute. "What are you playing at in there?"

"Can't you stop being such a moody cow for once?" James shouted back. "You're so damned ugly; I bet you've never had a man near you."

A brighter person might have seen through James's

ruse, but Georgie was a hothead who had very little going on in the brains department.

"You'd better watch that tongue, young man!" Georgie yelled as she bowled into the bathroom.

James stepped out from behind the open door. The cistern lid weighed a ton and it strained James's biceps as it smashed into the back of Georgie's head. It didn't knock her out, but she lost her footing and toppled like a great tree, so stunned that she didn't even put out her arms to save herself. As Georgie moaned, James grabbed the gun off her shoulder. He couldn't help grinning as he stepped over her legs and slammed the bathroom door: Georgie took such delight in being mean to kids that he reckoned she totally deserved a taste of her own medicine.

He ran into the corridor, pulled shut the reinforced metal door, and turned the key in the lock. Lauren, Rat, and the little kids were waiting.

"What happened to Georgie?" Joseph asked as they turned the strollers around and set off briskly towards the sewer. "Why have you got her gun?"

The two little lads were old enough to understand some of the Survivors' beliefs. James realized they'd start going nuts if they realized they weren't really heading for the church, but he couldn't think up a good excuse.

Fortunately Rat butted in. "We discovered that Georgie's a devil," he explained. "James had to deal with her."

Joseph and Ed broke into big smiles. "She's always *so* mean to us," Joseph said.

Rat nodded. "Exactly. Someone that horrible couldn't really be an angel."

This explanation proved very satisfactory to the two

small boys, who'd been terrorized by Georgie their whole lives. The three toddlers, one pushed by Rat and two by Lauren, were asleep. As the strollers clattered rapidly over the tunnel floor, James dropped behind, so that Joseph and Ed didn't overhear his attempts to radio Chloe.

"No signal," James said, looking at Lauren when he caught up.

While James had fallen behind, Ed had started asking questions about why they were going the wrong way. He was only seven, but he'd lived in the Ark his whole life and he knew the way to the Holy Church.

As ever, Rat proved the master of excuses as he turned his stroller off the main underground walkway and into a gloomy tunnel that had a mass of explosive sticks wired up in its entrance.

"The soldiers are really close, Ed," Rat said. "They've taken over some of the Ark, so we've got to take a really long way around. Don't worry though, I know these tunnels. Once we get under the church you'll be safe."

The corridor ended at the base of a spiral staircase. James gave Lauren a filthy look as he picked Annabel and Martin out of the double stroller. It was a huge palaver, taking the toddlers out of the strollers, folding them up, carrying them up the stairs, unfolding the strollers again, and then putting the three toddlers back in their seats and doing the whole thing gently so as not to wake them up.

Unfortunately, Rat misjudged a step and stumbled as he carried Joel. The blond-haired kid woke with a start and realized that he was in a strange place in the arms of a strange person. It was all the excuse he needed for a good scream up.

As they set off again, Joseph pushed the empty single stroller and Rat struggled to hold Joel in his arms as the toddler wriggled and kicked for all he was worth.

"Where's everyone else?" Ed asked. "Are you sure we're not lost?"

Lauren was losing her patience with the kids and she'd realized that their racket was echoing for hundreds of meters, giving away their position. She turned sharply and practically bit Ed's head off. "Shut up," she said fiercely.

"Who are *you*?" Ed said. "You can't boss me. You're not even a grown-up."

Rat stole one of Georgie's favorite lines. "Shut up the pair of you, or I'll knock your bloody heads together."

A couple of minutes after the staircase, they turned into a maintenance corridor with bare bulbs instead of fluorescent tubes. It had bunches of pipes and electrical cables running along the walls and a damp stone floor. Fifty meters along, Rat dumped a slightly calmer Joel back into his stroller and scowled at Joseph.

"Don't let him run off," Rat said firmly, before taking a few steps forwards and pointing at a metal hatch in the floor.

"There it is," Rat said. "Sewage tank's right under our feet."

James squeezed past the strollers as Rat pushed his fingers under the hatch and tugged it open. James felt himself heave as he caught a blast of warm air and the most intense stench he'd ever encountered.

"Oh my *God*."

Rat managed a grin. "So that's what three hundred people's crap smells like."

"Is there anywhere near here where we might get a

torch or something?" James asked. "It's pitch-black down there."

"There might be something in one of the storage cupboards, but they're all kept locked," Rat said. "You'll have to climb down the ladder and feel your way around the walls. Keep walking straight until you get to the other end. There's probably another ladder and the exit hatch should be right above your head."

"I suppose," James said, before something occurred to him. "Hang on," he said angrily. "Who said I had to be the first one to go down there?"

"You're senior," Lauren said.

James shook his head. "You ignore me all day, but *now* my rank counts for something."

"What's down there?" Joseph asked, sounding scared. "I don't want to go down that hole."

Lauren tousled his hair. "Don't worry, we'll carry you."

"I *don't* want to," he repeated firmly. "It stinks."

"You want to get to the church, don't you?" Lauren said. "This is the only way. It's probably not that bad once you're used to it."

James slid the gun off his shoulder and handed it to Lauren. "Safety's on. Do you know how to use that if the devils come after us?"

"Course." Lauren nodded.

James took a deep breath and stood with one foot on either side of the hatch. As he stepped down onto the first rung of a metal ladder, he tried not to think too deeply about where he was about to put his feet.

CHAPTER 42

LIGHT

James couldn't see how many steps down, or how deep the sewage was. Hopefully it was only a few centimeters, then it wouldn't even run inside his shoe. At least the fumes got better as he stepped down, though he was still fighting back puke every time he took a breath.

His trainer touched a layer of bubbles. All the Survivors' contaminated water ended up here, whether it was from a toilet, or the soapy discharge from a dishwasher or washing machine. The next rung brought a trickle over the top of his trainer and in a couple of seconds he could feel the cold liquid squelching under his sock.

He had a horrible thought: *What if this is so deep I*

have to swim through it? What's it gonna be like if it runs in my ears and gets in my mouth.

He felt relieved as his sole touched concrete. It had a worrying coating of slime on it, but at least it wasn't that deep, barely reaching over his ankle.

He felt blindly along the wall behind the ladder until he reached the corner. He turned away and took a step forwards, but his foot didn't touch anything. By the time James realized he'd stepped off a ledge, it was too late to pull back. He felt his body topple forwards and gain momentum. His trainer finally hit the floor, half a meter below where he'd started, and he felt it glide through something slippery. He swung his back leg forwards and put out his arms to save himself as he felt the sewage swill up his legs and soak into the bottom of his shorts.

Lauren heard the splash and yelled out anxiously, "You OK?"

Somehow, James managed to stop himself from falling on his face, but the putrid water had splashed up his arms and there were even a few trickles running down his face.

"This is it!" James shouted furiously. "I quit. If we get out of this alive, I'm *never* going on another mission."

He heard Joseph sobbing up above, "I'm not going down there."

Then another voice, belonging to an adult. As the metal ceiling hatch clanged shut, James realized Lauren and Rat were in trouble. He thought about climbing back up the ladder, but they had the gun. There wasn't much he could do to help.

• • •

"What the hell are you kids doing down there?" Ernie shouted, pointing his gun at Lauren and Rat as he looked in the corridor entrance.

Lauren was startled and let go of the hatch so fast that she almost caught Rat's fingers as it slammed shut.

"I just went down to double check the explosives," Ernie continued, as he stepped towards them. "Georgie was thumping on the door. Head bleeding, she's in a real bad way."

"Stay *back*!" Lauren shouted, picking up the M16 and noisily clicking the safety to emphasise that she meant business.

"*Whoa*, little lady," Ernie said, grinning like the move was a big joke. "Put that thing down. It's not a toy."

"Don't patronize me," Lauren said, pointing the gun up high, selecting single shot and firing a round at the ceiling. It made a hell of a racket in the enclosed tunnel, enough to rouse the three toddlers.

Ernie caught a dose of reality and backed off a little. "Well, what's your plan? If you stay here, you'll get done by the explosives."

Lauren didn't know what to say. Rat got off the floor and stepped forwards with his hands in the air. "Hey, Ernie. You know who I am, don't you?"

"Sure, Rathbone. Why don't you both come over to me so we can talk about this? We've got to get you and the little guys to the church quickly. Once Eleanor's ordered the doors closed, nobody gets in or out until she's received the message from God."

"Listen to me," Rat said. "This is the truth, Ernie: I swear as an angel on pain of eternity in a fiery hell. My

342

father called me to his bedside before he died. He'd spoken to God and received a final message. He knew that Susie was going to kill him in a few hours. He told me that the Ark had been penetrated by devils and would be destroyed tonight, not from without but from within. He told me to leave and go into hiding. He said that when I'm older, God will contact *me* and tell me how to gather the angels and rebuild the Ark."

By the time Rat finished speaking, he'd walked to within a few steps of Ernie and was holding his arms out wide, demanding acceptance. Lauren couldn't help being impressed by Rat's speech and the sheer balls he showed, facing off a man pointing a gun at him.

"Give me the gun, Ernie," Rat boomed, sounding eerily similar to one of Joel Regan's taped speeches. "My father told me that this Ark has been poisoned by devils. Give it to me."

Ernie looked uncertainly at the end of his gun. Rat wanted to appear strong and hoped Ernie couldn't see how badly his hands were shaking.

James had shuffled ten meters across the tank when he heard Lauren's warning shot. He was scared that someone had been hit and thought about going back, but finding the exit was the most useful thing he could do.

His eyes were slowly adjusting to the dark and he could now discern reflections off the water and a crack of light coming through the hatch at the far end. Not wanting to fall again, he slid cautiously across the oily floor, feeling out the ground with his toes before shifting his weight.

It took James two minutes to reach the corner, though it seemed way longer. There was a ledge, like the one he'd fallen off at the other end. He stepped up and shuffled along. The TAG units had a searchlight sweeping the compound and the cracks along the edge of the exit hatch lit up every time the beam swung past.

He felt around, growing increasingly frustrated as he realized that there wasn't any ladder. He reached up, and even went on tiptoes. The metal rectangle was out of reach, but the darkness made it hard to tell how much extra height he needed. Maybe Joseph or Ed would be able to reach up and open it if he gave them a piggyback, but even then how would he get out without help from outside?

James was only just below the surface and figured there was a decent chance he'd get a signal out from here. As he reached down into his shorts his heart sank. He'd totally forgotten about the radio and it had gone under-water when he'd stumbled off the ledge. Still, it had been designed to live inside a sweaty training shoe, so there was still a chance it was OK.

James put the unit up to his ear and switched it on. He couldn't hear the usual static and the low battery indicator flickered when he pressed the transmit button.

Some days you just don't get the breaks.

Lauren was overwhelmed: dripping with sweat as she held the gun, watching Rat face off Ernie, and trying to keep the toddlers in their pushchairs while Ed asked awkward questions and Joseph screamed that he wasn't going down the dark hole.

"I'm of the blood, Ernie," Rat said firmly. "To save the Survivors, you *must* believe what I'm saying."

The old man looked confused. "How can you get out from here?"

"The sewage tank," Rat explained. "My father told me about it. We were trying to get over here when you caught us the first time."

"I was a plumber before I became an angel." Ernie nodded, deep in thought. "I've had to go down there and unblock it a couple of times. It's pretty foul, but you *can* get out."

"I know," Rat said as Ernic dithered, trying to figure out what to believe. "My father told me to do this, Ernie. Look into your heart and ask God. Then you'll *know* I'm telling the truth."

The old man's face suddenly lit up. "Yes!" he shouted euphorically. "That's why I'm here, isn't it? Only me and two others have ever been down inside that tank. It's no coincidence: The Lord sent me here to help you."

Rat broke into a big smile. "*Wow*, Ernie, I didn't know that. He *must* have done."

Lauren couldn't hear exactly over the bawling kids, but she realized Rat had pulled off a miracle as she saw him step forwards and embrace Ernie.

"My God," Ernie said, grinning like a man who'd discovered the meaning of life. "Thank you for choosing me, Lord. Thank you, Rathbone."

"Do you know how to get out of there, Ernie?" Lauren asked as she pulled up the hatch. "My brother's already down there somewhere."

Ed seemed reassured by the presence of an adult, but

Joseph was bawling as hard as ever. "*Not* going down that hole," he sobbed.

Ernie stood over the hatch and pulled it up a few centimeters. "You say James is already down there?"

Lauren nodded. "Yeah."

Ernie looked mystified as he opened the hatch up. He reached behind one of the pipes running along the wall and flipped a partially obscured switch.

"Why didn't you turn the lights on?"

CHAPTER 49

BOATS

Under different circumstances, mastering the controls of a thirty-meter, twenty-thousand-horsepower catamaran might have been fun, but Dana was shattered and her foot was agony. She'd lost a lot of blood and as she sat in the captain's chair watching the radar screen, she had to keep pinching herself to stay conscious.

Barry was in a bad way, still out cold. Nina came around, hurled some abuse and fought her ropes for a while, but Dana wasn't in a sympathetic mood and aimed Barry's gun at her.

"Unless you want a hole in your head to match the one you put in my foot, I'd suggest you shut up."

"You've betrayed the Survivors, devil."

Dana smiled. "You're no more of a Survivor than I am."

The sea was pitch-dark, so all Dana could do was watch the radar screen and the GPS as the cat blasted through the water towards a liaison with an Australian coastguard vessel. It was a huge relief when she saw its searchlight flash across the twin bows. She cut the turbines and left the tricky business of coming alongside to the experts.

A coastguard officer pulled off a hair-raising stunt, leaping over the side of his ship and dropping several meters onto the slippery deck of the low-slung catamaran. Once he was aboard, Dana watched him scramble to his feet and secure a rope between the two vessels. After a trial run with a container of medical supplies, two more officers hooked themselves to a pulley and slid along the rope onto the deck of the catamaran.

As two male officers took down the rope, a woman headed up to the bridge. She was taken aback by the amount of blood smeared over the decking.

"Oh, sweetheart," the woman gushed, as she saw Dana slumped in the captain's chair, hardly able to keep her head up. "How do you feel?"

"Faint," Dana said weakly. "I didn't take my shoe off in case it made the bleeding worse."

"That's good," the woman nodded. "I'm Dr. Goshen. I'll get one of the lads to carry you down to the mess, then I'll take a proper look at you where there's a bit more room."

The larger of the two male officers scooped Dana into his arms and took her on an unsteady trip downstairs, laying her out on one of the sofas at the back of the mess.

He smiled as he put her down. "You're a heavy old lump."

Dana struggled to smile back. "I do triathlons. It's all muscle."

"I can believe that." The officer nodded. "He's a heck of a size, that fellow you tackled up there."

"What about the dinghy?" Dana asked. "Did you find Eve?"

The man shook his head. "They're rubber and plastic, virtually impossible to pick up on radar, even when the sea's as calm as it is tonight. I doubt she'll last more than a couple of hours out there with an open hull. One big wave will flood her out. Even if she makes it to Indonesia, they've anchored the tankers a couple of kilometers offshore and vented off the gas in the jetty."

"That's good," Dana said, sniffing involuntarily as she imagined Eve plowing through the sea, desperately bailing out her tiny boat.

The coastguard officer looked anxiously at his colleague, as if to say *I didn't mean to make her cry*.

"Try not to worry, we're doing all we can to find her."

Dana waved her hand in front of her face. "It's not your fault." She sniffed. "It's . . . My foot really hurts, and I'm tired and Eve . . . Eve isn't really a bad person, you know. She's only fifteen. It was just the lot she got in with."

As Dana said this, the light-headedness suddenly overcame her. She heard one of the coastguard officers shouting for the doctor, then everything went black.

James looked at the row of flickering lights and Ernie's desert boot on the bottom rung of the ladder. He stared down at his clothes: his shorts and trainers were soaked in brown water and there was a humongous cockroach crawling up his arm.

"*I . . .*," he gasped, unable to curse, unable to think; angrier than he'd ever been in his life before. "There's a *light switch*," he spluttered finally.

As he looked around, he realized that the switch also powered a fan that was venting off the fumes. He also made a final discovery that made him totally insane: a gantry. If James had gone left instead of right when he'd stepped off the ladder, he'd have found the metal gantry stretching over the sewage from one ledge to the other. You wouldn't have wanted to eat your dinner off it, but it beat wading through filth by about a billion percent.

"This *better* be a dream," James groaned.

Ernie hopped from the ladder onto gantry without so much as getting his boot wet.

"James," he gasped, "what in the blazes are you doing down there? Look at the state of you."

Lauren's head popped down through the hatch and James thought he saw a tiny grin. He pointed at her. "Don't you *dare* laugh."

Lauren screwed up her face in horror. "Is that toilet paper stuck on your leg?"

Ernie walked along the gantry and grabbed a ladder that hung horizontally from two hooks on the wall.

"I don't know what kind of welcome we can expect when we get out there," he said gravely.

James realized he had to forget his personal embarrassment and focus on the mission. "Lauren!" he shouted. "My radio's knackered. Get yours out and try telling

350

Chloe what's going on; we don't want TAG units shooting when they see us."

"Gotcha." Lauren nodded.

She squatted down in the damp passageway and pulled off her trainer. Meanwhile, in the tank, Ernie was using the top of the ladder to push the hatch open.

"Chloe, do you copy me?" Lauren shouted.

Chloe came back in her ear: "Loud and clear, Lauren."

"We're about to head out via the sewage tank. We're between the fourth and fifth turrets. Can you make sure nobody starts shooting at us?"

Chloe sounded elated. "You're getting out? Thank *God*. I think you'll be OK. The TAG teams are all over the other side by the airport and as far as we can tell, the Survivors have abandoned the turrets."

"Makes sense." Lauren nodded. "Everyone's been ordered to get into the strong rooms beneath the Holy Church. But you've got to tell the soldiers not to come steaming in here. The whole joint has been wired up with explosives."

"Got that," Chloe said. "I tell you what, head out of the Ark and run for at least a few hundred meters, just in case someone tries to take a pot shot from inside. I'll drive over to meet you in my car. I should be there to pick up in a few minutes."

"We've got company," Lauren said. "There's nine of us altogether."

"*Nine* . . . ," Chloe gasped, pausing briefly before realizing that there would be time for explanations when her agents were out of danger. "Right, I'm on it."

Lauren tucked the radio in her shorts and looked across

351

at Rat. "You go; I'll start passing down the little ones."

At the other end of the tank, the hatch was open and the ladder was in place. Ernie held his gun out to James, "You go first, take this to cover yourself."

"OK, boss," James said as he hooked the gun over his shoulder and stepped onto the ladder.

He was shitting himself as he poked his head out above ground, but it was a relief seeing the running track and the outer wall of the Ark behind him.

"Looks good, mate," James said as he clambered out. He crawled for the first thirty meters before breaking into a sprint over the baked ground.

Joseph and Ed had both now realized that they were leaving the Ark, but Ernie was around and the small boys instinctively trusted him because he was an adult. The two little lads made their own way down the ladder and pinched their noses theatrically as they ran across the gantry. When they reached the other side, Ernie lifted them up all but the last couple of rungs and told them to run in a straight line until they met James on the outside.

Once the boys were out, Lauren lowered the three sleepy toddlers down to Ernie. He ran each one across the gantry, before handing them up to Rat who leaned into the outer hatch and grabbed them on the other side.

By the time everyone met up, Chloe was approaching in her car and a big Toyota 4x4 driven by a TAG officer ran close behind. James had stripped to his boxers and used the dry part of his T-shirt to wipe away the worst of the filth stuck to his skin. While he slumped on the ground feeling sorry for himself, Lauren and Ernie tried to calm down the overwrought toddlers. Joseph and Ed couldn't understand what had just happened and stood in stunned silence.

Rat stood a few places from the others and shuddered with excitement as he looked back at the three glowing spires.

"I'm never going back," he promised himself quietly as he grabbed the leather strap from around his neck and gave it an almighty tug. It felt beautiful watching the beads slide off and bounce on the hard ground.

Then the Ark exploded.

CHAPTER 44

TV

LIVE TV BROADCAST—Good Morning, Australia!
"Good morning, it's exactly seven a.m. and I'm Mick Hammond standing at the smoldering remains of The Survivors' Ark. Linda Levitt is back at the studio in Sydney.

"We have just one headline this morning. Australia is waking up to one of the most sensational stories in its history. The colorful religious guru Joel Regan is dead, believed murdered by his own wife, Susie. His world-famous Ark has been devastated by an explosion, killing many of his most devoted followers."

The picture cut to a studio set and a newsreader in a peach-colored blouse.

"Thank you, Michael. Here's a rundown of the last

twelve dramatic hours. The story began some time after seven last night, when Joel Regan was found dead by his eldest daughter, Eleanor. At the same time, four Australian army helicopters containing Tactical Assault Group commandos set off from an airbase in Queensland. Their aim was to launch a surprise raid on the Ark, seize documents, and arrest senior cult members in connection with atrocities committed by the terrorist group Help Earth.

"It still isn't clear if Susie Regan was tipped off about the impending raid. But the coincidence of Joel Regan's murder and the helicopter assault sowed the seeds of an extraordinary tragedy.

"At eight p.m., four army helicopters reached the Survivors' Ark, only to find that Susie Regan had fled and Eleanor Regan had ordered her followers to arm themselves and booby-trap sections of the Ark with explosives.

"As the helicopters tried to land, they came under intense fire. One was hit by a rocket-propelled grenade, resulting in the deaths of two commandos who had been preparing to leap from the aircraft. Six others suffered burns and one remains in critical condition. Moments later, a second helicopter was destroyed, killing its entire compliment of eighteen men and three women. The TAG units were forced to withdraw.

"As military and police reinforcements arrived by air and road, many believed that Australia faced the prospect of a lengthy standoff between the Survivors and the authorities. Accounts vary as to what happened next. What is certain is that at half past midnight a huge explosion erupted inside the Ark. Some claim this was sabotage by allies of Susie Regan or a deliberate suicide bid, but most

now agree that the blast was caused when explosive charges were triggered accidentally."

The screen showed grainy video footage of three Survivor children staggering through rubble in the darkness.

"At least fifty died instantly in the explosion. More than half were children making their way from the Ark's boarding school towards Regan's bunker. As parts of the perimeter and a one-hundred-and-fifty-meter-high spire collapsed, Survivors began emerging from the underground tunnels, many suffering from burns and smoke inhalation. Soldiers entering the damaged perimeter to assist victims of the blast then came under small-arms fire, resulting in the death of another TAG commando and injuries to two more."

The screen cut to an aerial film of a sunrise over the smoldering Ark.

"As day broke, it became clear that the army had taken control of the area. Specialist units had disabled the remaining explosives. The death toll had reached ninety-three, including thirty-seven children and twenty-four military personnel. More than fifty others have been flown to hospital and at least a dozen of these are reported to be in life-threatening condition. Among the bodies recovered inside the Ark are two of Joel Regan's children: his oldest daughter, Eleanor, and his youngest son, eleven-year-old Rathbone.

"Now . . . Sorry—I'm sorry, I'm hearing something in my earpiece. I believe Mick has more breaking news from the Ark, so let's head straight back over to him."

The image cut back to Mick Hammond, standing in the outback with the two remaining spires of the Ark and a few tufts of smoke in the background.

"Yes, Linda. Information is flooding in all the time. I've

just been having a conversation with a senior intelligence official about Susie Regan. As you know, her jet was intercepted by two F-16 fighters and it was then forced to land at Perth International Airport in the early hours of this morning. I've been told that when Susie Regan was arrested, she was accompanied by none other than Brian "Bungle" Evans. Brian Evans was the mastermind behind Help Earth's attempted anthrax attack in the United Kingdom a couple of years back.

"The official also said that if the military hadn't already been on raised-alert status because of the terrorist threat, there is every possibility that Susie Regan and Brian Evans would have been able to escape Australian airspace. Back over to you in the studio, Linda."

The newsreader looked stunned as the director cut back to her chair.

"Well," she said, smiling uneasily, "we're doing our best to keep on top of things here. Right now it's over to our Brisbane studio, where we have Professor Miriam Longford. Professor Longford is an expert on religious cults and the effects that they have on the minds of their followers. Good morning, Professor. What do you make of the events of the last twelve hours? Could anyone possibly have foreseen a tragedy such as this?"

CHAPTER 45

DEAD

Two days after the calamitous helicopter assault on the Ark, Rat—who was very much alive—spent the morning shopping with Lauren in Townsville, 1,300 kilometers north of Brisbane. It was a crummy mall, the type of place where locals came for groceries and household stuff, but Rat hadn't been shopping since his mother died eight years earlier and he loved every minute.

He got excited over every little thing: seeing a toddler rocking back and forth on the fifty-cent ride, pushing a trolley through every aisle of a supermarket, even though they were only picking up chocolate bars and a loaf of bread. The video game shop was a thrill, but it was the bargain bookshop that sent him over the edge, buying a flurry of three-dollar paperbacks.

They ended up in a food court. Rat couldn't decide between KFC and McDonalds, so they got one of each to share and Rat scoffed most of both.

"What are you grinning at?" Rat asked as he looked at Lauren across the plastic table. She had a big black scab and three stitches in her bottom lip.

Lauren shrugged, "It's nice watching you have so much fun."

"Don't you like shopping?"

"Sure," Lauren said. "If it's somewhere ritzy and I've got money to spend."

"So there's places better than this?"

"Rat, this place is a dump. My best shopping center is Bluewater near London. It's like a big triangle, there's two floors, a massive cinema, and it takes a whole day to see everything. When my mum was alive, she used to take us there every November and she'd make a big list of everything we wanted stolen for our Christmas presents."

"Stolen." Rat grinned.

"Oh, that's a long story. She ran the biggest shoplifting gang in North London before she died."

"Can I ask you a question?" Rat said, his face turning serious as he flicked away a piece of chicken skin stuck to his fingertip.

Lauren nodded. "Sure."

"Do you think I'm weird?"

Lauren shook her head and laughed out loud. "Rat, you're funny and clever. I like you a lot. What made you ask that?"

Rat blushed. "Well . . . I've spent a lot of time watching girls in the shower, but we weren't allowed to mix inside the Ark. You're sort of . . . You're the first girl I've *ever* actually had a conversation with and I wondered if you thought I was normal."

Lauren reached across the table and put her hand on top of Rat's. "You don't need to worry." She grinned. "Most boys drive me nuts, but you're really nice. Mind you, there is one thing."

"What?" Rat asked anxiously.

Lauren twisted her face like she didn't really want to broach the subject. "I know you've had a weird upbringing, but not everybody will understand. The whole thing about spying on girls in the shower is *creepy*. I'd try keeping it out of the conversation."

"Right," Rat said. "I'll remember that—oh, there's John."

Lauren glanced over her shoulder, then at her watch. "John's Mr. Punctuality. You can set your watch by him."

Dressed uncharacteristically in shorts and T-shirt, John Jones slid onto the bench alongside Lauren and peered down at Rat's two shopping bags.

"Looks like my fifty bucks didn't last long. What did you get?"

"Books mostly. I got a new copy of *Oliver Twist* and four other Charles Dickens novels. Plus that *Lord of the Rings* book that Dana raved about at the hospital."

"Pretty brave attempting *Lord of the Rings*," John said. "Never managed to plow through it all myself."

"I love reading, but we never got good books inside the Ark."

"You and James can stop squabbling over that hand-held PlayStation doo-dah now you've got those to read."

Lauren shook her head. "I wouldn't bet on it."

"Anyway," John said, "while I was over at the hospital visiting Dana, I had a phone call from the chairman back at campus."

Lauren and Rat both straightened up, looking nervous.

"I'm pleased to say . . ."

"*Yessssssssss!*" Rat screamed.

John raised his hand, but couldn't help smiling. "Let me finish, Rat. Dr. McAfferty has read James's report on what you did inside the Ark and says he's happy to waive the standard CHERUB recruitment tests. The doctor who examined you said you're in perfect health and the results of your IQ test were outstanding. You're being offered a place at CHERUB, with basic training to commence in three weeks."

Lauren leaned across the table and gave Rat a hug. "Well done, mate. Basic training is rough, but once you get through that, you're gonna *love* being a cherub."

James sat in the living room of a beachfront house, holding a cordless phone up to his ear.

"Kerry, at *last*," he said, breaking into a grin. "I've been calling for two days."

"I just got back from a mission down in Devon."

"Right," James said. "Anything exciting?"

"Not really. Kyle said you were in the Survivors' Ark when it went bang. Are you OK?"

"Yeah, not bad. We managed to escape through a sewage pipe. It's lucky we did, 'cos the explosion was right near the room where we'd been holed up. I picked up some nasty stomach bug in the sewer, so I'm on antibiotics."

"Poor you."

"Yeah, I've got my appetite back today, but I'm still weak. So, has the Survivor thing been on the news over there?"

"Just a *bit*," Kerry said. "It's still the top story, even today."

"Oh, and you'll never guess who we're staying with."

Kerry laughed, "Better tell me, then."

"They didn't want us going back to Brisbane in case we were recognized by Survivors collecting money in the street, so they flew us all up to Townsville. We're staying with Amy Collins and her brother John."

"Cool," Kerry said. "I haven't seen Amy since she retired from CHERUB. How's she doing these days?"

"Seems good, but she's at university and I think they're short of money. Amy's gone bohemian: you know, beads in her hair and grubby jeans. She's got this hippy boyfriend who's like thirty five, or something."

"Jealous, are we?"

"You know I only have eyes for you, Kerry."

"*Riiiiight*," she sneered. "That reminds me, I think Gabrielle wants to kick your arse."

"Eh?"

"Me and the girls got gossiping the other day, and I *might* have let it slip that you said you only asked her out because you were drunk."

James tutted. "Nice one, Kerry."

"So, when are you coming home?"

"We're staying out here for another couple of weeks,

having a rest and a bit of a holiday. The doctor who examined us says we're really run down from living with the Survivors. They eat bad food and you only get six or seven hours' sleep a night. My skin's disgusting: I've got about twenty zits on my back."

"*Eww,*" Kerry said. "I hope they're gone by the time I see you."

"I wish you were here with us. I missed you every day."

"I missed you, James. I'm really looking forward to us being back together again."

James giggled. "I'm looking forward to getting my hand up your top."

"Maybe I won't be wearing a top."

James's eyeballs practically sprung out on stalks. "Are you *serious*?"

"Might be," Kerry teased. "I've picked up loads of tricks from the guys I cheated on you with while you were away."

"Same here." James grinned. "This mission's just been one hot religious babe after another."

"Anyway, James, it's great hearing from you, but it's one in the morning and I'm helping Miss Takada coach some red-shirts in the dojo at half six. I'd better get to sleep."

"Right," James said. "I'll call you again tomorrow, OK?"

"Cool," Kerry said, as she blew a couple of kisses into the phone. "Have a good rest. Can't wait to see you."

"Speak tomorrow," James said, blowing a few back before hitting the end call button.

He strolled through to the kitchen, imagining Kerry taking her top off and hoping that she wasn't kidding. Amy stood at the counter mixing a giant bowl of salad.

"Do you think this will be enough for everyone?" she asked.

James smirked. "I think you could feed a small army with all that."

"You seem to be getting on well with Kerry these days."

"Yeah," James said. "I always miss her when I'm away. It's a pity it never works as well when we're both on the same continent."

Amy grinned. "She's worth the effort, James. I've always said you two complement each other."

"So, do you need a hand with anything here?"

"Nah, I reckon it's covered." Amy shrugged. "My brother John's setting the barbecue up outside, and John Jones is supposed to be stopping off at the grog shop to pick up some booze."

James noticed a car moving up the driveway outside. "That's Dana and Chloe."

He strolled out onto the drive with Amy and helped Dana out of the back of the car. Once she was standing on her crutches, James gave her a hug.

"So, how you feeling?" James asked. "I'm glad you made it in one piece."

Dana smiled. "Minus the tip of my middle toe."

"Look on the bright side," James grinned. "You've shaved ten percent off the time it takes to cut your toe-nails."

"Every cloud, eh, James?"

"Sorry I couldn't visit you in the hospital with the others, but the doctor said it was best if I stayed away while I was sick."

"But you're OK now?" Dana asked as she stepped towards the back door.

"Pretty much."

"Lauren said your face was a real picture when the light came on in that sewer. Says you threatened to quit CHERUB and everything."

James tutted. "She's gonna tell *everyone* on campus. I'm never gonna hear the end of it."

"So you're not quitting?"

James shook his head. "You know what missions are like: You don't always exactly enjoy it while you're there, but as soon as you've recovered, you're itching for another one."

An hour later, the house was full of barbecue smells and the gathering was in full swing out on the patio. It was Saturday afternoon and Amy's brother John— another ex-cherub—manned the grill. Everyone else stood around, eating, chatting, and holding drinks: John Jones, Chloe, Abigail, Dana, James, Amy, and Lauren.

John Jones put his glass of wine on a plastic table and clapped his hands together. "I'm sorry everyone, but while you're all gathered together like this, I'm going to have to inflict a speech on you—hang on, where's Rat?"

All the heads on the patio turned around, mystified.

"I'll get him," Lauren groaned.

She put her paper plate down and stepped through the patio doors into the living room. Rat sat on the couch, with a look of intense concentration on his face, scowling at James's PSP.

"Come on, you unsociable git," Lauren said. "You can't sit here playing computer games when we're having a party."

Rat glanced up anxiously. "Let me finish this race. James says I get the Mitsubishi Evo if I win this track."

Lauren tutted as she snatched the handheld and turned it off.

"Hey," Rat gasped.

Lauren grabbed his arm and tugged him off the couch. Everyone smiled as Rat was dragged out into the sunlight.

"Thank you, Lauren," John said, before resuming his speech. "I know that our memories of this mission will be tinged with sadness, because of the people who died in the Ark. But I don't want that to detract from the outstanding work done by the people gathered here."

John paused to take a mouthful of wine. "I had a long conversation with our chairman, Dr. McAfferty, this morning. You've all heard the news that Rathbone has been accepted as a CHERUB recruit."

A splutter of clapping broke out and Rat smiled.

"Mac also offered thanks to Abigail for her assistance. I'm sure we all wish her success in her ongoing ASIS career.

"I'm afraid that Mac's second piece of news makes me rather sad. It seems that young Chloe will no longer be my assistant. Dr. McAfferty has offered her a position as a full mission controller. She'll even be getting her own assistant to boss around."

Chloe looked happy as Amy gave her a rub on the back.

"But this mission would never have got anywhere without the work of three brilliant youngsters. In fact, the first thing that Dr. McAfferty said when I spoke to him this morning was that he was delighted finally to have an opportunity to promote Dana Smith to a navy shirt. We now know that over a hundred people would have died if Help Earth had successfully destroyed the Indonesian LNG facility. Each of them owes their lives to Dana's extraordinary bravery."

Everyone clapped as Dana broke into an uncharacteristic smile and turned bright red.

"Long overdue!" James shouted and everyone murmured in agreement.

John smiled. "James, Mac also expressed his thanks for another solid performance from you.

"However, the chairman singled out our youngest agent for the strongest praise of all. Despite being just eleven years of age, Lauren behaved almost immaculately over the space of two months under extremely difficult circumstances. Not only that, but when the mission reached its climax, she not only kept her cool, but instigated the rescue of five young children who would almost certainly have perished in the explosion.

"Lauren Adams, I'm absolutely delighted to say that you have been awarded a black shirt. I'm told that this will make you the third youngest cherub ever to wear it."

James was stunned as Lauren put her hands over her eyes and squealed, "Are you *kidding* me?"

Chloe stepped up behind Lauren and pulled her into a big hug. James was happy, but at the same time he resented it slightly. It *had* been Lauren's idea to rescue the little kids, but he'd been through everything else with Lauren and hadn't got anything.

Amy jabbed a finger in his back. "Go and congratulate your sister, then."

James stepped forward and got caught up in the happy mood as he hugged his sister, who had tears streaking down her face.

"I don't believe it," she sniffed happily. "None of my mates are even navy shirts. The other black shirts are all fifteen and sixteen. I—I just . . ."

John grinned at her. "It's ability not age that counts at CHERUB."

As James headed over to the barbecue to replenish his plate, he caught a sly glance from Dana.

"What are you grinning at?" James asked.

"Oh," Dana said, shrugging casually, "I just think it's going to be a hoot watching Lauren boss you around on training exercises and stuff. I mean, now that your little sister outranks you. . . ."

epilogue

Help Earth

The arrests of BRIAN EVANS, SUSIE REGAN, NINA WILLIAMS, and BARRY COX represented a huge step in the fight against the terrorist group Help Earth.

Although the four are initially expected to stand trial in Australia, they are also wanted for questioning in Hong Kong, the United Kingdom, America, and Venezuela. It is expected that they will spend the rest of their lives in prison.

In the days after the Survivors' Ark tragedy, several more arrests were made, including that of ARNOS LOMBORG, who is now believed to have been the financial mastermind behind Help Earth.

MIKE EVANS has not been sighted since his beachfront encounter with Dana Smith and remains at large.

Although these arrests struck a major blow against Help Earth, it is thought that the terrorist group has a decentralized structure made up of small cells located throughout the world. Many of these cells remain a threat, especially as much of the $400 million stolen from the Survivors by Susie Regan has not been traced.

The Survivors

Many commentators thought that the death of Joel Regan and the Ark tragedy would spell the end of the Survivor cult; this did not prove to be the case.

While the Survivors were bankrupted by the financial implications of the failed terrorist attack, the movement itself restructured. Most Survivors now believe that God will select a new messenger to lead them and build another Ark.

ELLIOT MOSS fully recovered from his stab wound. Together with WEEN he set up the *New Survivor Foundation*, known as the NSF. Using a mixture of bank loans and money raised by commune members, the NSF was able to purchase the Brisbane mall and the adjoining warehouse from creditors.

Although four Survivor communes around the world closed after the *fall of the first Ark*—as NSF members call it—nineteen others used the earning power and ingenuity of their residents to stay in business.

ERNIE CRAIG was arrested in the wake of the Ark tragedy and cautioned for various firearms offenses. Other
members of the NSF did not accept his repeated claims
that he escaped the Ark with Rathbone Regan and that
the boy will one day return to lead the Survivors. After
a series of heated arguments he was forced to leave the
Brisbane commune.

GEORGIE GOLDMAN was found among the dead inside
a collapsed tunnel within the Ark.

The body of EVE STANNIS washed up on an Indonesian
island. No trace was ever found of the dinghy or explosives. She was flown back to Brisbane and buried in a
Survivor ceremony. Eve's parents and two younger sisters are believed to have left the NSF shortly afterwards.

The Others
ABIGAIL SANDERS went back to her real family and her
regular job with ASIS. She is currently working to identify the remaining Help Earth cells and trace the money
stolen by Susie Regan.

MIRIAM LONGFORD attained brief celebrity in the
aftermath of the Ark tragedy. As the pre-eminent expert
on the Survivors, she appeared on more than a dozen
TV shows and was quoted in hundreds of newspapers
around the world. Once the attention died down, she
resumed her work counseling former cult members and
is currently writing a biography, *From Supermodel to
Terrorist: The Sensational Life of Susie Regan*.

Following the Ark tragedy, EMILY WILDMAN changed her will again, this time leaving one quarter of her money to her son RONNIE and three quarters to the Australian Red Cross. She remains in reasonable health and recently celebrated her eighty-eighth birthday.

The Cherubs
RATHBONE REGAN changed his name to Greg Rathbone. He has started basic training alongside eleven other recruits and is said to be doing exceptionally well. Despite begging everyone on CHERUB campus to call him Greg, he is still known as Rat.

Despite the injury to her toe, DANA SMITH has resumed light training and has set herself a target to compete in her first adult triathlon in August 2006.

After ten days' rest in Townsville, JAMES and LAUREN ADAMS returned to CHERUB campus. They will be eligible for another mission once they have caught up on their schoolwork.

CHERUB:
A HISTORY
(1941-1996)

1941 In the middle of the Second World War, Charles Henderson, a British agent working in occupied France, sent a report to his headquarters in London. It was full of praise for the way the French Resistance used children to sneak past Nazi checkpoints and wangle information out of German soldiers.

1942 Henderson formed a small undercover detachment of children, under the command of British Military Intelligence. Henderson's Boys were all thirteen or fourteen years old, mostly French refugees. They were given basic espionage training before being parachuted into occupied France. The boys gathered vital intelligence in the run-up to the D-Day invasions of 1944.

1946 Henderson's Boys disbanded at the end of the war. Most of them returned to France. Their existence has never been officially acknowledged.

Charles Henderson believed that children would make effective intelligence agents during peacetime. In May 1946, he was given permission to create CHERUB in a disused village school. The first twenty CHERUB recruits, all boys, lived in wooden huts at the back of the playground.

1951 For its first five years, CHERUB struggled along with limited resources. Its fortunes changed following its first major success: Two agents uncovered a ring of Russian spies who were stealing information on the British nuclear weapons program.

The government of the day was delighted. CHERUB was given funding to expand. Better facilities were built and the number of agents was increased from twenty to sixty.

1954 Two CHERUB agents, Jason Lennox and Johan Urminski, were killed while operating undercover in East Germany. Nobody knows how the boys died. The government considered shutting CHERUB down, but there were now over seventy active CHERUB agents performing vital missions around the world.

An inquiry into the boys' deaths led to the introduction of new safeguards:

(1) The creation of the ethics panel. From now on, every mission had to be approved by a three-person committee.

(2) Jason Lennox was only nine years old. A minimum mission age of ten years and four months was introduced.

(3) A more rigorous approach to training was brought in. A version of the 100-day basic training program began.

1956 Although many believed that girls would be unsuitable for intelligence work, CHERUB admitted five girls as an experiment. They were a huge success. The number of girls in CHERUB was upped to twenty the following year. Within ten years, the number of girls and boys was equal.

1957 CHERUB introduced its system of colored T-shirts.

1960 Following several successes, CHERUB was allowed to expand again, this time to 130 students. The farmland surrounding headquarters was purchased and fenced off, about a third of the area that is now known as CHERUB campus.

1967 Katherine Field became the third CHERUB agent to die on an operation. She was bitten by a snake on a mission in India. She reached hospital within half an hour, but tragically the snake species was wrongly identified and Katherine was given the wrong antivenom.

1973 Over the years, CHERUB had become a hotchpotch of small buildings. Construction began on a new nine-story headquarters.

1977 All CHERUBs are either orphans, or children who have been abandoned by their family. Max Weaver was one of the first CHERUB agents. He made a fortune building office blocks in London and New York. When he died in 1977, aged just forty-one, without a wife or children, Max Weaver left his fortune for the benefit of the children at CHERUB.

The Max Weaver Trust Fund has paid for many of the buildings on CHERUB campus. These include the indoor athletics facilities and library. The trust fund now holds assets worth over £1 billion.

1982 Thomas Webb was killed by a landmine on the Falkland Islands, becoming the fourth CHERUB to die on a mission. He was one of nine agents used in various roles during the Falklands conflict.

1986 The government gave CHERUB permission to expand up to four hundred pupils. Despite this, numbers have stalled some way below this. CHERUB requires intelligent, physically robust agents who have no family ties. Children who meet all these admission criteria are extremely hard to find.

1990 CHERUB purchased additional land, expanding both the size and security of campus. Campus is marked on all British maps as an army firing range. Surrounding roads are routed so that there is only one road onto campus. The perimeter walls cannot be seen from nearby roads. Helicopters are banned from the area and airplanes must stay above ten thousand meters. Anyone breaching the CHERUB perimeter faces life imprisonment under the State Secrets Act.

1996 CHERUB celebrated its fiftieth anniversary with the opening of a diving pool and an indoor shooting range.

Every retired member of CHERUB was invited to the celebration. No guests were allowed. Over nine hundred people made it, flying from all over the world. Among the retired agents were a former prime minister and a rock guitarist who had sold 80 million albums.

After a firework display, the guests pitched tents and slept on campus. Before leaving the following morning, everyone gathered outside the chapel and remembered the four children who had given CHERUB their lives.